'I swear I didn't breathe the [...]
it. Gripping, pacy, [...]
CLARE MAC[...]

'I had an unrelentingly pleasurable and a thrilling
for-God's-sake-tell-me-what-happened sensation in
my stomach for the entire read . . . Stupendous!'
RUTH JONES

'A twisty and engrossing story of betrayal and redemption.
Reminiscent of Donna Tartt in scope and quality.'
IAN RANKIN

'Few writers of psychological suspense devise such swift,
slippery plots; fewer still people their stories with characters
so human and complex. Lisa Jewell's *The Family Upstairs*
glitters like a blade and cuts even deeper.'
AJ FINN

'Rich, dark and intricately twisted, this enthralling
whodunnit mixes family saga with domestic noir
to brilliantly chilling effect.'
RUTH WARE

'The perfect poolside read. The perfect anywhere read, to
be honest. *The Family Upstairs* is riveting, moving and
gets the highest possible level of recommendation.'
SOPHIE HANNAH

'Absolutely brilliant. Great characterisation, a fascinating
and dark set up and a great conclusion. Lisa Jewell is
always great but this is next level stuff.'
SARAH PINBOROUGH

'Compelling, immersive and unputdownable . . . *The
Family Upstairs* is one of her very best. An intriguing,
claustrophobic and compelling mystery about a family
that comes to stay and refuses to leave.'
C L TAYLOR

THE
FAMILY
UPSTAIRS

LISA JEWELL

PENGUIN BOOKS

UK | USA | Canada | Ireland | Australia
India | New Zealand | South Africa

Penguin Books is part of the Penguin Random House group of companies
whose addresses can be found at global.penguinrandomhouse.com.

Penguin
Random House
UK

First published in the UK by Century in 2019
First published in paperback by Arrow Books in 2020
Published in Penguin Books 2022

32

Typeset by Jouve (UK), Milton Keynes
Printed and bound in Great Britain by Clays Ltd, Elcograf S.p.A.

The authorised representative in the EEA is Penguin Random House Ireland,
Morrison Chambers, 32 Nassau Street, Dublin D02 YH68

A CIP catalogue record for this book is available from the British Library

ISBN: 978–1–787–46148–2
ISBN: 978–1–787–46149–9 (export)

www.greenpenguin.co.uk

This book is dedicated to my readers,
with love and gratitude

A note on the character name of 'Cerian Tahany'

The name 'Cerian Tahany' was given to me by a real life Cerian Tahany, one of this year's winners of the Get In Character campaign.

CLIC Sargent is the UK's leading cancer charity for children and young people. Their mission is to change what it means to be diagnosed with cancer when you're young. They believe that children and young people with cancer have the right to the best possible treatment, care and support, throughout their cancer journey and beyond. The Get In Character campaign has been running since 2014 and has been supported by many of the UK's most well-known authors. To date, the campaign has raised over £40,000.

I have been very happy to support the Get In Character campaign over the years, and it will launch again on eBay in 2020, running from 9th–5th March.

Further details can be found at www.clicsargent.org.uk

It would be inaccurate to say that my childhood was normal before they came. It was far from normal, but it felt normal because it was all I'd known. It's only now, with decades of hindsight, that I can see how odd it was.

I was nearly eleven when they came, and my sister was nine.

They lived with us for more than five years and they turned everything very, very dark. My sister and I had to learn how to survive.

And when I was sixteen, and my sister was fourteen, the baby came.

I

1

Libby picks the letter up off the doormat. She turns it in her hands. It looks very formal; the envelope is cream in colour, made of high-grade paper, and feels as though it might even be lined with tissue. The postal frank says 'Smithkin Rudd & Royle Solicitors Chelsea Manor Street SW3'.

She takes the letter into the kitchen and sits it on the table while she fills the kettle and puts a teabag in a mug. Libby is pretty sure she knows what's in the envelope. She turned twenty-five last month. She's been subconsciously waiting for this envelope. But now it's here she's not sure she can face opening it.

She picks up her phone and calls her mother.

'Mum,' she says. 'It's here. The letter from the trustees.'

She hears a silence at the other end of the line. She pictures her mum in her own kitchen, a thousand miles away in Dénia: pristine white units, lime-green colour-coordinated kitchen accessories, sliding glass doors on to a small terrace with a distant view to the Mediterranean, her phone held to her ear in the crystal-studded case that she refers to as her *bling*.

'Oh,' she says. 'Right. Gosh. Have you opened it?'

'No. Not yet. I'm just having a cup of tea first.'

'Right,' she says again. Then she says, 'Shall I stay on the line? While you do it?'

'Yes,' says Libby. 'Please.'

She feels a little breathless, as she sometimes does when she's just about to stand up and give a sales pres-entation at work, like she's had a strong coffee. She takes the teabag out of the mug and sits down. Her fingers caress the corner of the envelope and she inhales.

'OK,' she says to her mother, 'I'm doing it. I'm doing it right now.'

Her mum knows what's in here. Or at least she has an idea, though she was never told formally what was in the trust. It might, as she has always said, be a tea-pot and a ten-pound note.

Libby clears her throat and slides her finger under

the flap. She pulls out a sheet of thick cream paper and scans it quickly:

To Miss Libby Louise Jones

As trustee of the Henry and Martina Lamb Trust created on 12 July 1977, I propose to make the distribution from it to you described in the attached schedule . . .

She puts down the covering letter and pulls out the accompanying paperwork.

'Well?' says her mum, breathlessly

'Still reading,' she replies.

She skims and her eye is caught by the name of a property. Sixteen Cheyne Walk, SW3. She assumes it is the property her birth parents were living in when they died. She knows it was in Chelsea. She knows it was big. She had assumed it was long gone. Boarded up. Sold. Her breath catches hard at the back of her throat when she realises what she's just read.

'Er,' she says.

'What?'

'It looks like . . . No, that can't be right.'

'What!'

'The house. They've left me the house.'

'The Chelsea house?'

'Yes,' she says.

'The whole house?'

'I think so.' There's a covering letter, something about nobody else named on the trust coming forward in due time. She can't digest it at all.

'My God. I mean, that must be worth . . .'

Libby breathes in sharply and raises her gaze to the ceiling. 'This must be wrong,' she says. 'This must be a mistake.'

'Go and see the solicitors,' says her mother. 'Call them. Make an appointment. Make sure it's not a mistake.'

'But what if it's not a mistake? What if it's true?'

'Well then, my angel,' says her mother – and Libby can hear her smile from all these miles away, 'you'll be a very rich woman indeed.'

Libby ends the call and stares around her kitchen. Five minutes ago, this kitchen had been the only kitchen she could afford, this flat the only one she could buy, here in this quiet street of terraced cottages in the backwaters of St Albans. She remembers the flats and houses she'd seen during her online searches, the little intakes of breath as her eye caught upon the perfect place: a suntrap terrace, an eat-in kitchen, a five-minute walk to the station, a bulge of ancient leaded window, the suggestion of cathedral bells from across a green, and then she would see the price and feel herself a fool for ever thinking it might be for her.

She'd compromised on everything in the end to find a place that was close to her job and not too far from the train station. There'd been no gut instinct as she stepped across the threshold; her heart said nothing to her as the estate agent showed her around. But she'd made it a home to be proud of, painstakingly creaming off the best that TK Maxx had to offer, and now her badly converted, slightly awkward one-bedroom flat makes her feel happy. She'd bought it; she'd adorned it. It belonged to her.

But now it appears she is the owner of a house on the finest street in Chelsea and suddenly her flat looks like a ridiculous joke and so does everything else that was important to her five minutes ago – the £1500-a-year rise she'd just been awarded at work, the hen weekend in Barcelona next month that had taken her six months to save for, the Mac eye shadow she'd 'allowed' herself to buy last weekend as a treat for getting the pay rise – the soft frisson of abandoning her tightly managed monthly budget for just one glossy, sweet-smelling moment in House of Fraser, the weight-lessness of the tiny MAC bag swinging from her hand, the shiver of placing the little black capsule in her make-up bag, of knowing that she owned it, that she might in fact wear it in Barcelona, where she might also wear the dress her mother bought her for Christmas, the one from French Connection with the lace panels she'd wanted for ages. Five minutes ago her joys in life had been small, anticipated, longed-for, hard-earned and saved-up-for, inconsequential little splurges that meant nothing in the scheme of things but gave the flat surface of her life enough sparkles to make it worth getting out of bed every morning to go and do a job which she liked but didn't love.

Now she owns a house in Chelsea and the proportions of her existence have been blown apart.

She slides the letter back into its expensive envelope and finishes her tea.

2

There is a storm brewing over the Côte d'Azur; it sits dark as damsons on the horizon, lying heavy on the crown of Lucy's head. She cups her skull with one hand, grabs her daughter's empty plate with the other and lowers it to the floor so that the dog can lick off the gravy stains and crumbs of chicken.

'Marco,' she says to her son, 'finish your food.'

'I'm not hungry,' he replies.

Lucy feels rage pulse and throb at her temples. The storm is edging closer; she can feel the moisture cooling in the hot air. 'This is it,' she says, her voice clipped with the effort of not shouting. 'This is all there is to eat today. This is the end of the money.

No more. No telling me you're hungry at bedtime. It'll be too late then. Eat it. Please.'

Marco shakes his head long-sufferingly and cuts into his chicken schnitzel. She stares at the top of his head, the thick chestnut hair swirling from a double-crown. She tries to remember the last time they all washed their hair and she can't.

Stella says, 'Mama, can I have a dessert?'

Lucy glances down at her. Stella is five years old and the best mistake Lucy ever made. She should say no; she's so hard on Marco, she should not be so soft on his sister. But Stella is so good, so yielding and easy. How can she deny her something sweet to eat?

'If Marco finishes his schnitzel,' she says evenly, 'we can get an ice cream to share.'

This is clearly unfair on Stella, who finished her chicken ten minutes ago and shouldn't have to wait for her brother to finish his. But Stella's sense of injustice seems still to be unformed and she nods and says, 'Eat quickly, Marco!'

Lucy takes Marco's plate from him when he is done and puts it on the pavement for the dog. The ice cream comes. It is three flavours in a glass bowl with hot chocolate sauce, crumbled praline and a pink foil palm tree on a cocktail stick.

Lucy's head throbs again and she eyes the horizon. They need to find shelter and they need to do it soon.

She asks for the bill, places her card on the saucer, taps her number into the card reader, her breath held against the knowledge that now there is no money in that account, that there is no money anywhere.

She waits while Stella licks out the glass bowl, then she unties the dog's lead from the table leg and collects their bags, handing two to Marco, one to Stella.

'Where are we going?' asks Marco.

His brown eyes are serious, his gaze is heavy with anxiety.

She sighs. She looks up the street towards Nice's old town, down the street towards the ocean. She even looks at the dog, as though he might have a good suggestion to make. He looks at her eagerly as though there might be another plate to lick. There's only one place to go and it's the last place she wants to be. But she finds a smile.

'I know,' she says, 'let's go and see Mémé!'

Marco groans. Stella looks uncertain. They both remember how it was last time they stayed with Stella's grandmother. Samia was once a film star in Algeria. Now she is seventy years old, blind in one eye and living in a scruffy seventh-floor apartment in a tower block in l'Ariane with her disabled adult daughter. Her husband died when she was just fifty-five and her only son, Stella's father, disappeared three years ago and hasn't been in touch since. Samia is angry and raw and

13

Lisa Jewell

rightly so. But she has a roof and a floor; she has pillows and running water. She has everything right now that Lucy can't offer her children.

'Just for one night,' she says. 'Just tonight and then I'll sort something out for tomorrow. I promise.'

They reach Samia's estate just as the rain starts to fall, tiny water bombs exploding on to the hot pavement. In the graffiti-daubed lift on the way to the seventh floor, Lucy can smell them: the humid aroma of unwashed clothes, of greasy hair, of trainers that have been worn too long. The dog, with his coat of dense wiry hair, smells particularly horrible.

'I can't,' says Samia at her front door, blocking their entrance. 'I just can't. Mazie is sick. The carer needs to sleep here tonight. There is no room. There is just no room.'

A crack of thunder booms overhead. The sky behind them turns brilliant white. Sheets of rain sluice from the sky. Lucy stares at Samia desperately. 'We have nowhere else to go,' she says.

'I know,' says Samia. 'I know that. I can take Stella. But you and the boy and the dog, I'm sorry. You'll have to find somewhere else.'

Lucy feels Stella push against her leg, a shiver of unease run through her small body. 'I want to stay with you,' she whispers to Lucy. 'I don't want to stay without you.'

Lucy crouches down and takes Stella's hands. Stella's eyes are green, like her father's, her dark hair is streaked hazel-blond, her face tanned dark brown from the long hot summer. She is a beautiful child; people stop Lucy on the street sometimes to tell her so, with a soft gasp.

'Baby,' she says. 'You'll be dry here. You can have a shower; Mémé will read you a story . . .'

Samia nods. 'I'll read you the one you like,' she says, 'about the moon.'

Stella presses herself tighter against Lucy. Lucy feels her patience ebbing. She would give anything to be allowed to sleep in Mémé's bed, to be read the book about the moon, to shower and slip into clean pyjamas.

'Just one night, baby. I'll be here first thing tomorrow to collect you. OK?'

She feels the flutter of Stella's head nodding against her shoulder, the intake of her breath against tears. 'OK, Mama,' says Stella, and Lucy bundles her into Samia's flat before either of them can change their mind. Then it is just her and Marco and the dog, yoga mats rolled up on their backs, heading into the heavy rain, into the darkening night, with nowhere to go.

For a while they take shelter beneath the flyover. The constant fizz of car tyres over hot wet tarmac is deafening. The rain keeps falling.

Marco has the dog held in his lap, his face pressed against the dog's back.

He looks up at Lucy. 'Why is our life so shit?' he asks.

'You know why our life is shit,' she snaps.

'But why can't you do something about it?'

'I'm trying,' she says.

'No you're not. You're letting us go under.'

'*I am trying*,' she hisses, fixing him with a furious gaze. 'Every single minute of every single day.'

He looks at her doubtfully. He is too, too clever and knows her too, too well. She sighs. 'I'll get my fiddle back tomorrow. I can start making money again.'

'How are you going to pay for the repairs?' He narrows his eyes at her.

'I'll find a way.'

'What way?'

'I don't know, all right? I don't know. Something will come up. It always does.'

She turns from her son then and stares into the parallel lines of headlights burning towards her. A huge cannon of thunder explodes overhead, the sky lights up again, the rain becomes, if it is possible, even heavier. She pulls her battered smartphone from the outside pocket of her rucksack, turns it on. She sees that she has 8 per cent battery charge left and is about to switch it off again when she notices her phone has sent her a notification from her calendar. It's been there for weeks now but she can't bring herself to cancel it.

It says, simply: *The baby is 25.*

3

My name, like my father's name, is Henry. This dupli-
cation was the cause of occasional confusion, but as
my mother called my father *darling* and my sister called
him *Daddy* and pretty much everyone else called him
Mr Lamb or *sir*, we got by.

My father was the sole beneficiary of his own
father's fortune, made from slot machines. I never
knew my grandfather, he was very old when my dad
was born, but he was from Blackpool and his name
was Harry. My father never worked a day in his life,
just sat around waiting for Harry to die so that he
could be rich in his own right.

He bought our house on Cheyne Walk in Chelsea
the very same day he got his hands on the money. He'd

been house-hunting during Harry's dying days, had his eye on the place for a few weeks, was terrified that someone else was going to put an offer in on it before he could claim his inheritance.

The house was empty when he bought it and he spent years and thousands filling it with what he used to call *objets*: moose heads looming off panelled walls, hunting swords hanging crossed above doorways, mahogany thrones with barley twist backs, a medieval-style banqueting table for sixteen, replete with scars and wormholes, cabinets full of pistols and bullwhips, a twenty-foot tapestry, sinister oil portraits of other people's ancestors, reams of gold-blocked leather-bound books that no one would ever read and a full-size cannon in the front garden. There were no comfortable chairs in our house, no cosy corners. Everything was wood and leather and metal and glass. Everything was hard. Especially my father.

He lifted weights in our basement and drank Guinness from his own private keg in his own private bar. He wore £800 handmade suits from Mayfair that barely accommodated his muscles and his girth. He had hair the colour of old pennies and raw-looking hands with tight red knuckles. He drove a Jaguar. He played golf although he hated it because he wasn't designed to swing a golf club; he was too solid, too unyielding. He went on shoots at the weekends:

disappeared on Saturday morning wearing a tight-fitting tweed jacket with a boot full of guns and came home on Sunday evening with a brace of wood pigeons in an ice box. Once, when I was about five, he brought home an English Bulldog he'd bought from a man on the street using the mint-fresh fifty-pound notes he kept rolled up in his jacket pocket. He said it reminded him of himself. Then it shat on an antique rug and he got rid of it.

My mother was a *rare beauty*.

Not my words. My father's.

Your mother is a rare beauty.

She was half-German, half-Turkish. Her name was Martina. She was twelve years younger than my dad, and back then, before they came, she was a style icon. She would put on a pair of dark sunglasses and take herself off to Sloane Street to spend my father's money on bright silk scarves and gold-encased lipsticks and intense French perfume and she would be photographed sometimes, her wrists encircled with bag handles, and put in the posh papers. They called her a socialite. She wasn't really. She went to glamorous parties and wore beautiful clothes but when she was at home she was just our mum. Not the best mum, but not the worst, and certainly a relatively soft spot in our big, masculine, machete-adorned Chelsea mansion.

She'd once had a job, for a year or so, introducing important fashion people to each other. Or at least that was my impression. She had little silver business cards in her purse, printed with the words 'Martina Lamb Associates' in hot pink. She had an office on the King's Road, a bright loft room over a shop, with a glass table and leather chairs and a telex machine, rails of clothes in clear plastic, a vase of white lilies on a plinth. She would take me and my sister into work with her on school holidays and give us crisp piles of tantalisingly white paper from a ream in a box, and a handful of Magic Markers. The phone would ring occasionally, and Mummy would say, 'Good morning, Martina Lamb Associates.' Sometimes a visitor would be buzzed in via the intercom – my sister and I fighting over whose turn it was to press the button. The visitors were shrill, very thin women who only wanted to talk about clothes and famous people. There were no 'associates', just our mother and the occasional wide-eyed teenage girl on work experience. I don't know what happened to it all. I just know that the loft office disappeared, and the silver business cards disappeared, and Mummy just carried on being a housewife again.

My sister and I went to school in Knightsbridge – quite possibly the most expensive school in London. Our father was not afraid of spending money then. He loved spending money. The more the better. Our uniform was shit brown and bile yellow with knicker-bocker-style trousers for the boys. Thankfully, by the time I was old enough to be humiliated by the attire, my father had no money left to pay for school fees, let alone for corduroy knickerbockers from the Harrods school uniform department.

It all happened so slowly, yet so extraordinarily quickly, the change to our parents, to our home, to our lives after they arrived. But that first night, when Birdie appeared on our front step with two large suitcases and a cat in a wicker box, we could never have guessed the impact she would have, the other people she would bring into our lives, that it would all end the way it did.

We thought she had just come to stay for the weekend.

4

Libby can hear the whisper of every moment that this room has existed, feel every breath of every person who has ever sat where she is sitting.

'Seventeen ninety-nine,' Mr Royle had replied in answer to her earlier question. 'One of the oldest legal practices in the capital.'

Mr Royle looks at her now across his heavily waxed desk top. A smile flickers across his lips and he says, 'Well, well, well. This is some birthday present, no?'

Libby smiles nervously. 'I'm still not convinced it's really true,' she says. 'I keep expecting someone to tell me it's a big wind-up.'

Her choice of words – *big wind-up* – feels wrong in this venerable and ancient setting. She wishes she'd used a different turn of phrase. But Mr Royle doesn't seem concerned. His smile stays in place as he leans forward and passes Libby a thick pile of paperwork. 'No winding up, I can assure you, Miss Jones.

'Here,' he says, pulling something from the pile of paper. 'I wasn't sure whether to give this to you now. Or maybe I should have sent it to you. With the letter. I don't know – it's all so awkward. It was in the file and I kept it back, just in case it didn't feel right. But it does seem the right thing to do. So here. I don't know how much your adoptive parents were able to tell you about your birth family. But you might want to take a minute to read this.'

She unfolds the piece of newsprint and lays it out on the table in front of her.

Socialite and husband dead in suicide pact
Teenage children missing; baby found alive

Police yesterday were called to the Chelsea home of former socialite Martina Lamb and her husband Henry after reports of a possible triple suicide. Police arrived at lunchtime and found the bodies of Mr and Mrs Lamb side by side on the floor of the kitchen. A second man, who has yet to be identified, was also found dead. A baby, believed to be female and ten months old, was found in a room on the first floor.

The baby has been taken into care and is said to be in good health. Neighbours have observed that there had been numerous children living in the house in recent years and there are varying reports of other adults living at the property, but no trace was found of any other residents.

The cause of death is still to be ascertained, but early blood samples tested appear to suggest that the trio may have poisoned themselves.

Henry Lamb, 48, was the sole beneficiary of the estate of his father, Mr Harry Lamb, of Blackpool, Lancashire. He had suffered from ill health in recent years and was said to be wheelchair-bound.

Police are now trawling the country for sightings of the couple's son and daughter who are described as roughly fourteen to sixteen years old. Anyone with any information about the whereabouts of the children is invited to contact the Metropolitan Police at the earliest possible juncture. Anyone who may have spent time living at the property with the family in recent years is also of great interest to the police.

She stares at Mr Royle. 'Is that . . .? The baby left behind – is that me?'

He nods. She can see genuine sadness in his eyes. 'Yes,' he says. 'Such a tragic story, isn't it? And such a mystery. The children, I mean. The house was in trust for them, too, but neither of them ever came forward. I can only assume, well, that they're . . . anyway.' He leans forward, clutches his tie and smiles, painfully. 'May I offer you a pen?'

He tips a wooden pot of expensive-looking ball-point pens towards her and she takes one. It has the name of the firm printed on its barrel in gold script.

Libby stares at it blankly for a moment.

A brother.

A sister.

A suicide pact.

She shakes her head, very slightly; then she clears her throat and says, 'Thank you.'

Her fingers clutch the solid pen tightly. She can barely remember what her signature is supposed to look like. There are sticky plastic arrows attached to the edges of the pages she is expected to sign, pointing her in the right direction. The sound of the pen against the paper is almost excruciating. Mr Royle watches benignly; he pushes his teacup across the desk a few inches, then back again.

As she signs, she feels very strongly the import of this moment, this invisible turning in her life taking her from *here* to *there*. On one side of this pile of papers is careful trolley trips round Lidl, one week away a year and an eleven-year-old Vauxhall Corsa. On the other is the keys to an eight-bedroom house in Chelsea.

'Good,' he says, almost with a sigh of relief, as Libby passes him back the paperwork. 'Good, good, good.' He flicks through it, casting his gaze over the spaces next to the plastic arrows and then he looks up at Libby and smiles and says, 'Right. I think it's time for you to take ownership of the keys.' He pulls a small white jiffy bag from a drawer in his desk. The label on the packet says '16 Cheyne Walk'.

Libby peers inside. Three sets of keys. One with a metal keyring with the Jaguar logo on it. One with a brass keyring with a cigarette lighter built into it. And one set without a keyring.

He gets to his feet. 'Shall we go?' he says. 'We can walk. It's only just around the corner.'

It's a violently hot summer's day. Libby can feel the heat of the paving stones through the soles of her slip-on canvas shoes, the glare of the midday sun burning through the thin film of cloud. They walk down a street filled with restaurants, all open to the pavement, fully laid-up tables set on special platforms and protected from the sun by vast rectangular parasols. Women in oversized sunglasses sit in twos and threes drinking wine. Some of them are as young as her and she marvels at how they can afford to sit drinking wine in a posh restaurant on a Monday afternoon.

'So,' says Mr Royle, 'this could be your new neighbourhood, I suppose. If you decided to live in the house.'

She shakes her head and issues a small nervous laugh. She can't form a proper reply. It's all just too silly.

They pass tiny boutiques and antique shops filled with bronzes of foxes and bears, vast twinkling chandeliers the size of her bathtub. Then they are by the river and Libby can smell it before she sees it, the wet-dog tang of it. Wide boats slip by each other; a smaller boat with more rich people on it bubbles past: champagne in a silver cooler, a windswept golden retriever at the prow squinting against the sun.

'It's just down here,' says Mr Royle. 'Another minute or two.'

Libby's thighs are chafing and she wishes she'd worn shorts instead of a skirt. She can feel sweat being absorbed by the fabric of her bra where the cups meet in the middle and she can tell that Mr Royle, in his tight-fitting suit and shirt, is finding the heat unbearable too.

'Here we are,' he says, turning to face a terrace of five or six red-brick houses, all of differing heights and widths. Libby guesses immediately which is hers, even before she sees the number sixteen painted on the fanlight in a curly script. The house is three floors high, four windows wide. It is beautiful. But it is, just as she'd imagined it would be, boarded up. The chimney pots and gutters are overgrown with weeds. The house is an eyesore.

But such a beautiful eyesore. Libby inhales sharply. 'It's very big,' she says.

'Yes,' says Mr Royle. 'Twelve rooms in total. Not including the basement.'

The house stands well back from the pavement behind ornate metal railings and an overgrown parterre garden. There is a wrought-iron canopy running towards the front door and to the left is a full-size cannon set on a concrete block.

'Would you like me to do the honours?' Mr Royle indicates the padlock securing the board over the front door.

Libby nods and he unlocks it, hefting the hoarding away by looping his fingers around it. It comes away with a terrible groan and behind it is a huge black door. He rubs his fingertips together and then goes through the keys methodically until he finds the one that opens the door.

'When was the last time anyone was in this house?' she asks.

'Gosh, I suppose a few years back now when something flooded. We had to get in with the emergency plumbers. Repair some damage. That sort of thing. Right, here we are.'

Lisa Jewell

They step into the hallway. The heat of outdoors, the hum of traffic, the echo of the river all fades away. It's cool in here. The floor is a soft dark parquet, scarred and dusty. A staircase ahead has a dark wood barley-twist banister, with an overflowing bowl of fruit carved into the top of the newel post. The doors are carved with linen folds and have ornate bronze handles. The walls are half panelled with more dark wood and papered with tatty wine-red flock wallpaper, which has vast bald patches where the moths have eaten it away. The air is dense and full of dust motes. The only light comes from the fanlights above each doorway.

Libby shudders. There's too much wood. Not enough light. Not enough air. She feels like she's in a coffin. 'Can I?' She puts her hand to one of the doors.

'You can do whatever you like. It's your house.'

The door opens up into a long rectangular room at the back of the house with four windows overlooking a dense tangle of trees and bushes. More wooden panelling. Wooden shutters. More parquet underfoot.

'Where does that go?' she asks Mr Royle pointing at a narrow door built into the panelling.

'That', he replies, 'is the door to the staff staircase. It leads directly to the smaller rooms on the attic floor, with another hidden door on the first-floor landing. Very normal in these old houses. Built like hamster cages.'

They explore the house room by room, floor by floor.

'What happened to all the furniture? All the fittings?' Libby asks.

'Long gone. The family sold everything to keep afloat. They all slept on mattresses. Made their own clothes.'

'So they were poor?'

'Yes,' he says. 'I suppose, in effect, they were poor.'

Libby nods. She hadn't imagined her birth parents as poor. Of course she had allowed herself to create fantasy birth parents. Even children who aren't adopted create fantasy birth parents. Her fantasy parents were young and gregarious. Their house by the river had two full walls of plate-glass windows and a wrap-around terrace. They had dogs, small ones, both girls, with diamonds on their collars. Her fantasy mother worked in fashion PR, her fantasy father was a graphic designer. When she was their baby they would take her for breakfast and put her in a high chair and break up brioches for her and play footsie with each other under the table where the small dogs lay curled together. They had died driving back from a cocktail party. Most probably in a crash involving a sports car.

'Was there anything else?' she says. 'Apart from the suicide note?'

Mr Royle shakes his head. 'Well, nothing official.

31

But there was one thing. When you were found. Something in your cot with you. I believe it's still here. In your nursery. Shall we . . . ?'

She follows Mr Royle into a big room on the first floor. Here there are two large sash windows overlooking the river; the air is stagnant and dense, the high corners of the room filled with thick curtains of cobweb and dust. There is an opening at the other end of the room and they turn the corner into a small room. It's fitted as a dressing room, three walls of wardrobes and drawers decorated with ornate beading and painted white. In the centre of the room is a cot.

'Is that . . . ?'

'Yes. That's where you were found. Gurgling and chirruping by all accounts, happy as Larry.'

The cot is a rocking design with metal levers for pushing back and forth. It is painted a thick buttermilk cream with a scattering of pale blue roses. There is a small metal badge on the front with the Harrods logo on it.

Mr Royle reaches for a shelf on the back wall and picks up a small box. 'Here,' he says, 'this was tucked away inside your blankets. We assumed, we all assumed, us and the police, that it was meant for you. The police held it as evidence for years then sent it back to us when the case ran dry.'

'What is it?'

'Open it and see.'

She takes the little cardboard box from him and pulls the flaps apart. It is filled with shreds of torn newspaper. Her fingers find something solid and silky. She brings it from the box and lets it dangle from between her fingertips. It's a rabbit's foot hanging from a gold chain. Libby recoils slightly and the chain slithers from her grasp and on to the wooden floor. She reaches down to pick it up.

Her fingers draw over the rabbit's foot, feeling the cold deathliness of its sleek fur, the sharp nibs of its claws. She runs the chain through her other hand. Her head, which a week ago had been filled with new sandals, a hen night, her split ends, the houseplants that needed watering, was now filled with people sleeping on mattresses and dead rabbits and a big, scary house, empty but for a large rocking crib from Harrods with strangely sinister pale blue roses painted on the sides. She puts the rabbit's foot back into the box and holds it, awkwardly. Then slowly she lowers her hand on to the mattress at the base of the crib, feels for the echo of her small, sleeping body, for the ghost of the person who last laid her down there, tucked her in safe with a blanket and a rabbit's foot. But there is nothing there of course. Just an empty bed, the smell of must.

'What was my name?' she says. 'Did anyone know?'

'Yes,' says Mr Royle. 'Your name was written on the note that your parents left behind. It was Serenity.'

'Serenity?'

'Yes,' he says. 'Pretty name. I think. If a little . . . bohemian?'

Suddenly she feels claustrophobic. She wants to run dramatically from the room, but it is not her way to be dramatic.

Instead she says, 'Can we see the garden now, please? I could do with some fresh air.'

5

Lucy turns off her phone. She needs to keep the charge in case Samia tries to get in touch. She turns to Marco, who is looking at her curiously.

'What?' she says.

'What was that message? On your phone?'

'What message?'

'I saw it. Just now. It said *The baby is twenty-five*. What does that mean?'

'It doesn't mean anything.'

'It must mean *something*.'

'It doesn't. It's just a friend's baby. Just a reminder that they turned twenty-five. I must send a card.'

'What friend?'

'A friend in England.'

'But you haven't got any friends in England.'

'Of course I have friends in England. I was brought up in England.'

'Well, what's her name?'

'Whose name?'

Marco roars with frustration. 'Your *friend's* name, of course.'

'What does it matter?' she replies sharply.

'It matters because you're my mum and I want to know stuff about you. I like, literally, don't know anything about you.'

'That's ridiculous. You know loads about me.'

He gazes at her wide-eyed and stupefied. 'Like *what*? I mean, I know your parents died when you were a baby. I know you grew up in London with your aunt and that she brought you to France and taught you to play the fiddle and died when you were eighteen. So I know, like, the *story* of you. But I don't know the details. Like where you went to school or who your friends were and what you did at the weekends or funny things that happened or anything normal.'

'It's complicated,' she says.

'I know it's complicated,' he says. 'But I'm twelve years old now and you can't treat me like a little baby any more. You have to tell me things.'

Lucy stares at her son. He's right. He's twelve and he is not interested in fairy stories any more. He knows there's more to life than five major events, that life is made up of all the moments in between.

She sighs. 'I can't,' she says. 'Not yet.'

'Then when?'

'Soon,' she says. 'If we ever get to London, I'll tell you everything.'

'Are we going?'

She sighs and pulls her hair away from her hairline. 'I just don't know. I've got no money. You and Stella don't have passports. The dog. It's all just . . .'

'Dad,' says Marco, cutting her off. 'Call Dad.'

'No way.'

'We can meet somewhere public. He wouldn't try anything then.'

'Marco. We don't even know where your father is.'

There is a strange silence. She can sense her son fidgeting edgily, burying his face into the dog's fur again.

'I do.'

She turns again, sharply, to look at him.

He closes his eyes, then opens them again. 'He collected me from school.'

'When!'

Marco shrugs. 'A couple of times. Towards the end of term.'

'And you didn't tell me?'

'He told me not to.'

'Fuck, Marco. Fuck.' She punches the ground with her fists. 'What happened? Where did he take you?'

'Nowhere. Just sort of walked with me.'

'And?'

'And what?'

'What did he say? What is he doing?'

'Nothing. Just on holiday. With his wife.'

'And where is he now?'

'Still here. He's here for the whole summer. In the house.'

'The house?'

'Yes.'

'God, Marco! Why didn't you tell me before?'

'Because I knew you'd go mental.'

'I'm not going mental. Look at me. Totally not mental. Totally just sitting here on the hard, wet ground under a flyover with nowhere to sleep while your father is a mile up the road living in the lap of luxury. Why would I go mental?'

'Sor-ry.' He tuts. 'You said you never wanted to see him again.'

'That was when I wasn't sleeping under a motorway.'

'So you *do* want to see him again?'

'I don't want to see *him*. But I need a way out of this mess. And he's the only option. At the very least he can pay to get my fiddle back.'

'Oh, yeah, cos then we'll be really rich, won't we?'

Lucy clenches her hands into fists. Her son always puts the unpalatable bottom line into words, then slaps her round the face with it.

'It's the middle of July. All the UK and German schools will be breaking up about now. There'll be twice as many tourists. It shouldn't take long to make enough to get to the UK.'

'Why can't you ask Dad to pay for us to go? Then we can just go. I really want to go to London. I want to get away from here. Just ask Dad to pay. Why can't you?'

'Because I don't want him to know we're going. No one can know we're going. Not even Mémé. OK?'

He nods. 'OK.'

His chin falls against his chest and she sees the clumps of matted hair that have formed at the back of his head in the week that they've been homeless. Her heart aches and she cups her hand around the back of his slender boy neck, squeezes it gently. 'I'm so sorry, my lovely boy,' she says, 'I'm so sorry about everything. Tomorrow we'll see your father and then everything will start getting better, I swear.'

'Yes,' he snaps, 'but nothing will ever be normal, will it?'

No, she thinks to herself. No. It probably won't.

6

Birdie came first. Birdie Dunlop-Evers.

My mother had met her somewhere or other. At a *do*. Birdie played the fiddle in a pop band called the Original Version and was, I suppose, vaguely famous. There'd been a jangly single that had almost got to number one and they'd been on *Top of the Pops* twice. Not that I cared much about such things. I never really liked pop music and the deification of celebrities slightly disgusts me.

She was sitting in our kitchen drinking tea out of one of our brown mugs. I jumped slightly when I saw her there. A woman with long thin hair down to her waist, men's trousers tied round with a belt, a striped shirt and braces, a long grey overcoat and green fingerless gloves. She looked so wrong in our house, I thought. The only people who came to our house wore hand-stitched suits and bias-cut satin; they smelled of Christian Dior aftershave and l'Air du Temps.

Birdie glanced up at me as I walked in, small blue eyes with thin pencil lines of eyebrow above, a hard mouth which didn't close quite properly over a row of small teeth, a rather weak chin that appeared to have buckled under the joylessness of her face. I thought she might smile, but she didn't.

'Henry,' said my mother, 'this is Birdie! The lady I was telling you about, from the pop group.'

'Hello,' I said.

'Hello,' she replied. I couldn't make sense of her. She sounded like my headmistress but looked like a tramp.

'Birdie's group want to use the house to film a pop video!' said my mother.

I admit, at this point I did have to feign disinterest somewhat. I held my features straight and said nothing, heading silently to the biscuit barrel on the counter for my daily back-from-school snack. I selected two Malted Milks and poured myself a glass of milk. Then and only then did I say, 'When?'

'Next week,' said Birdie. 'We had a location chosen, but they had a flood or some such disaster. *Bouf.* Cancelled.'

'So I said, come and look at our house, see what you think,' my mother continued.

'And here I am.'

'And here she is.'

I nodded casually. I wanted to ask when they were coming and could I take the day off school and could I help but I was not then, and never have been, a person to show enthusiasm for anything. So I dipped my Malted Milk biscuit in my milk, the exact way I always did, just to the T in 'Malted', where the end of the standing cow meets the end of the lying down cow, and ate it silently.

'I think it's brilliant,' said Birdie, gesturing around her. 'Better than the other place in fact. Just perfect. I think there'd be things to sign.' She rolled her eyes. 'You know, waivers, etc. In case we set fire to your house. Or one of your moose heads lands on one of us and kills us. That sort of thing.'

'Yes, yes,' said my mother as if she had to sign waivers for accidental moose-head fatalities all the time. 'That makes sense. And obviously I'd need to discuss it with my husband first. But I know he'll be happy. He loves your music.'

This I suspected was untrue. My father liked rugby songs and bawdy opera. But he did like fuss and attention and he did like his house and anyone who liked his house was always going to go down well with him.

Birdie left a few minutes later. I noticed a small pile of dry skin pickings on the table by her mug and felt a bit sick.

The shoot for the video lasted two days and was much more boring than I'd thought it would be. There was endless time spent finessing light readings and getting the scruffy band members to repeat actions over and over again. They were all dressed alike in brownish clothes that looked like they might smell, but didn't because a lady with a clothes rail had brought them along in clear plastic bags. By the end of the day the song was embedded inside my head like a trapped fly. It was a terrible song but it went to number one and stayed there for nine long, dreadful weeks. The video was on every TV screen you passed, *our house*, there, on view to millions.

It was a good video. I'll give it that. And I got a minor thrill from telling people that it was my house in the video. But the thrill faded as the weeks passed, because long after the film crew had left, long after the single had dropped out of the charts, long after their next single dropped out of the charts, Birdie Dunlop-Evers, with her bead eyes and her tiny teeth, was still in our house.

7

Libby works for an expensive kitchen design company. She's head of sales, based in a showroom in the centre of St Albans, near to the cathedral. She has two sales managers and two assistant sales managers beneath her and an assistant sales director, a senior sales director and a managing director above her. She's halfway up the ladder, the ladder that has been the focus of her existence for the past five years. In her head Libby has been building a bridge towards a life that will begin when she is thirty. When she is thirty she will be the director of sales and if she is not then she will go elsewhere for a promotion. Then she will marry the man whom she is currently trying to find both online and in real life, the man with the smile lines and the dog and/or cat, the man with an interesting surname that she can double-barrel with Jones, the man who earns the same as or more than her, the man who likes hugs more than sex and has nice shoes and beautiful skin and no tattoos and a lovely mum and attractive feet. The man who is at least five feet ten, but preferably five feet eleven or over. The man who has no baggage and a good car and a suggestion of abdominal definition although a flat stomach would suffice.

This man has yet to materialise and Libby is aware that she is possibly a little over proscriptive. But she has five years to find him and marry him and then another five years to have a baby, maybe two if she likes the first one. She's not in a rush. Not yet. She'll just keep swiping left, keep looking nice when she goes out, keep accepting invitations to social events, keep positive, keep slim, keep herself together, keep going.

It's still hot when Libby gets up for work and there's a kind of pearlescent shimmer in the air even at eight in the morning.

She'd slept all night with the bedroom window open even though she knew women were advised not to. She'd arranged glasses in a row along her windowsill so that if a man did break in at least she would have some warning. But still she'd tossed and turned all night, the sheets twisted and cloying beneath her body.

The sun had woken her up from a brief slumber,

laser bright through a tiny gap in her curtains, heating the room up again in minutes. For a moment everything had felt normal. And then it hadn't. Her thoughts switched violently to yesterday. To the dark house and the linen-fold panels, the secret staircase, the rabbit's foot, the pale blue roses on the side of the crib. Had that really happened? Was that house still there or had it turned to particles in her wake?

She's the second to arrive at work that morning. Dido, the head designer, is already behind her desk and has got the air conditioner running. The iced air feels exquisite against her clammy skin, but she knows in half an hour she'll be freezing and wishing she'd brought a cardigan.

'Good morning,' says Dido, not looking up from her keyboard. 'How did it go?'

She'd told Dido yesterday in confidence that she needed the day off to visit a solicitor about an inheritance. She didn't tell her about being adopted or the possibility of the inheritance being a house. She'd said it was an elderly relative and suggested that she might be in line for a few hundred pounds. Dido had got very excited about the possibility of a few hundred pounds and at the time Libby wasn't sure she'd be able to face her reaction if she told her the truth. But now that she's here, and it's just the two of them and it's Tuesday morning and she won't be seeing her best friend April until the weekend and she hasn't really got anyone else she can tell, she decides maybe it would be good to share, that maybe Dido, who is twelve years older than her, will have something wise or useful to impart to help her make sense of the whole ridiculous thing.

'I've inherited a house,' Libby says, running water into the Nespresso machine.

'Ha ha,' says Dido, clearly not believing her.

'No. I have. It's in Chelsea, by the river.'

'Chelsea, London?' says Dido, her mouth hanging open.

'Yes.'

'As in *Made In*?'

'Yes,' Libby says again. 'By the river. It's huge.'

'Are you winding me up?'

She shakes her head. 'No,' she says.

'Oh my God,' says Dido. 'So you're basically a millionaire?'

'I guess.'

'And yet here you are, at Northbone Kitchens on a Tuesday morning, acting like a normal person.'

'I'm letting it sink in.'

'God, Libby, if I were you I would be letting it sink in right now drinking champagne in the garden at St Michael's Manor.'

'It's twenty to nine.'

47

'Well, tea then. And Eggs Benedict. What on earth are you doing here?'

Libby feels her seams loosen and begin to come apart at the thought that she need not be here, that the sturdy ladder she's been gripping on to for dear life has just dissolved into a heap of golden coins, that everything has changed.

'I only found out yesterday! I haven't sold it yet,' she says. 'I might not be able to.'

'Yeah, right, because nobody wants a house in Chelsea overlooking the Thames.'

Roughly six or seven million pounds. That was the estimate that the solicitor had given her yesterday when she'd finally got up the nerve to ask. Minus, he'd said, expenses and fees owed to the firm. And then there would be inheritance taxes to pay. You'll end up with about three and half million, he'd said. Or thereabouts.

He'd given her a high five. Confused her with a young person like the ones he read about in the newspapers. It had been quite disconcerting.

'It's in a bad state,' Libby says, now. 'And it has a history.'

'History?'

'Yes. Some people died there. A bit shady. Distant relatives.' She was about to mention the baby left behind in the cot but stopped.

'No way!'

'Yeah. All a bit shocking. So for now I'm just going to act like everything's normal.'

'You're going to keep on selling kitchens? In St Albans?'

'Yes,' says Libby, feeling her equilibrium start to re-balance itself at the thought of nothing changing. 'I'm going to keep on selling kitchens in St Albans.'

8

Marco and Lucy spent the night on the beach in the end. The rain had stopped at about 2 a.m. and they'd gathered their things and walked the twenty minutes across town to the Promenade des Anglais where they'd unrolled their yoga mats on the wet pebbles, tucked themselves under sarongs and watched shreds of spent grey rain clouds chase each other across a big pink moon until the sun started to leak through the line between the sea and the sky.

At eight o'clock Lucy collected together all the cents from the bottom of her rucksack and the bottom of her purse and found she had enough to buy croissants and a coffee. They ate them on a bench, both stultified by lack of sleep and the awfulness of the night before.

The Family Upstairs

Then they'd walked back across town to Samia's flat to collect Stella, and Samia had not invited them in for lunch despite the fact that it was midday and they had clearly not slept in beds. Stella had been bathed and redressed in clean clothes, her soft curls brushed out and pinned back with pink fluffy clips and, as they walked back across town yet again, Lucy pondered that it probably looked like she and Marco had kidnapped her.

'I can keep her for another night,' Samia had said, her hand on Stella's shoulder. Lucy had seen Stella shrug against Samia's hand, almost imperceptibly, a tiny shake of her head.

'That's kind of you, but I've found us somewhere to sleep tonight.' She'd felt Marco's eyes burning into her shoulder at her lie. 'But I am so, so grateful to you. Really.'

Samia had tilted her head slightly and narrowed her eyes, processing some silent account of Lucy's situation. Lucy had held her breath, awaiting some damning pronouncement on her appearance, her parenting, the part she'd played in Samia's precious son's moonlight flit. Instead Samia had moved slowly towards the table halfway up the hallway and pulled a small purse from her shoulder bag. She'd peered into the purse and pulled out a twenty-euro note which she passed to Lucy.

'It's all I have,' she'd said. 'There is no more.'

Lucy had taken it and then leaned into Samia and hugged her. 'Thank you,' she'd said. 'God bless you.'

Now she and the children and the dog are walking along the Promenade des Anglais in the burning afternoon sun with a bag full of clean clothes from the laundromat and bellies full of bread and cheese and Coca-Cola. They head towards one of the many beach clubs that line the beaches here in Nice: le Beach Club Bleu et Blanc.

Lucy has eaten here, in the past. She has sat at these tables with Marco's dad, worked her way through piles of fruits de mer, a glass of champagne at her elbow or a white wine spritzer, whilst being cooled by intermittent puffs of chilled water squirted from tiny nozzles. They wouldn't recognise her now, those jaded old waiters in their incongruously trendy blue and white polo shirts. She'd been a sight for sore eyes twelve years ago.

A woman sits on a perch at the entrance to the restaurant. She is blonde in that way that only women in the south of France can be blonde, something to do with the contrast between vanilla hair and darkly toasted skin. She glances at Lucy, indifferently, taking in the state of Lucy and Marco and the dog, before returning her gaze to her computer screen. Lucy pretends that she is waiting for someone to join her from the beach, cupping her eyes with her hand and peering towards the horizon until the woman is distracted by a party of five people arriving for lunch.

'Now,' she hisses, 'now.'

She collects the dog into her arms and pushes Stella ahead of her. Her heart races as she strides as nonchalantly as she can down the wooden platform that runs behind the restaurant towards the shower block. She looks straight ahead. 'Keep moving,' she hisses at Stella as she stops, inexplicably, halfway down. Then finally they are there, in the dank, humid gloom of the shower block.

'Reserved exclusively for the use of patrons of le Beach Club Bleu et Blanc', say numerous signs nailed to the wooden walls. The concrete floor is sandy and damp underfoot; the air is fusty. Lucy guides Stella to the right. If they can get through the wooden saloon doors to the showers without being spotted, then they will be fine.

And then they are in. The showers are empty. She and Marco strip off their clothes for the first time in nearly eight days. She finds a bin for her knickers. She never wants to wear them again. She pulls shampoo and conditioner from her rucksack, a bar of soap, a towel. She takes the dog in with her, massages shampoo all through his fur, under his tail, under his collar, behind his ears. He stands steady and still, almost as though he knows that this is needed. Then she passes him to Stella who is waiting outside. He shakes himself off and Stella giggles as she is splattered with droplets from his fur. And then Lucy stands under the flow of warm water and lets it run over her head, into her eyes and ears, under her arms, between her legs and toes, feels the hell of the past week start to dissolve along with the dust and the mud and the salt. She shampoos her hair, pulling her fingers through the length of it until it squeaks. Then she passes the bottle under the stall to Marco. She watches their combined suds meeting in the gap between them, the sad, grey tinge of it.

'Really get into the hair at the back of your neck, Marco,' she says. 'It's all clumpy there. And armpits. Really do your armpits.'

After, they sit side by side on a wooden bench, wrapped in towels. They can see people passing by on the other side through gaps in the wood, see slices of shimmering blue sky, smell sun-warmed wood and fried garlic. Lucy sighs. She feels unburdened, almost, but still not quite ready to do the next thing.

They put on clean clothes and deodorant and Lucy rubs moisturiser into her face and gives the children sun cream for theirs. She has a small bottle of perfume in the bottom of her toiletry bag which she sprays behind her ears and into her cleavage. She twists her damp hair into a roll at the back of her head and clips it with a plastic claw. She looks at herself in the mirror. Nearly forty years old. Homeless. Single. Penniless. Not even who she says she is. Even her name is fake. She is a ghost. A living, breathing ghost.

She puts on some mascara, some lip gloss, adjusts the pendant of her golden necklace so that it sits in her sun-burnished cleavage. She looks at her children: they are beautiful. The dog looks nice. Everyone smells good. They have eaten. This is as good as things have been in days.

'Right,' she says to Marco, shoving her dirty clothes back into her rucksack and pulling it closed. 'Let's go and see your dad.'

9

CHELSEA, 1988

I'd been watching from the stairs, so I already knew. A man with dark curls, a hat with a brim, a donkey jacket, tweed trousers tucked into big lace-up boots. Old suitcases that looked like props from an olden-days movie and a wickerwork cat box held together with a worn leather strap. And Birdie standing by his side, in a dress that looked like a nightie.

'Darling!' I heard my mother call out to my father. 'Come and meet Justin!'

I watched my father appear from the drawing room. He had a cigar clenched between his teeth and was wearing a hairy green jumper.

'So,' he said, squeezing the man's hand too hard, 'you're Birdie's boyfriend?'

'Partner,' Birdie interjected. 'Justin is my partner.'

My father looked at her in that way he had when he thought someone was deliberately making him look a fool, as though he was considering violence. But the look passed quickly and I saw him push through it with a smile. 'Yes,' he said. 'Of course. That's the modern way, isn't it?'

Birdie had told my mother that she and her *partner* needed somewhere to stay for a few days. Their landlord had kicked them out because they'd got a cat – what sort of idiot gets a cat without checking the terms of their lease? I was not even eleven years old and had never lived in a rental and I knew that much – and Birdie hadn't known whom else to turn to. As an adult man now of forty-one years old I have often used this refrain to get people to do what I want them to do. *I didn't know who else to turn to.* It gives the person you're trying to manipulate nowhere to go. Their only option is to capitulate. Which is exactly what my mother had done.

'But we have so many rooms,' she'd said when I complained about the upcoming arrangement. 'And it's only for a few days.'

My mother, in my opinion, just wanted a pop star living in her house.

My sister passed me on the stairs and stopped with a small intake of breath when she saw the cat basket in the hall. 'What's it called?' she said, dropping to her knees to peer through the grille.

'It's a girl. She's called Suki,' said Birdie.

'Suki,' she said, tucking the knuckles of her fingers between the bars. The cat pushed itself against her hand and purred loudly.

The man called Justin picked up his stage prop suitcase and said, 'Where shall we put our things, Martina?'

'We've got a lovely room for you at the top of the house. Children, show our guests to the yellow room, will you?'

My sister led the way. She was by far the more gregarious of the two of us. I found grown-ups relatively terrifying whereas she seemed to quite like them. She was wearing green pyjamas. I was wearing a tartan dressing gown and blue felt slippers. It was nearly nine and we'd been on a countdown to bedtime.

'Oh,' said Birdie as my sister pushed open the hidden door in the wood panelling that led to the stairs to the top floor. 'Where on earth are you taking us?'

'It's the back stairs,' my sister said. 'To the yellow room.'

'You mean the servants' entrance?' Birdie replied sniffily.

'Yes,' my sister replied brightly because although she was only a year and a half younger than me she was too young to understand that not everyone thought sleeping in secret rooms at the top of secret staircases was an adventure; that some people might think they deserved proper big bedrooms and would be offended.

At the top of the secret staircase there was a wooden door leading to a long thin corridor where the walls were sort of wonky and lumpy and the floorboards warped and bouncy and it felt a bit like walking along a moving train. The yellow room was the nicest of the four up there. It had three windows in the ceiling and a big bed with a yellow duvet cover to match the yellow Laura Ashley wallpaper and modern table lamps with blue glass shades. Our mother had arranged yellow and red tulips in a vase. I watched Birdie's face as she took it all in, a sort of grudging tilt of her chin as if to say: I suppose it will do.

We left them there, and I followed behind my sister as she skipped down the stairs, through the drawing room and into the kitchen.

Dad was uncorking wine. Mum was wearing her frilled apron and tossing a salad. 'How long are those people staying for?' I couldn't help blurting out. I saw a shadow pass across my father's face at the note of impudence I'd failed to mask.

'Oh. Not for long.' My mother pushed the cork back into a bottle of red wine vinegar and placed it to one side, smiling benignly.

'Can we stay up?' my sister asked, not looking at the bigger picture, not looking beyond the nose on her face.

'Not tonight,' my mother replied. 'Tomorrow maybe, when it's the weekend.'

'And then, will they go?' I asked, very gently nudging the line between me and my father's patience with me. 'After the weekend?'

I turned then as I sensed my mother's gaze drift across my shoulder. Birdie was standing in the doorway with the cat in her arms. It was brown and white with a face like an Egyptian queen. Birdie looked at me and said, 'We shan't be staying long, little boy. Just until Justin and I have found a place of our own.'

'My name is Henry,' I said, hugely taken aback that a grown-up in my own home had just called me 'little boy'.

'Henry,' repeated Birdie, looking at me sharply. 'Yes, of course.'

My sister was staring greedily at the cat and Birdie said, 'Would you like to hold her?'

She nodded and the cat was placed into her arms where it immediately twisted itself round 180 degrees like a piece of unfurled elastic and escaped leaving her with a terrible red scratch on the inside of her arm. I saw her eyes fill with tears and her mouth twist into a brave smile.

'It's OK,' she said, as my mother fussed over her, dabbing at her arm with a wet cloth.

'Henry, fetch some Germolene, will you, from my bathroom cupboard.'

I threw Birdie a look as I passed, wanting her to see that I knew she hadn't taken enough care passing the cat to my sister. She looked back at me, her eyes so small I could barely make out their colour.

I was a strange boy. I can see that now. I've since met boys like me: slow to smile, intense, guarded and watchful. I suspect that Birdie had probably been a very strange little girl. Maybe she recognised herself in me. But I could tell she hated me, even then. It was obvious. And it was very much mutual.

I passed Justin as I crossed the hallway. He was holding a battered box of Black Magic and looking lost. 'Your parents that way?' he asked, pointing in the general direction of the kitchen.

'Yes,' I said. 'In the kitchen. Through that arch.'

'Merci beaucoup,' he said, and although I was only ten I was old enough to know that he was being pretentious.

We were sent to bed shortly after that, my sister with a plaster on the inside of her arm, me with the beginnings of an upset stomach. I was one of those children: my emotions made themselves felt in my gut.

I could hear them shuffling about upstairs later that

night. I put a pillow over my head and went back to sleep.

The Black Magic sat unopened on the kitchen table the next morning, when I came down extra early. I was tempted to unpeel the cellophane and open them. A small act of rebellion that would have made me feel better in the short term but way, way worse in the long. I felt a movement behind me and saw the cat squeezing through the door behind me. I thought about the scratch on my sister's arm and remembered Birdie's impatient tut: 'It was an accident, she wasn't holding her properly, Suki would never scratch on purpose.'

A bubble of hot red anger passed right through me at the memory and I hissed loudly at the cat and chased it out of the room.

It was almost a relief to go to school that day, to feel normal for a few hours. I'd just started my last term of primary school. I would turn eleven the following month, one of the youngest boys in my year, and then I would be moved on to a bigger school, closer to home, with no knickerbockers. I was very fixated on it at this point. I had very much outgrown the knickerbocker school and all the children I'd grown up with. I could tell I was different. Completely different. There was no one like me there and I had fantasies about going to the big school and finding myself surrounded by people like me. Everything would be better at the big school. I just had ten weeks to get through, then a long boring summer, and then it would all begin.

I had no idea, none whatsoever, how different the landscape of my life would look by the end of that summer and how all the things I'd been waiting for would soon feel like distant dreams.

10

Libby sits at her kitchen table. Her back door is open on to her courtyard, which is overcast in the late afternoon sun, but still too humid to sit in. She has a Diet Coke poured into a tumbler full of ice to hand and is barefooted, her sandals cast aside moments after walking into her flat. She flips open the lid of her rose-gold laptop and brings up her Chrome browser. She is almost surprised to see that the last thing she'd browsed, four days ago, before the letter had arrived and upturned everything, was local classes in salsa dancing. She can barely imagine what she'd been thinking. Something to do with meeting men, she supposes.

She opens up a new tab and slowly, nervously, types in the words *Martina and Henry Lamb*.

She immediately finds a link to an article in the *Guardian* from 2015. She clicks it. The article is called: 'The Mysterious Case of Serenity Lamb and the Rabbit's Foot'.

Serenity Lamb, she thinks, that was me, that *is* me. I am Serenity Lamb. I am also Libby Jones. Libby Jones sells kitchens in St Albans and wants to go salsa dancing. Serenity Lamb lies in a painted cot in a wood-panelled room in Chelsea with a rabbit's foot tucked inside her blanket.

She finds it hard to locate the overlap, the point at which one becomes the other. When her adoptive mother first held her in her arms, she imagines. But she wasn't sentient then. She wasn't aware of the transition from Serenity to Libby, the silent twisting and untwisting of the filaments of her identity.

She takes a sip of her Coke and starts to read.

11

The house in Antibes is the colour of dead roses: a dusty, muted red, with shutters painted bright blue. It is the house where Lucy once lived, a lifetime ago, when she was married to Marco's father. Ten years after their divorce she can still barely bring herself to use his name. The feel of it on her tongue, on her lips, makes her feel nauseous. But here she stands, outside his house, and his name is Michael. Michael Rimmer.

There is a red Maserati parked on the driveway, leased no doubt as Michael is many things but *as rich as he thinks he should be* is not one of them. She sees Marco's gaze hover intently on the car. She can see the naked desire written on his features, his held breath, his awe.

'It's not his,' she mutters, 'he's just renting it.'

'How do you know?'

'I just do, all right?'

She squeezes Stella's hand reassuringly. Stella has never met Marco's father before, but she knows full well how Lucy feels about him. They approach the door and Lucy presses the brass bell. A maid comes to the door, wearing white overalls and latex gloves. She smiles. *'Bonjour, madame,'* she says.

'Is Mr Rimmer at home?' asks Lucy, using her best and clearest English accent.

'Oui,' says the maid. 'Yes. He is in the garden. Wait one minute.' She pulls a small black Nokia from the pocket of her overalls, pulls off one of her latex gloves and dials a number. She glances up at her. 'Who shall I say is here?'

'Lucy,' she says. 'And Marco.'

'Sir, Mr Rimmer, there is a lady here called Lucy. And a boy called Marco.' She nods. 'OK. Yes. OK. OK.' She hangs up and slips the phone back into her pocket. 'Mr Rimmer says to bring you to him. Come.'

Lucy follows the tiny woman through the hallway. She averts her gaze as she walks, away from the spot at the foot of the stone staircase where she'd ended up with a broken arm and a fractured rib when Michael pushed her when she was four months pregnant with Marco. She averts it from the spot on the wall in the corridor where Michael banged her head repeatedly because he'd had a bad day at work – or so he explained an hour later when he was trying to stop her from leaving because he loved her so much, because he *couldn't live without her*. Oh, the irony. Because here he is, married to someone else and utterly and entirely alive.

Lucy's hands shake as they near the back entrance, the one she knows so well, the vast wooden double doors that swing open into the tropical splendour of the garden, where hummingbird moths sip from horn-shaped flowers and banana trees grow in shady corners, where a small waterfall trickles through a flowery rockery and a sparkling rectangle of azure-blue water sits in the southernmost point, basking in the afternoon sun. And there he is. There is Michael Rimmer. Sitting at a table by the pool, a wireless headpiece in one ear, a laptop open in front of him and two phones, a small bottle of beer belying the hectic business-guy act he's clearly portraying.

'Lucy!' he says, beaming, getting to his feet, sucking in his tanned stomach, trying to cover up the fact that at forty-eight he no longer has the gym-sculpted physique of the thirty-eight-year-old man she'd escaped from ten years earlier. He pulls the earpiece from his ear and heads towards her. 'Lucy!' he says again, with added warmth, his arms outstretched.

Lucy recoils.

'Michael,' she responds circumspectly, moving away from him.

He takes his outstretched arms to Marco instead and gives him a bear hug. 'So you told her then?'

Marco nods.

Michael gives him a mock-withering look.

'And who is this?' says Michael, turning his attention to Stella who is clinging to Lucy's leg.

'This is Stella,' says Lucy. 'My daughter.'

'Wow,' says Michael. 'What a beautiful little girl. Lovely to meet you, Stella.' He offers his hand for her to shake and Lucy resists the temptation to pull Stella from its path.

'And this is?' He peers down at the dog.

'This is Fitzgerald. Or Fitz for short.'

'For F. Scott?'

'Yes, for F. Scott.' She feels the small shot of adrenaline: the memory of the question-and-answer sessions he'd once subjected her to, to show her that she was stupid and uneducated, unworthy of him, lucky to have him. But there had always been something small and hard and certain at her very core reminding her that he was wrong, reminding her that one day she would find her escape and that once she did she would never ever look back. And now here she is nervously answering his questions, about to ask him for money, almost back where she started.

'Well, hello, Fitz,' he says, scruffing the dog under his chin. 'Aren't you a cute little guy.' Then he stands back and appraises Lucy and her little family. It's the same way he used to appraise Lucy when he was considering the possibility of punishing her. That knife edge of time that could end with a laugh and a hug or could end with a broken finger or a Chinese burn.

'Well, well, well,' he says, 'look at you all. You are all just adorable. Can I get you anything? Some juice?' He looks at Lucy. 'Are they allowed juice?'

She nods and Michael looks up at the maid who is hanging behind in the shade of the terrace at the back of the house. 'Joy! Some juice for the children! Thank you! And you, Lucy? Wine? Beer?'

Lucy hasn't had a drink for weeks. She would die for a beer. But she can't. She has to keep all her wits about her for the next half an hour or so. She shakes her head. 'No, thank you. Juice would be fine for me too.'

'Three juices, Joy. Thank you. And I'll have another beer. Oh, and some potato chips. Those, erm what are they called, you know, with the ridges? Great.'

He turns his gaze back to Lucy, still playing it wide-eyed and boyish. 'Sit down, sit down.'

He rearranges the chairs, they sit. 'So,' he says, 'Lucy Lou, how the hell have you been?'

She shrugs and smiles. 'You know. Getting on with it. Getting older. Getting wiser.'

'And you've been out here, all this time?'

'Yup.'

'Never went back to the UK?'

'Nope.'

'And your daughter . . . her father? Are you married?'

'Nope,' she says again. 'We lived together for a couple of years. Then he went back to Algeria to "visit family" about three years ago and we haven't heard from him since.'

Michael winces as though Stella's dad's disappearance was a physical assault upon her. Too ironic to bear. 'Tough,' he says. 'That's tough. So you're a single mom?'

'Yes. I am. Very much so.'

Joy returns with a tray laid with a carafe of chilled orange juice, three glasses on paper coasters, crisps in small silver bowls, tiny paper napkins, straws. Michael pours the juice and passes the glasses to each of them, offers them the ridged crisps. The children pounce on them eagerly.

'Slow down,' she hisses.

'It's fine,' says Michael. 'I have packets and packets of the things. So, where are you living?'

'Here and there.'

'And are you still . . . ?' He mimes playing the fiddle.

She smiles wryly. 'Well, I was. Yes. Until some drunk English dick on a stag night decided to snatch it off me and then made me chase him and his mates around for half an hour trying to get it back before tossing it over a wall. Now it's being repaired. Or at least, it has been repaired. But . . .' The insides of her mouth are dry with dread. 'I don't have the money to pay to collect it.'

He throws her his *oh, poor baby* look, the one he used to give her after he'd hurt her.

'How much?' he says, and he's already twisting in his seat to locate his wallet in his back pocket.

'A hundred and ten euros,' she says, her voice catching slightly.

She watches him peeling off the notes. He folds them in half and passes them to her. 'There,' he says. 'And a little extra. Maybe for a haircut for my boy.' He scruffs Marco's hair again. 'And maybe you too.' And it's there, when he glances at her hair, that terrible dark look of disappointment. *You've let yourself go. You're not trying hard enough. How can I love you when. You. Don't. Make. Any. Fucking. Effort.*

She takes the folded notes from his hand and feels the almost imperceptible tug as he grips them a little tighter, the hint of a nasty game of control and power. He smiles and loosens his grip. She puts the notes in her shoulder bag and says, 'Thank you. I'm very grateful. I'll get it back to you in a couple of weeks. I promise.'

'No,' he says, leaning back, spreading his legs a little, smiling darkly. 'I don't want it back. But . . .'

A trickle of coldness runs down Lucy's spine.

'Promise me one thing.'

Her smile freezes.

'I'd love to see you. I mean, more of you. You and Marco. And you too of course.' He switches his grim gaze to Stella, winking at her. 'I'm here all summer. Until mid-September. Between jobs. You know.'

'And your wife, is she . . . ?'

'Rachel had to go back. She has *important business to attend to in the UK*.' He says this in a dismissive tone of voice. Rachel could be a brain surgeon or a politician for all Lucy knows, she might hold the lives of hundreds, thousands in her hands. But as far as Michael is concerned, anything that distracts a woman's attention away from him for even a moment is some kind of pathetic joke. Including babies.

'Oh,' she says. 'That's a shame.'

'Not really,' he says. 'I needed some space. Because guess what I'm doing . . . ?'

Lucy shakes her head briskly, and smiles.

'I am writing a book. Or in fact, *a memoir*. Or possibly a blend of the two. A semi-autobiographical kind of thing. I don't know yet.'

God, he looks so pleased with himself, Lucy thinks, like he wants her to say, Oh wow, Michael, that's amazing, you are so clever. Instead she wants to laugh in his face and say, Ha, you, writing a book? Are you serious?

'That's great,' she says. 'How exciting.'

'Should be, yes. Although quite a bit of downtime too, I shouldn't wonder. So it would be just great to see more of you guys. Hang out a bit. Make some use of the pool.'

Lucy's gaze follows his, towards the pool. She feels her breath catch hard, her lungs expand then shrink, her heart pound at the memory of her head under that perfect teal water, the pressure of his hands on her crown. Pushing her. Pushing her until her lungs nearly exploded. Then suddenly letting her bob to the top, choking, rasping, while he pulled himself from the pool, snatched a towel from a sun lounger, wrapped it around himself and strode back into the house without a backward glance.

'I could have killed you,' he said about it afterwards. 'If I'd wanted. You know that, don't you? I could have killed you.'

'Why didn't you?' she'd asked.

'Because I couldn't be bothered.'

'Well,' she says now, 'maybe. Though we're pretty busy ourselves this summer.'

'Yes,' he says patronisingly. 'I'm sure you are.'

'You know,' she says, turning to look at the house, 'I always thought you must have sold this place. I've seen other people living here over the years.'

'Holiday let,' he says. And she can hear the shame in his voice, the idea of shiny, incredible, successful, wealthy Michael Rimmer having to stoop so low as to rent out his Antibes holiday home to strangers. 'Seemed a shame' – he rallies – 'to have it sitting empty all the time. When other people could be enjoying it.'

She nods. Lets him hold on to his pathetic little lie. He hates 'other people'. He will have had the place disinfected from top to bottom before he could have faced returning.

'Well,' she says, turning to smile at the children, 'I think it's probably time for us to hit the road.'

'No,' says Michael. 'Stay a while! Why not? I can open a bottle of something. The kids can splash in the pool. It'll be fun.'

'The music shop will be shutting soon,' she says, trying not to sound nervous. 'I really need to pick up my fiddle now, so I can work tonight. But thank you. Thank you so much. What do you say, children?'

They say thank you and Michael beams at them. 'Beautiful kids,' he says, 'really beautiful.'

He sees them to the front door. He looks like he wants to hug Lucy and she rapidly drops to her knees to rearrange the dog's collar. Michael watches them from the doorway, across the bonnet of his ridiculous car, a smile still playing on his lips.

For a moment Lucy thinks she is going to be sick. She stops and breathes in hard. And then, as they are about to turn the corner, the dog suddenly squats and produces a small pile of crap up against the wall of Michael's house, right in the path of the afternoon sun. Lucy reaches into her bag for a plastic bag to pick it up with. Then she stops. In an hour the shit will be baked and bubbling like a brie. It will be the first thing he sees next time he leaves his house. He might even step in it.

She leaves it there.

12

Libby was supposed to be going to a friend's barbecue on Saturday. She'd been looking forward to it. Her friend, April, had told her she was inviting a 'fit bloke from work. I think you'll really like him. He's called Danny.'

But as Saturday dawns, another hot day with a sky full of nothing but blue, the windowpanes already red hot beneath her hand as she pushes them open, Libby has no thoughts of hot Danny or of April's famous spicy couscous salad or of a glowing orange globe of Aperol Spritz in her hand and her feet in a rubber paddling pool. She has no thoughts of anything other than the mysterious case of Serenity Lamb and the rabbit's foot.

She texts April.

I'm so so so so sorry. Have an amazing day. Let me know if you're still going strong this evening and I'll pop in for a sundowner.

Then she showers and puts on a tropical-print playsuit and open sandals made of gold leather, rubs sun cream into her arms and shoulders, sits her sunglasses on her head, checks her bag for the door keys to the house, and gets the train into London.

Libby puts the key into the padlock on the wooden hoarding and turns it. The padlock slides open and she puts another key into the front door. She half expects a hand on her shoulder, someone to ask her what she's doing, if she has permission to open this door with these keys.

Then she is in the house. Her house. And she is alone.

She closes the door behind her and the sound of the morning traffic dies away immediately; the burn on her neck cools.

For a moment she stands entirely still.

She pictures the police here, where she stands. They are wearing old-fashioned helmets. She knows what they look like because there were pictures of them in the *Guardian* article. PCs Ali Shah and John Robbin. They were following up on an anonymous call to the station from a 'concerned neighbour'. The concerned neighbour had never been traced.

She follows Shah and Robbin's vanished footsteps into the kitchen. She imagines the smell growing stronger now.

PC Shah recalled the sound of flies. He said he thought someone had left a pair of clippers running, or an electric toothbrush. The bodies, they said, were in the very earliest stages of decay, still recognisable as an attractive, dark-haired, thirty-something woman and an older man with salt and pepper hair. Their hands were linked. Next to them lay the corpse of another man. Fortyish. Tall. Dark hair. They all wore black: the woman a tunic and leggings, the men a kind of robe. The items, it transpired, had been homemade. They'd later found a sewing machine in the back room, remnants of black fabric in a bin.

Apart from the buzzing flies, the house was deathly quiet. The police said they wouldn't have thought to look for a baby if it hadn't been for the mention of her on the note left on the dining table. They'd almost missed the dressing room off the master bedroom, but then they'd heard a noise, an 'ooh', PC Shah had said.

An 'ooh'.

Libby steps slowly up the staircase and into the bedroom. She peers around the corner of the door into the dressing room.

And there she'd been! Bonny as anything! That's what PC Robbin had said. *Bonny as anything!*

Her flesh crawls slightly at the sight of the painted crib. But she breaks through the discomfort and stares at the crib until she is desensitised. After a moment she feels neutral enough to lay a hand upon it. She pictures the two young policemen, peering over the top of the crib. She imagines herself, in her pure white Babygro, her hair already a full helmet of Shirley Temple curls even at only ten months old, her feet kicking up and down with excitement at the sight of the two friendly faces staring down at her.

'She tried to stand up,' said Robbin. 'She was pulling up at the sides of the cot. Desperate to be taken out. We didn't know what to do. She was evidence. Should we touch her? Should we call for back-up? We were flummoxed.'

Apparently, they'd decided not to pick her up. PC Shah sang songs to her while they waited to hear what they should do. Libby wished she could remember it; what songs had he sung to her, this kind young policeman? Had he enjoyed singing her the songs? Had he felt embarrassed? According to the article, he'd gone on to have five children of his own, but when he found Serenity Lamb in her crib, he'd had no experience of babies.

A crime scene team soon arrived in the house, including a special officer to collect the baby. Her name was Felicity Measures. She was forty-one at the time.

Now she is sixty-five and newly retired, living in the Algarve with her third husband. 'She was the dearest baby,' the article quoted her. 'Golden curls, well fed and cared for. Very smiley and cuddly. Incongruous given the setting in which she'd been left. Which was gothic, really. Yes, it was quite, quite gothic.'

Libby pushes the cot and it creaks pathetically, evidencing its great age. Who was it bought for? she wonders. Was it bought for her? Or for generations of babies before her? Because she now knows there are other players in the story of her. Not just Martina and Henry Lamb, and the mystery man. Not just the missing children. Neighbours had spoken of not two, but 'numerous' children, of other people 'coming and going'. The house was filled with untraceable bloodstains and DNA, with fibres and dropped hairs and strange notes and scribbles on walls and secret panels and a garden full of medicinal herbs, some of which had been used in her parents' apparent suicide pact.

'We are setting ourselves free from these broken bodies, from this despicable world, from pain and disappointment. Our baby is called Serenity Lamb. She is ten months old. Please make sure she goes to nice people. Peace, always, HL, ML, DT', the note by their decaying bodies had said.

Libby leaves the room and slowly wanders the house, seeking out some of the strange things found in the aftermath of the deaths. Whoever else had been in the house the night of the suicides had run, the article said, leaving wardrobe doors flung open, food in the fridge, half-read books open on the floor, pieces of paper torn from walls leaving behind their Sellotaped corners.

She finds one of these strips of Sellotape on the wall in the kitchen, yellowed and crisp. She tugs the small shred of paper from it and stares at it for a moment in the palm of her hand. What had been on the piece of paper that the people fleeing this sinking ship had not wanted other eyes to see?

There is a fridge in the country-style kitchen, a huge rusting American-style fridge, cream and beige, probably quite unusual in the UK in the eighties, she imagines. She pulls it open and peers inside. Speckles of mould, a pair of cracked and broken plastic ice trays, nothing more. In the kitchen cupboards she finds empty enamelled tins, a packet of flour so old that it has turned to a brick. There is a set of white teacups, a chrome tea-pot, ancient pots of herbs and spices, a toast rack, a large tray, painted black. She scratches at the black paint to reveal the silver beneath. She wonders why someone would paint a silver tray black.

And then she stops. She has heard something. Some sort of movement from upstairs. She slides the tray back into the cupboard and stands at the foot of the stairs. She hears the sound again, a sort of dull *thump*.

Her heart quickens. She tiptoes to the landing. There it is again. And again. And then – her heart rate doubles at the sound – someone clears their throat.

Mr Royle, she thinks, it must be Mr Royle, the solicitor. It couldn't be anyone else. She'd shut the door behind her when she arrived. Definitely.

'Hello?' she calls out. 'Hello. Mr Royle!'

But there is silence. An immediate, deliberate silence.

'Hello!' she calls out again.

The silence sits like a still bear at the top of the house. She can almost hear the thump of someone's pulse.

She thinks of all the other mysteries the magazine article had revealed: the children who fled this house, the person who stayed behind to care for her; she thinks of the scribbles on the walls and the fabric strip hanging from the radiator and the scratches gouged into walls, the awkward note left by her parents, the blue painted roses on the creaking crib, the sheets of paper torn from walls, the bloodstains and the locks on the outsides of the children's rooms.

Then she thinks again of her friend April's neat lawn, her spicy couscous, the neon orange of an Aperol Spritz, her sticky feet in an icy paddling pool. She thinks of hot Danny and the potential babies they might have when she is thirty. Or earlier. Yes, why not earlier? Why put it off? She can sell this house with its bleak, dreadful legacy, its mouldy fridge and dead garden, its throat-clearing, thumping person in the attic. She can sell it now and be rich and marry Danny and have his babies. She doesn't care any more about what happened here. She doesn't want to know.

She fiddles for the door keys in her handbag and she locks up the big wooden front door and the padlocked hoarding and she emerges with relief on to the hot pavement and pulls her phone from her bag.

Save some couscous for me. I'll be there in an hour.

13

Lucy turns her fiddle this way and that in the muted light of the music repair shop.

She places it under her chin and quickly plays a three-octave A major scale and arpeggio, checking for evenness of sound quality and for wolf notes or whistles.

She beams at Monsieur Vincent.

'It's amazing,' she says, in French. 'It's better than it was before.'

Her heart softens in her chest. She hadn't realised, in the dreadfulness of sleeping on beaches and under motorway flyovers, just how hard she'd found it to be parted from her instrument and how much anger she'd been harbouring towards the drunken dickheads who'd broken it. But more than that, she hadn't realised just how much she'd missed playing it.

She counts out the twenty-euro notes on to the counter and Monsieur Vincent writes her out a receipt, tears it from a pad, hands it to her. Then he pulls two Chupa Chups lollipops from a display on his counter and hands one to each of the children.

'Look after your mother,' he says to Marco. 'And your sister.'

In the just-cooling evening air outside the shop, Lucy untwists the cellophane wrapper from Stella's lollipop and hands it to her. Then they walk towards the touristic centre, her children sucking their sweets, the dog snuffling at the hot pavement looking for discarded chicken bones or spilt ice creams. Lucy still has no appetite. The meeting with Michael killed it off completely.

The early diners have just arrived: older holidaymakers or ones with small children. This is a tougher crowd than the later one. The later crowd has been drinking; they're not embarrassed to approach the lady in the floaty voile skirt and strappy vest, with the tanned sinewy arms, the large breasts, the nose stud and ankle bracelet, with the two beautiful, tired-looking children sitting on a yoga mat behind her in the shade, the scruffy Jack Russell with its head on its paws. They're not distracted by irritable toddlers up past their bedtimes. Or cynically wondering if she'll spend the money on drugs or booze, if the children and the dog are just for show, if she'll beat them when they get home if she hasn't made enough money. She's heard everything over the years. She's been accused of it all. She's grown a very thick skin.

She takes the hat from her rucksack, the one that Marco used to call the 'money hat'; now he calls it the 'begging hat'. He hates that hat.

She places it on the ground in front of her and she unclips her fiddle case. She checks behind her that her children are settled. Marco has a book to read. Stella is colouring in. Marco looks up at her wearily. 'How long are we going to be here?'

So much teenage attitude, so many months yet to go before he turns thirteen.

'Until I've made enough money for a week at the Blue House.'

'How much is that?'

'Fifteen euros a night.'

'I don't know why you didn't just ask my dad for some more money. He could have spared it. He could have given you another hundred. So easily.'

'Marco. You know why. Now please, just let me get on with it.'

Lisa Jewell

Marco tuts and raises his eyebrows; then he lets his gaze drop to his book.

Lucy lifts her fiddle to her chin, points her right foot away from her body, closes her eyes, breathes in deep, and plays.

It is a good night; the passing of the storm last night has calmed the ether, it's not quite so hot and people are more relaxed. Lots of people stop tonight to stand and watch Lucy play her fiddle. She plays Pogues songs and Dexys Midnight Runners' songs; during her rendition of 'Come On Eileen' alone she calculates roughly fifteen euros being thrown into her hat. People dance and smile; one couple in their thirties give her a ten-euro note because they just got engaged. An older woman gives her five because her father used to play the fiddle and it reminded her of a happy childhood. By nine thirty Lucy has played in three locations and has nearly seventy euros.

She gathers the children, the dog, their bags. Stella can barely keep her eyes open and Lucy feels nostalgic for the days of the buggy when she could just scoop Stella into it at the end of the night and then scoop her out and straight into bed. But now she has to wake her hard, force her to walk, try not to shout when she whines that she's too tired.

The Blue House is a ten-minute walk away, halfway

up the hill to Castle Park. It's a long thin house, originally painted baby blue, a once elegant townhouse, constructed for its views across the Mediterranean, now peeling and grey and weather-beaten with cracked windowpanes and ivy clinging to drainpipes. A man called Giuseppe bought it in the 1960s, let it go to rack and ruin and then sold it to a landlord who filled it up with itinerants, a family to a room, shared bathrooms, cockroaches, no facilities, cash only. The landlord lets Giuseppe stay on in a studio apartment on the ground floor in return for maintenance and management and a small rent.

Giuseppe loves Lucy. 'If I had had a daughter,' he always says, 'she would have been like you. I swear it.'

For a few weeks after her fiddle was broken Lucy had not paid any rent and had been waiting, waiting for the landlord to kick her out. Then another tenant had told her that Giuseppe had been paying her rent for her. She'd packed a bag that same day and left without saying goodbye.

Lucy feels nervous now as they reach the turning for the Blue House; she starts to panic. What if Giuseppe doesn't have a room for her? What if he is angry that she left without saying goodbye and slams the door in her face? What if he's gone? Died? The house has burned down?

But he comes to the door, peers through the gap left

by the security chain and he smiles, a wall of brown teeth glimpsed through a bush of salt and pepper beard. He spies her fiddle in its case and smiles wider still. 'My girl,' he says, unclipping the chain and opening the door. 'My children. My dog! Come in!'

The dog goes mad with joy, jumps into Giuseppe's arms and nearly knocks him backwards. Stella wraps her arms around his legs and Marco pushes himself against Giuseppe and lets him kiss the top of his head.

'I have seventy euros,' she says. 'Enough for a few nights.'

'You have your fiddle. You stay as long as you like. You look thin. You all look thin. I only have bread. And some ham. It's not good ham though, but I have good butter, so . . .'

They follow him into his apartment on the ground floor. The dog immediately jumps on to the sofa and curls himself into a ball, looks at Lucy as if to say, *Finally*. Giuseppe goes to his tiny kitchenette and returns with bread and ham and three tiny dimpled glass bottles of Orangina. Lucy sits next to the dog and strokes his neck and breathes out, feels her insides untwist and unfurl and settle into place. And then she puts her hand into her rucksack to feel for her phone. The battery died some time during the night. She finds her charger and says to Giovanni, 'Is it OK if I charge my phone?'

'Of course, my love. There's an empty socket here.'

She plugs it in and holds the on button down, waiting for it to spring into life.

The notification is still there.

The baby is 25.

She sits with the children over the coffee table and watches them eat the bread and ham. The humiliations of the last week start to wash away, like footprints on the shore. Her children are safe. There is food. She has her fiddle. She has a bed to sleep in. She has money in her purse.

Giuseppe watches the children eat too. He glances at her and smiles. 'I was so worried about you all. Where have you been?'

'Oh,' she says lightly, 'staying with a friend.'

'N—' Marco begins.

She prods him with her elbow and turns to Giuseppe. 'A little bird told me what you'd been doing, you naughty man. And I couldn't have that. I just couldn't. And I knew if I told you I was going you'd have persuaded me to stay. So I had to sneak off and, honestly, we've been fine. We've been absolutely fine. I mean, look at us! We're all fine.' She pulls the dog on to her lap and squeezes him.

'And you have your fiddle back?'

'Yes, I have my fiddle back. So . . . is there a room? It doesn't have to be our usual room. It can be any room. Any room at all.'

'There is a room. It's at the back though, so no view. And a little dark. And the shower is broken, just a tap. You can have it for twelve euros a night.'

'Yes,' Lucy says, 'yes please!' She puts the dog down and gets to her feet and hugs Giuseppe. He smells dusty and old, a little dirty, but she doesn't care. 'Thank you,' she says, 'thank you so much.'

That night the three of them sleep in a tiny double bed in the dark room at the back of the house where the sound of tyres hissing on the hot tarmac outside competes with the creaking of a crappy plastic fan as it oscillates across the room, the television of the people in the room next door and a fly caught somewhere in between the curtains and the window. Stella has her fist in Lucy's face, Marco is moaning gently in his sleep and the dog is snoring. But Lucy sleeps hard and deep and long for the first time in over a week.

14

That day, 8 September 1988, should have been my second day at big school, but you've probably already guessed by now that I did not get to go to my long-anticipated big school that year, the school where I would meet my soulmates, my lifelong friends, my people. At intervals that summer I would ask my mother, 'When are we going to Harrods to buy my uniform?' And she would say, 'Let's wait until the end of the holidays, in case you have a growth spurt.' And then the end of the holidays approached and still we had not been to Harrods.

Neither had we been to Germany. We usually went for a week or two to stay with my grandmother in her big airy house in the Black Forest with its dank

above-ground swimming pool and silken pine nee-
dles underfoot. But this summer we could not afford
it, apparently, and if we couldn't afford to fly to Germany then how on earth, I wondered, were we going
to be able to afford school fees?

By the beginning of September my parents were
making applications to local state schools and putting
our names on to waiting lists. They never specifically
said that we had financial problems, but it was obvious
that we did. I had a stomach ache for days, worrying
about being bullied at a rough comprehensive.

Oh, such petty, tiny concerns. Such trifling worries.
I look back at eleven-year-old me: a slightly odd boy of
average height, skinny build, my mother's blue eyes,
my father's chestnut hair, knees like potatoes wedged
on to sticks, a disapproving tightness to my narrow
lips, a slightly haughty demeanour, a spoiled boy convinced that the chapters of his life had already been
neatly written out and would follow accordingly; I
look back at him and I want to slap his stupid, super-
cilious, starry-eyed little face.

Justin was crouched in the garden fingering the plants
he'd been growing out there.

'Apothecarial herbs; the planting of, growing of and
use of,' he explained to me in his almost comatose
drawl. 'The big pharmaceutical companies are out to

corrupt the planet. In twenty years' time we'll be a nation of prescription drug addicts and the NHS will be on its knees trying to pay for a sick nation's candy. I want to turn back the clock and use what the soil provides to treat everyday ailments. You don't need eight different types of chemical to cure a headache. Your mother says she wants to stop using pills and start using my tinctures.'

I gazed at him. We were a family of pill takers. Pills for hay fever, pills for colds, pills for tummy aches and headaches and growing pains and hangovers. My mum even had some pills for what she called her 'sad feelings'. My dad had pills for his heart and pills to stop his hair falling out. Pills everywhere. And now we were, apparently, to grow herbs and make our own medicine. It beggared belief.

My father had had a small stroke during the summer holidays. It left him with a limp and a slight slur and no longer himself in some kind of barely definable way. To see him diminished in this way made me feel strangely unprotected, as though there was now a small but significant gap in the family's defences.

His physician, a dry-as-they-come man of indeterminate age called Dr Broughton who lived and ran his practice in a six-storey house around the corner, came to visit after my father got back from an overnight stay in hospital. He and my father smoked cigars in the garden and talked about his prognosis. 'I'd say, Henry, that what you need are the services of a really good rehabilitation physiotherapist. Unfortunately, all the rehabilitation physiotherapists I know are bloody awful.'

They laughed and my father said, 'I'm not sure, any more, I'm not sure about anything. But I'd happily try it. Try anything really, just to get myself back to myself.'

Birdie was tending Justin's herb garden. It was hot and she was wearing a muslin top through which her nipples were plainly visible. She took off a floppy canvas hat and stood in front of my father and his doctor.

'I know someone,' she said, her hands on her hips. 'I know someone amazing. He's a miracle worker. He uses energy. He can move chi around people's bodies. He's cured people I know of bad backs. Of migraines. I'll get him to come and visit.'

I heard my father begin to protest. But Birdie just said, 'No. Honestly, Henry. It's the least I can do. The very least. I'll call him right now. His name's David. David Thomsen.'

I was in the kitchen with my mother watching her make cheese scones when the doorbell chimed that morning. My mother wiped her hands on her apron, nervously adjusted the ends of her permed and scrunch-dried bob and said, 'Ah, that must be the Thomsens.'

'Who', I asked, not remembering Birdie's recommendation of the week before, 'are the Thomsens?'

'Friends,' she said brightly. 'Of Birdie and Justin. The husband is a physiotherapist. He's going to work with your father, try and get him back into shape. And the mother is a trained teacher. She's going to home school you both, just for a short while. Isn't that good?'

I had no chance to ask my mother to expand on this rapidly introduced and rather shocking development before she'd pulled open the door.

With my jaw slightly ajar, I watched them troop in.

First, a girl, around nine or ten. Black hair cut into a bob, cut-off dungarees, scratched-up knees, a blob of chocolate swept across her cheek, a faint air of pent-up energy. Her name, apparently, was Clemency.

And then a boy, my age, maybe older, blond, tall, dark feathered lashes that swept the edges of steel-cut cheekbones, hands in the pockets of smart blue shorts, a fringe flicked out of his eyes effortlessly and with more than a little attitude. His name was Phineas. Phin, we were told, for short.

Their mother followed next. Big-boned, pale, flat-chested, with long blond hair and a slightly nervous demeanour. This, I was to discover, was Sally Thomsen.

And behind them all, tall, broad-shouldered, slim, tanned, with short black hair, intense blue eyes and a full mouth, was the father. David Thomsen. He gripped my hand hard inside his and cupped it with the other. 'Good to meet you, young man,' he said in a low, smooth voice.

Then he let my hand go and held his arms aloft.

He smiled at each of us in turn and said, 'Good to meet you all.'

David insisted on taking us all out for dinner that night. It was a Thursday, still warm around the edges. I spent quite some time that night finessing my appearance, not merely in the way I usually did of ensuring my clothes were clean and my parting sharp and my cuffs straight, but more foppishly; the boy called Phineas was fascinating to me, not only in terms of his great beauty, but also in terms of his style of dressing. Along with the casual blue shorts, he'd worn a red polo shirt with white stripes down the collars and bright white Adidas sports shoes with white ankle socks. I searched my wardrobe that evening for something equally effortless. All my socks reached my calves; only my sister had ankle socks. All my shorts were made out of wool and all my shirts had buttons. I even considered my old PE kit for a moment, but quickly dismissed the idea when I realised it was still bunched up in my PE bag from my very last PE lesson. Eventually I settled on a plain blue T-shirt and jeans, with my plimsolls. I tried to make the lick of hair that grew from my hairline fall upon my brow, as Phineas's did, but it stubbornly refused to move out of place. I stared at myself for a full twenty seconds before I left the room, hating the awfulness of my stupid face, the plainness of my T-shirt, the sad cut of my John Lewis for Boys jeans. I made a strangulated noise under my breath, kicked the wall and then headed downstairs.

Phin was there, in the hallway, sitting on one of the two huge wooden chairs that sat either side of the staircase. He was reading a book. I stared at him through the balustrade for a moment before making my entrance. He really was the most beautiful thing I had ever seen in my life. I felt my cheeks flush red as I took in the lines of him: the delicate outline of a mouth that looked like it had been moulded out of the softest reddest clay, as if a fingertip would leave an imprint in it. His skin was like chamois pulled across cheekbones that looked as though they might tear through it. He even had the thrilling suggestion of a moustache.

He tossed his fringe once more and then glanced up at me disinterestedly as I descended, his eyes falling immediately back to his book. I wanted to ask him what he was reading but I didn't. I felt awkward, not sure where to put myself or how to stand. But others quickly appeared: first my mother and father, then the girl called Clemency, who was with my sister, the two of them already chatting easily with each other, then Sally, then Justin and Birdie, and then finally, and virtually encased in a circle of light at the top of the staircase, David Thomsen.

What can I tell you about David Thomsen from my perspective then, as a young boy? Well, I can tell you that he was very handsome. Not in the soft, almost feminine way that his son was handsome, but in a more traditional way. He had a dense five o'clock shadow that looked as if it had been painted on, a heavy, defined brow, an animal energy, a potent power. He had a way of making anyone who stood next to him appear somewhat lesser than him, even when they weren't. I can tell you that he appalled me and fascinated me in equal measure. And I can tell you that my mother acted strangely in his presence, not flirtatiously but, if anything, more guardedly, as though she didn't trust herself around him. He was both puffed-up and down-to-earth, warm yet cold. I hated him, yet I could see why others loved him. But all that was yet to come. First of all was that very first dinner on that very first night when everyone was showing their very best selves.

* * *

We sat squashed around a long table in the Chelsea Kitchen, which was really only meant for eight. The children had all been put at one end which meant I found myself elbow to elbow with Phineas. I was so electrified by my proximity to him, my nerve endings so raw, my body so primed and aching for something that I was too young to even begin to understand, that I had no choice but to turn my back to him.

I glanced down the length of the table towards my father who sat at the head.

At the sight of him I felt something inside me plummeting, like an untethered lift hurtling down a shaft. I didn't quite understand what I was feeling, but I can tell you now that what I had experienced was a terrifying moment of prescience. I had seen my father suddenly rendered short in the company of David Thomsen, who was unusually tall, and I had seen that his hold on the head of the table, once so unquestionable and defined, was flimsy. Even without the damage that the stroke had caused, everyone at the table was cleverer than him, even me. He was dressed wrong, in his too-tight jacket, the flourish of a dark pink handkerchief in his breast pocket that clashed with the rust of his hair. I saw him shuffle in his seat; I saw the conversation dash across the top of his head like clouds on a windy day. I saw him stare at the menu for longer than was necessary. I saw David Thomsen lean across the table towards my mother to emphasise a point and then lean back again to observe my mother's response.

I saw all this, I saw all this, and I knew already on some subliminal but incredibly uncomfortable level that a power struggle had started under my very nose and that even then, at moment zero, my father was already losing.

15

On Monday morning Libby gets into work twenty minutes late.

Dido looks up at her in surprise. Libby is never late for work.

'I was about to call you,' she says. 'Is everything OK?'

Libby nods, takes her phone out of her bag, then her lip balm and her cardigan, tucks the bag under her desk, unties her hair, ties it up again, pulls out her chair and sits down heavily. 'Sorry,' she says eventually. 'I didn't sleep last night.'

'I was going to say,' says Dido. 'You look awful. The heat?'

She nods. But it wasn't the heat. It was the insides of her head.

'Well, let me get you a nice strong coffee.'

Normally Libby would say no, no, no, I can get my own coffee. But today her legs are so heavy, her head so woolly, she nods and says thank you. She watches Dido as she makes her coffee, feeling reassured by the sheen of her dyed black hair, the way she stands with one hand in the pocket of her black tunic dress, her tiny feet planted wide apart in chunky dark green velvet trainers.

'There,' says Dido, resting the cup on Libby's table. 'Hope that does the trick.'

Libby has known Dido for five years. She knows all sorts of things about her. She knows that her mother was a famous poet, her father was a famous newspaper editor, that she grew up in one of the most illustrious houses in St Albans and was taught at home by a governess. She knows her younger brother died when he was twenty and that she hasn't had sex for eleven years. She knows that she lives in a tiny cottage on the edge of her parents' estate and that she still has the horse she rode as a teenager and that that horse is called Spangles. She knows that the illustrious house has been left in Dido's parents' will not to her but to the National Trust and that she is fine about that.

She knows that Dido likes PG Tips, Benedict Cumberbatch, horses, Gianduja, coconut water, *Doctor Who*, expensive mattress toppers, Jo Malone Orange Blossom, stir fries, Nando's and facials. But she has never been to Dido's house or met Dido's family or friends. She has never seen Dido outside of work hours apart from at the annual Christmas party at the posh hotel up the road and the occasional leaving drinks. She doesn't actually know who Dido *is*.

But she looks at Dido now and it is suddenly, blindingly obvious to her that Dido is exactly the person she needs right now. She'd sat in April's back garden on Saturday night flirting mildly with Danny – who was not really all that hot, had a face like an eight-year-old boy and very small hands – and she'd looked around for someone she could talk to about the crazy things happening to her, about the house and the magazine article and the dead parents and the person coughing in the attic. But all she'd seen was people like her, normal people, with normal lives, people who still lived at home with their parents or in tiny flats with partners and friends, people with unpaid-off student loans, unexceptional jobs, unexceptional dreams, fake tans, handbag dogs, white teeth, clean hair. She'd felt caught between two painfully disparate places and had left before eleven, come home to her laptop and back to the internet's take on what had happened to Serenity Lamb.

But this had raised more questions than it had answered and she'd finally slammed down the lid of her laptop at 2 a.m. and gone to bed where her sleep had been disturbed, her dreams filled with strange leit-motifs and encounters.

'I need some advice,' she says to Dido now. 'About the Chelsea thing.'

'Oh yes,' says Dido, rubbing the oversized silver disc that hangs from a chain around her neck. 'What sort of advice?'

'Well, just to talk about it, really. You know about . . . *houses*. I thought you'd know about houses.'

'Well, I know about *a* house. Not houses in general. But sure, yes, why not. Come for supper.'

'When?' ·

'Tonight?'

'Yes,' Libby says, 'yes, please.'

Dido's cottage is beautiful. It's double-fronted with leaded windows, tiny pink roses growing across the doorway and there, outside, her shiny black Fiat Spider with its tan convertible roof. The car complements the cottage and the cottage complements the car and Libby can't help herself from taking her phone from her bag and photographing it for her Instagram page. Dido greets her at the door in wide floral trousers and a black vest top. Her hair is held from her face by large red sunglasses and she is barefoot. Libby has only ever seen her in clumpy work shoes so it's a surprise to see two small, white, perfectly pedicured feet with rose-pink nails.

'This is so lovely,' she says, stepping through the small door into a white hallway with a terracotta tiled floor. 'Just beautiful.'

Dido's house is full of what Libby assumes must be heirlooms and inheritances; nothing here from TK Maxx. The walls are hung with bright abstract art and Libby remembers Dido once mentioning that her mother was also an artist. Dido takes them through French doors at the back of the cottage and they sit in her perfect little country garden on old-fashioned Lloyd Loom rattan chairs, upholstered with floral cushions. It occurs to Libby as she takes in the back of Dido's beautiful house that maybe Dido doesn't actually need to work. That maybe her job designing posh kitchens is just a nice little hobby.

Dido brings out a bowl of quinoa and avocado salad, another bowl of buttered potatoes, a loaf of dark bread and two champagne glasses for the Prosecco that Libby brought with her.

'How long have you lived here?' Libby asks, buttering some of the dark bread.

'Since I was twenty-three, when I moved back from Hong Kong. It was my mother's cottage. She kept it for me. My brother, of course, was set to inherit the house, but then, well, things changed . . .'

Libby smiles, blankly. 'The house'. 'The cottage'. Another world entirely. 'So sad,' she says.

'Yes,' Dido agrees. 'But the house is a curse. I'm glad it's nothing to do with me.'

Libby nods. A week ago she'd have had no notion of big beautiful houses being curses, now she is closer to understanding.

'So, tell me about *your* house? Tell me everything.'

Libby sips her Prosecco, places the glass on the table and then leans back into her chair. 'I found an article,' she begins, 'in the *Guardian*. About the house. About my parents. About me.'

'You?'

'Yes,' says Libby, rubbing at the points of her elbows. 'It's all a bit bizarre. You see, I was adopted as a baby, when I was nearly a year old. The house in Chelsea, it belonged to my birth parents. And according to the article I was born into a cult.'

The word sounds horrible leaving her mouth. It's a word she's been trying her hardest to avoid using, to avoid even thinking about. It's so at odds with the pathetic fantasy she'd spent her life wallowing in. She sees Dido bristle slightly with excitement.

'What!'

'A cult. According to this article there was a sort of cult in the house in Chelsea. Lots of people lived there. They were all living spartanly. Sleeping on the floor.

Wearing robes that they made themselves. Yet . . .' She reaches into her bag and pulls out the printout of the article. 'Look, this was my mum and dad, six years before I was born, at a charity ball. I mean, look at them.'

Dido takes the article from her hands and looks. 'Gosh,' she says, 'very glamorous.'

'I know! My mother was a socialite. She ran a fashion PR company. She was once engaged to an Austrian prince. She's just stunning.'

Seeing her mother's face had been extraordinary; there was something reminiscent of Priscilla Presley about the dyed black hair and piercing blue eyes. Her mother had lived up to every one of her childhood fantasies, right down to the job in PR. Her father . . . well, he was very well dressed, but smaller than she'd imagined, shorter than her mother, with a slightly arrogant tilt to his chin but something oddly defensive in the way he looked at the photographer, as though expecting trouble of some kind. He held his arm around Martina Lamb's waist, the tips of his fingers just visible in the shot; she gripped a silk shawl around her shoulders with ringed fingers and the edges of her hip bone made indents in the fabric of her evening dress. It was, according to the article, the last photo taken of the 'socialite couple' before they disappeared from view, only to be found dead on their kitchen floor seven years later.

'I had a brother and sister,' she says, feeling the fresh shock propelling the words from her mouth too fast, leaving no gaps between them.

Dido glances up at her. 'Wow,' she says. 'What happened to them?'

'No one knows. The solicitor seems to think they might be dead.'

And there it is. The heaviest of all the extremely heavy facts that have been weighing her down for days. It lands between them, heavy as a thrown hammer.

'God,' says Dido. 'That's . . . I mean, how can that be?'

She shrugs. 'The police came after a call from a neighbour. They found my parents and some other man dead in the kitchen. They'd committed suicide, some kind of pact. And there was me, ten months old, healthy and well in a cot upstairs. But no sign of my brother and sister.'

Dido falls back into her chair, her mouth agape. She says nothing for a moment. 'OK.' She sits forward and clamps her temples with the heels of her hands. 'So, there was a cult. And your parents carried out a suicide pact with some random man . . .'

Libby nods. 'They poisoned themselves with plants they'd grown in the garden.'

Dido's jaw falls again. 'Yes,' she says drily. 'Of course they did. Fuck. Then what?'

'There'd been other people living in the house. Possibly another family, with children. But when the police got there, there was nobody. Just the dead bodies and me. All the children had just . . . *disappeared*. Never been heard of since.'

Dido shivers and puts a hand to her chest. 'Including your brother and sister?'

'Yes,' she says. 'They'd barely been seen in years. The neighbours assumed they were away at boarding school. But no school ever came forward to say they'd been a student there. And one of them must have stayed on in the house after my parents died, because apparently someone had been looking after me for days. My nappy was fresh. And when they took me out of the cot, they found this.' She takes the rabbit's foot from her bag and passes it to Dido. 'It was tucked into my blankets.'

'For luck,' says Dido.

'I suppose so,' Libby replies.

'And the other guy who died,' Dido asks, 'who was he?'

'Nobody knows. There was no paperwork to identify him, just his initials on the suicide note. No one reported him missing, no one recognised him from police sketches. The theory is that he was an itinerant. A gypsy, maybe. Which would perhaps explain that.' She gestures at the rabbit's foot in Dido's hand.

'Gypsies.' Dido massages the word with relish. 'Gosh.'

'And the house, it's weird. It's dark. And I was there, on Saturday morning, and I heard something. Upstairs.'

'What sort of something?'

'Well, a someone. Someone moving. A cough.'

'And you're sure it wasn't the neighbours?'

'I suppose it could have been. But it really sounded like it was coming from the top of the house. And now I'm too scared to go back there. I feel like I should just put it on the market and get rid of it and move on. But . . .'

'Your brother and sister . . . ?'

'My brother and sister. The truth. My story. It's all bound up in that house and if I sell it, I may never find out what really happened.'

Dido stares for a moment at the newspaper article. Then she looks up at Libby.

'Here,' she says, tapping at the top of the newspaper article with her fingertip. 'Him. The journalist.' She squints at the byline. 'Miller Roe. He's your man. You need to get in touch with him. Just imagine how amazed he'll be after all his months of investigative journalism to suddenly find you in his inbox. Serenity Lamb herself. Complete with actual rabbit's foot.'

They both fall silent then for a moment and let their

gazes drop to the rabbit's foot where it sits on the garden table in a pool of soft dappled evening light.

Libby takes the article from Dido's hand and finds the byline. 'Miller Roe'. An unusual name. Easy enough to google. She pulls her phone from her bag and types it in. In under a minute she has his contact email address at the *Guardian*. She turns her phone to show it to Dido.

Dido nods sagely. 'Good work,' she says. Then she lifts her glass of Prosecco and holds it towards Libby. 'To Serenity Lamb,' she says, 'and to Miller Roe. May one beget the truth about the other.'

16

Lucy is awake at five thirty the next morning. She slides carefully off the bed and the dog jumps down and follows her to the kitchenette, his claws clacking against the linoleum. Giuseppe has put teabags, granulated coffee and a plastic bag of chocolate brioche fingers on the counter. There is also a bottle of milk in the fridge. Lucy puts a pan of water on to boil and then sits for a while on the plastic chair in the corner staring at the curtained window. After a moment she stands and tugs open the curtain, then sits and stares at the building opposite, the dark windows reflecting the orange of the early dawn, the grey walls briefly turned pink. The sky overhead is detergent blue and filled with circling birds. The traffic has not started yet and the only noise is the steady rumble of the water coming to the boil, the whine of the gas flame beneath.

Lucy looks at her phone. Nothing. The dog is staring at her meaningfully. She opens the door to her apartment, quietly opens the back door on to the street and gestures to the dog to go outside. He passes her, lifts his leg against the outside of the building for half a minute, then runs back inside.

Indoors, Lucy pulls her rucksack towards her and unzips an inside pocket. In there is her passport. She flips it open. As she'd suspected, it expired three years earlier. The last time she'd used it was when Marco was two and she and Michael had taken him to New York to meet Michael's parents. They'd split up shortly afterwards and Lucy hadn't used it since.

Michael had originally got the passport for her. He'd been booking their honeymoon in the Maldives. 'Give me your passport, honey,' he'd said, 'I need the details.'

'I don't have a passport,' she'd said.

'Well, you're going to need to renew it, asap, or there'll be no honeymoon.'

She'd sighed and looked up at him. 'Look,' she'd said. 'I don't have a passport. Full stop. I've never had a passport.'

He'd stopped then and gazed at her for a moment,

the machinations of his mind visible in the space between his top and bottom lips. 'But . . .'

'I came to France as a passenger, in a car. When I was much younger. No one asked to see my passport.'

'Whose car?'

'I don't know. Just a car.'

'So, like, a stranger's car?'

'Not quite. No.'

'But what was the plan? If they'd asked you for a passport, what would you have done?'

'I don't know.'

'So how have you been living? I mean . . .'

'Well, like you found me,' she'd replied tersely, 'playing a fiddle for cents. Paying by the night for lodgings.'

'Since you were a child?'

'Since I was a child.'

She'd trusted him then, the tall, genial American with the winning smile. Back then he'd been her hero, the man who'd come to watch her play every single night for almost a month, who'd told her she was the most beautiful fiddler he'd ever seen, who'd brought her to his elegant rose-pink house and handed her soft towels to dry herself with after half an hour in a shower cubicle tiled with gold mosaic, who'd combed out the wet strands of her hair and made her shudder when his fingertips brushed against her bare shoulders, who'd handed her grimy clothes to his maid to be washed and pressed and returned to her in an origami fan upon the counterpane of her bed in the guest suite. Back then he'd been nothing but soft touches and awe and gentleness. Of course she'd trusted him.

So she'd told him everything, the whole story, and he'd looked at her with shining hazel eyes and said, 'It's OK, you're safe now. You're safe now.' And then he'd got her a passport. She had no idea how or from whom. The information on it was not entirely accurate: it was not her correct name, nor was it her correct date of birth or her correct place of birth. But it was a good passport, a passport that had got her to the Maldives and back, that had got her to Barbados and back, to Italy and Spain and New York and back without anyone ever asking any questions.

And now it has expired and she has no means of getting another one and no means of getting back to England. Not to mention the fact that there are no passports for the children nor a pet passport for the dog.

She closes her passport and sighs. There are two ways around this obstacle and one of them is dangerous and illegal and the other is just plain dangerous. Her only other alternative is not to go at all.

At this thought her mind fills with images of leaving England twenty-four years ago. She replays those last moments as she's replayed them a thousand times: the sound of the door clicking behind her for the very last time, whispering, *I'll be back soon, I promise you, I promise you, I promise you,* under her breath a dozen times as she ran down Cheyne Walk in the dark of the middle of the night, her heart pounding, her breath catching, her nightmare both ending, and beginning.

17

It was almost two weeks before Phineas Thomsen deigned to talk to me. Or maybe it was the other way round, who knows. I'm sure he'd have his own take on it. But in my recollection (and this is of course entirely *my* recollection) it was him.

I was, as ever, hanging around the kitchen with my mother, eavesdropping on her conversation with the women who now seemed to live in our house. I'd subliminally determined at this point that the only way to really know what was going on in the world was to listen to women talk. Anyone who ignores the chatter of women is poorer by any measure.

By now Birdie and Justin had been living with us for almost five months, the Thomsens for nearly two weeks.

The conversation in the kitchen on this particular day was one that operated on a kind of forty-eight-hour rotating cycle: the vexing matter of where Sally and David were going to live. At this point I was still clinging pathetically to the fallacy that Sally and David were only staying for a short while. Every few days a possibility would appear on the horizon and be talked about at length and the feeling that Sally and David were about to move on would hang briefly, tantalisingly in the air until, *pop*, the 'possibility' would be found to have an inherent flaw and they'd be back to the drawing board. Right now the 'possibility' was a houseboat in Chiswick. It belonged to a patient of David's who was going backpacking for a year and needed someone to look after her bearded dragons.

'Only one bedroom, though,' Sally was saying to my mother and Birdie. 'And a tiny bedroom at that. Obviously David and I could sleep on the berths in the living room, but it's a bit cramped because of the vivariums.'

'Gosh,' said Birdie, picking, picking at the dry skin around her nails, the flakes landing on the cat's back. 'How many are there?'

'Vivariums?'

'Whatever. Yes.'

'No idea. Six or so. We might have to find a way to pile them up.'

'But what about the children?' my mother asked. 'Will they want to share? Especially a double bed. I mean, Phin's going to be a teenager . . .'

'Oh God, it would only be short term. Just until we find somewhere permanent.'

I glanced up. This was the point where the plan usually fell apart. The moment it became clear that it was in fact a *stupid* plan, Sally would say, stoically, 'Oh, well, it's not permanent,' and my mother would say, 'Well, that's ridiculous, we have so much space here. Don't feel you have to rush into anything.' And Sally's body language would soften and she'd smile and touch my mother's arm and say, 'I don't want to stretch your hospitality.' And my beautiful mother would say, in her beautiful German accent, 'Nonsense, Sally. Nonsense. Just you take your time. Something will come up. Something perfect.'

And so it came to pass, that afternoon in late September. The houseboat plan was mooted and dispatched within a cool, possibly record-breaking, eight minutes.

I was torn, it must be said, by the presence of the Thomsens. On the one hand they were cluttering up my house. Not with objects, per se, but just with themselves, their human forms, their sounds, their smells, their otherness. My sister and Clemency had come together like an unholy union of loud and louder.

They careered about the house from morning to bedtime ensconced in strange games of make-believe that all seemed to involve making as much noise as possible. Not only that, but Birdie was teaching them both to play the fiddle, which was utterly excruciating.

Then, of course, there was David Thomsen, whose charismatic presence seemed to permeate every stratum of our house. As well as his bedroom upstairs he had also somehow commandeered our front room, which housed my father's bar, as a sort of exercise room where I had once observed him through a crack in the door attempting to raise his entire body from the floor using just his fingertips.

And at the other end of everything was Phin. Phin who refused even to look at me, let alone talk to me; Phin who acted as though I was not even there. And the more he acted as though I was not there, the more I felt like I might die of him refusing to see me.

And then, finally, that day, it happened. I'd left the kitchen after it had been established that Sally and David would be staying and had almost bumped into Phin coming the other way. He wore a faded sweatshirt with lettering on it and jeans with tears in the knees. He stopped when he saw me and for the first time his eyes met mine. I caught my breath. I searched my tangled thoughts for something to say, but found nothing there. I moved to the left; he moved to his right. I said sorry and moved to my right. I thought he'd pass silently onwards, but then he said, 'You know we're here to stay, don't you?'

'I'm sorry?'

'Just ignore anything my parents say about moving out. We're not going anywhere. You know,' he continued, 'we ended up in that house in Brittany for two years. We were only supposed to be there for a holiday.' He paused and cocked an eyebrow.

I was clearly supposed to be responding in some way, but I was stupefied. I had never stood so close to someone so beautiful before. His breath smelled of spearmint.

He stared at me and I saw disappointment flicker across his face, or not even disappointment but resignation, as though I was simply confirming what he'd already suspected of me, that I was boring and pointless, not worth his attention.

'Why don't you have your own house?' I asked finally.

He shrugged. 'Because my dad's too tight to pay rent.'

'Have you never had your own house?'

'Yes. Once. He sold it so we could go travelling.'

'But what about school?'

'What about school?'

'When do you go to school?'

'Haven't been to school since I was six. Mum teaches me.'

'Wow,' I said. 'But what about friends?'

He looked at me askance.

'Don't you miss having friends?'

He narrowed his eyes. 'No,' he said simply. 'Not even slightly.'

He looked as though he was about to leave. I did not want him to leave. I wanted to smell his spearmint breath and find out more about him. My eyes dropped to the book in his hand. 'What are you reading?' I asked.

He glanced down and turned the book upwards. It was *The Dice Man* by Luke Rhinehart, a novel I had not heard of at the time, but which I have since read roughly thirty times. 'Is it good?'

'All books are good,' he said.

'That's not true,' I said. 'I've read some really bad books.' I was thinking specifically of *Anne of Green Gables*, which we'd been forced to read the term before and which was the most stupid, annoying book I'd ever encountered.

'They weren't bad books,' Phin countered patiently. 'They were books that you didn't enjoy. It's not the same thing at all. The only bad books are books that are so badly written that no one will publish them. Any book that has been published is going to be a "good book" for someone.'

I nodded. I couldn't fault his logic.

'I've nearly finished it,' he said, glancing down at the book in his hand. 'You can borrow it after me, if you want?'

I nodded again. 'OK,' I said. 'Thank you.'

And then he left. But I stood where I was, my head pulsating, my palms damp, my heart filled with something extraordinary and new.

18

Miller Roe stands as Libby approaches him. She recognises him from his photo on the internet, although he has grown a beard since he had his byline photo taken, and also gained some weight. He is halfway through a very messy sandwich and has a speck of yellow sauce in his beard. He wipes his fingers on a napkin before he takes Libby's hand to shake and says, 'Libby, wow, so good to meet you. So good to meet you!' He has a London accent and dark blue eyes. His hand around hers is huge. 'Here, sit down. What can I get you? The sandwiches are amazing.'

She glances down at his car crash sandwich and says, 'I only just had breakfast.'

'Coffee, tea?'

'A cappuccino would be nice. Thank you.'

She watches him at the counter of the trendy café on West End Lane where he'd suggested they meet as a midway point between St Albans and South Norwood. He's wearing low-slung jeans and a faded T-shirt, a green cotton jacket and walking boots. He has a big belly and a large head of thick dark brown hair. He's slightly overwhelming to look at, ursine but not unappealing.

He brings back her cappuccino and places it in front of her. 'So grateful to you for coming to meet me. I hope your journey was OK?' He pushes his sandwich to one side as though he has no intention of eating any more.

'No problem,' she says, 'fifteen minutes, straight through.'

'From St Albans, right?'

'Yes.'

'Nice place, St Albans.'

'Yes,' she agrees. 'I like it.'

'So,' he says, stopping and staring meaningfully at her, 'you're the baby.'

She laughs nervously. 'It seems I am.'

'And you've inherited that house?'

'I have, yes.'

'Wow,' he says. 'Game changer.'

'Complete,' she agrees.

'Have you been to see it?'

'The house?'

'Yeah.'

'Yes, a couple of times.'

'God.' He throws himself back into his chair. 'I tried so hard to get them to let me into that house. I was virtually offering the guy at the solicitors my firstborn. One night I even tried to break in.'

'So you never actually saw it?'

'No, I very much didn't.' He laughs wryly. 'I peered through windows; I even sweet-talked the neighbours round the back to be allowed to look out of their windows. But never actually got in the house. What's it like?'

'It's dark,' she says. 'Lots of wood panelling. Weird.'

'And you're going to sell it, I assume?'

'I am going to sell it. Yes. But . . .' She trails her fingertips around the rim of her coffee cup as she forms her next words. 'First I want to know what happened there.'

Miller Roe makes a sort of growling noise under his breath and rubs his beard with his hand, dislodging the speck of yellow sauce. 'God, you and me both. Two years of my life, that article took from me, two obsessed, insane, fucked-up years of my life. Destroyed my marriage and I still didn't get the answers I was looking for. Nowhere near.'

He smiles at her. He has, she thinks, a nice face. She tries to guess his age, but she can't. He could be anywhere between twenty-five and forty.

She reaches into her bag and pulls out the keys to Cheyne Walk, places them on the table in front of him.

His gaze drops on to them and she sees a wave of longing pass across his eyes. His hand reaches across the table. 'Oh my God. May I?'

'Sure,' she says. 'Go ahead.'

He stares at each key in turn, caresses the fobs. 'A Jag?' he says, looking up at her.

'Apparently.'

'You know, Henry Lamb, your dad, he used to be quite the Jack the Lad. Used to go screaming off hunting at the weekends, partying at Annabel's on school nights.'

'I know,' she replies sanguinely. 'I read your article.'

'Yes,' he says. 'Of course you did.'

There is a brief silence. Miller pulls the edge off his sandwich and puts it in his mouth. Libby takes a sip of her coffee.

'So,' he says, 'what next?'

'I want to find my brother and sister,' she says.

'So they've never tried to get in touch with you?'

'No. Never. What's your theory?'

'I have a million theories. But the big question is: Do they know the house was held in trust for you?

And if they knew, will they know that you've inherited it now?'

Libby sighs. 'I don't know. The solicitor said that the trust had been drawn up years before, when my brother was born. It was meant to go to him when he turned twenty-five. But he never came to claim it. Then to his sister, but she never came to claim it either . . . and of course the solicitors had no way of contacting either of them. But yes, I guess there's a chance they knew it would come to me. Assuming . . .' She was going to say *they're still alive*, but stops herself.

'And the guy,' she says. 'The man who died with my parents. In the article you said you followed a lot of dead leads. But you never managed to find out who it was?'

'No, frustratingly not.' Miller rubs his beard. 'Although there was one name that came up. I had to give up in my search for him. But it's nagged at me ever since. David Thomsen.'

Libby throws him a quizzical look.

'There were initials on the suicide note, remember? ML, HL, DT. So I asked police for names of missing person cases that had involved the initials DT. David Thomsen was one of thirty-eight that they unearthed. Thirty-eight missing persons with the initials DT. Ten within the John Doe's estimated age range. And one by one I eliminated all of them.

'But this one fascinated me. I don't know. There was just something about his story that rang true. Forty-two-year-old guy from Hampshire. Normal upbringing. But no record of him anywhere, not since he arrived back in the UK from France, in 1988, with a wife called Sally, and two children, Phineas and Clemency. The four of them arrive by ferry from Saint-Malo into Portsmouth in . . .' He flicks through a notebook for a moment. '. . . September 1988. And then there is literally no trace of any of them from that point onwards: no doctors' records, no tax, no school registers, no hospital visits, nothing. Their families described them as "loners" – there were rifts and grudges, a huge falling-out over an inheritance of some sort. So nobody wondered where they were. Not for years and years. Until David Thomsen's mother, nearing the end of her life, decides she wants a deathbed reconciliation and reports her son and his family as missing persons. The police run some perfunctory searches, find no trace of David or his family, then David's mother dies and no one asks about David or Sally Thomsen ever again. Until me, three years ago.' Miller sighs. 'I tried so hard to track them down. Phineas. Clemency. Unusual names. If they were out there they'd have been easy enough to find. But nothing. Not a trace. And I needed to file the article, I needed to get paid, I had to give up.' He shakes his head. 'Can you see now? Can you see why it took two years, why it nearly killed me? Why my wife left me? I was literally a research zombie. It was all I talked about, all I thought about.'

He sighs and runs his fingers across the bunch of keys. 'But yes. Let's do it. Let's find out what happened to all those people. Let's find out what happened to you.'

He holds his hand out to hers to shake. 'Are we on, Serenity Lamb?'

'Yes,' says Libby, putting her hand in his. 'We're on.'

Libby goes straight to the showroom from her breakfast with Miller Roe. It's only half past nine and Dido barely registers her lateness. When she does, she does a double take and says, in an urgent whisper, 'Oh God! The journalist! How did it go!'

'Amazing,' Libby replies. 'We're going to meet at the house this evening. Start our investigation.'

'Just you,' says Dido, her nose wrinkling slightly, 'and him?'

'Yes.'

'Hmm. Are you sure that's a good idea?'

'What? Why?'

'I don't know. Maybe he's not what he seems.' Dido narrows her eyes at her. 'I think I should come too.'

Libby blinks slowly and then smiles. 'You could have just asked.'

'I don't know what you mean.' Dido turns back to her laptop. 'I just want to look out for you.'

'Fine,' says Libby, still smiling. 'You can "look out" for me. I'm meeting him at seven. We'll need to be on the six eleven. OK?'

'Yes,' says Dido, her gaze resolutely on her computer screen. 'OK. And by the way' – she looks up suddenly – 'I've read every single Agatha Christie novel ever published. Twice. So I might even be quite useful.'

19

Lucy leaves the children sleeping with a note on the bedside table for Marco that says: 'I've gone to sort out passports. I'll be back in a couple of hours. Give your sister something to eat. The dog's with Giuseppe.'

She leaves the house at 8 a.m. and takes the long route across town to the Gare de Nice. She stops for a while and sits on a bench, letting the soft morning sun warm up her skin. At eight forty-five, she boards the train to Antibes.

Just after 9 a.m. she is in front of Michael's house. A metal jacket of bluebottles sits on Fitz's shit from the morning before. She smiles a tight smile. Then, very slowly, bile burning in the pit of her stomach, she rings on Michael's doorbell.

The maid answers. She smiles when she recognises Lucy and she says, 'Good morning to you! You are the wife of Michael! From before! The mother of Michael's son. I did not know before that Michael, he had a son!' She has her hand clasped to her chest and she looks genuinely joyful. 'Such beautiful boy. Come, come in.'

The house is silent. Lucy says, 'Is Michael available?'

'Yes, yes. He is having a shower. You wait for him on terrace. Is OK?'

Joy leads her on to the terrace and tells her to sit, insisting on bringing coffee with amaretti on the side, even when Lucy says water will be fine. Michael does not deserve such a woman, she thinks. Michael does not deserve anything.

She puts her hand into her shoulder bag and pulls out her old passport, and the tiny wallet with the photos of Stella and Marco tucked inside. She drinks her coffee but leaves the amaretti which she cannot stomach. A colourful bee-eater sits in a tree overhead surveying the garden for snacks. She breaks up the amaretti and drops it on the floor for him. He doesn't notice, and flies away. Lucy's stomach rolls and reels. It's half past nine.

Then finally he is there, immaculate in a white T-shirt and pea-green shorts, his thinning hair still wet from the shower and his feet bare.

'Well, my goodness me,' he says, brushing her cheek

with his on both sides. 'Twice in two days. It must be my birthday. No kids?'

'No. I left them sleeping. We had a very late night.'

'Next time.' He hits her with his big golden smile, sits and crosses his legs. 'So, to what do I owe the pleasure?'

'Well.' She lays her fingertips on top of her passport and his eyes fall to it. 'I need to go home,' she says. 'My friend is ill. Maybe dying. I want to see her, before she . . . in case . . . you know.' A tear falls from her left eye and lands wonderfully on top of her passport. She wipes it away. She hadn't planned to cry, but it had happened anyway.

'Oh, honey.' Michael puts his hand over hers.

She smiles tightly and tries to look grateful for the gesture.

'That's terrible. What is it? Is it cancer?'

She nods. 'Ovarian.' She takes her hand from under his and brings it to her mouth to stifle a small sob. 'I want to go next week,' she says, 'but my passport, it's expired. And I don't even have any for the children. And I'm so so sorry to ask you. And you were so generous yesterday with the money for my fiddle. And I really wouldn't ask if I had any other options. But do you still know the people? The ones who got me this passport?' She runs a finger under her eyes and then looks up at him, pathetically, but hopefully still alluringly.

'Well, gosh, not really. No. But, look, I'll try.' He pulls the passport towards him. 'Leave it with me.'

'Here. I brought photos. And, God, I know this might sound nuts, but I need one for the dog. He's overdue some vaccinations so I can't go the traditional route And God knows how long it would take, anyway . . .'

'You're taking the dog? To see a dying friend?'

'I don't really have any choice.'

'Well, I could have him?'

She tries not to look too appalled at the thought of her precious dog living here with this monster. 'But what would you do with a dog?'

'Er, gosh, I don't know. Play with it? Walk it? Feed it?'

'There's more to it than that. You have to get up every morning and take them to the toilet. And you have to pick up their shit.'

Michael rolls his eyes and says, 'Joy loves dogs. She'd love having him around. And so would I.'

Of course, thinks Lucy, Michael has people to pick up dog shit.

'Well,' she says, 'I'd rather take him with me. The children are attached to him, and so am I . . .'

'I'll see what I can do,' he says. 'I think dog passports are pushing the remit just a tad. But I'll try.'

'God,' she says, eyes wide with feigned gratitude. 'Thank you so much, Michael. I can't tell you how relieved I am. I literally just got the message about my friend last night and I couldn't sleep all night for worrying about how I was going to get to her. Thank you.'

'Well, I haven't done it yet.'

'I know,' she says. 'I know you haven't. But still, I'm so grateful.'

She sees his face turn from genial to creepy. 'Really, really grateful?'

She forces a smile. She knows where this is going; she was prepared for it. 'Really, really, really grateful,' she says.

'Ah.' He leans back into his chair and smiles. 'I like the sound of that.'

She returns his smile and runs her hand down her hair.

His eyes reach to the shuttered windows overhead, towards the master bedroom suite, location of multiple marital rapes. Then they return to her and she stifles a shudder. 'Maybe next time,' she says.

He cocks an eyebrow and slings one arm across the back of the chair to his right. 'Are you incentivising me?'

'Possibly,' she says.

'I like your style.'

She smiles. And then she sits straight and picks up the straps of her handbag. 'But right now,' she says, 'I need to get back to my sleeping children.'

They both get to their feet. 'When do you think . . .' she says hesitantly.

'I'll get on the case right now,' he says. 'Let me have your number, and I'll call you when I've got news.'

'I don't have a phone right now,' she says.

He grimaces. 'But you just said you got a message last night, about your friend?'

If sleeping on the beach for a week did anything for a person, it taught them to think on their feet. 'Oh, that was on the landline, in the hostel. Someone left it for me. On a piece of paper.'

'Right then, how will I get hold of you? Shall I call you at the hostel?'

'No,' she says coolly. 'No. Give me your number. I'll call you from the payphone. I'll call on Friday?'

He scribbles down his number and hands it to her. 'Yes, call me Friday. And here . . .' He puts his hand into his pocket and pulls out a folded wad of notes. He pulls off a few twenties and passes them to her. 'Get yourself a phone. For the love of God.'

She takes the twenties and says thank you. She has nothing left to lose now. She's just signed her soul away for a passport.

20

CHELSEA, 1989

Months and months passed. Phineas turned thirteen and grew an Adam's apple and a small blond moustache. I grew an inch and finally got my hair long enough to flop. My sister and Clemency became more and more insanely bonded, sharing a secret language and spending hours in a den made of bedsheets and upturned chairs in the empty bedroom on the attic floor. Birdie's band released a terrible single which got to number 48 in the charts, she left the band in a huff, nobody in the music press appeared to notice or care and she began to teach fiddle professionally in the music room.

Meanwhile, Justin turned my father's garden into a commercial enterprise, selling his herbal remedies through classified adverts in the backs of newspapers, Sally taught us all, for four hours every day, around the kitchen table and David ran three weekly classes for his alternative therapies in a church hall in World's End and came home with pockets full of cash.

Phin had been absolutely correct in his prediction all those months earlier.

The Thomsens were going nowhere.

I can look back at those years in the house on Cheyne Walk with the Thomsens and see exactly the tipping points, the pivots upon which fate twisted and turned, upon which the storyline warped so hideously. I remember the dinner at the Chelsea Kitchen and seeing my father already losing a power struggle he was too weak to realise had begun. And I remember my mother holding herself back from David, refusing to shine for fear of him desiring her. I remember where it started, but I have no idea how we'd got from that night to the point nine months later when strangers had taken over every corner of our home and my parents had let them.

My father feigned an interest in the various goings-on. He'd potter around the garden with Justin, pretending to be fascinated by his rows of herbs and plants; he'd pour two fingers of whiskey into two big tumblers every night at 7 p.m. and sit with David at the kitchen table and have strained conversations about politics and world affairs, his eyes bulging slightly with the effort of sounding as if he had a clue what he was talking about. (All my father's opinions were either black or white; things were either right or wrong, good or bad: there was no nuance to his world view. It was embarrassing.) He'd sit in on our classroom lessons in the kitchen sometimes and look terribly impressed by how clever we all were. I could not work out what had happened to my father. It was as though Henry Lamb had vacated the house but left his body behind.

I wanted desperately to talk to him about everything that was happening, the upending of my world, but I was scared that it would be like pulling a scab off his last remaining hold on his own sense of significance. He seemed so vulnerable, so broken. I saw him one lunchtime in early summer, clutching his mohair cap and his jacket, checking the contents of his wallet at the front door. We'd finished lessons for the day and I was bored.

'Where are you going?' I asked.

'To my club,' he replied.

Ah, his club. A set of smoky rooms in a side street off Piccadilly. I'd been there once before when my mother was out and our babysitter had failed to materialise. Rather than be stuck at home with two small, dull children to entertain, he'd put us into the back of a black cab and taken us to his club. Lucy and I had sat in a corner with lemonades and peanuts while my father sat smoking cigars and drinking whiskey with men I'd never seen before. I'd been enchanted by it, had wished never to leave, had prayed that our babysitters would fail to turn up for evermore.

'Can I come?'

He looked at me blankly, as though I'd asked him a hard maths question.

'Please. I'll be quiet. I won't talk.'

He glanced up the staircase as though the solution to his conundrum might be about to appear on the landing. 'You finished school?'

'Yes.'

'Fine.'

He waited while I put on my jacket; then we walked out on to the street together and he hailed a taxi.

In the club he found nobody he knew and while we waited for our drinks to be delivered he looked at me and said, 'So, how are you?'

'Confused,' I began.

'Confused?'

'Yes. About how our lives are turning out.' I held my breath. This was exactly the sort of impudent approach that would have had my father grimacing at me in the past, turning his gaze to my mother and asking her darkly if she thought this sort of behaviour

143

was acceptable, was this the sort of child they were bringing up.

But he looked at me with watery blue eyes and said, simply, 'Yes.'

His gaze left mine immediately.

'Are you confused too?'

'No, son, no. I'm not confused. I know exactly what's going on.'

I couldn't tell if he meant that he knew what was going on and was in control of it, or that he knew what was going on but could do nothing to stop it.

'So – what?' I said. 'What is it?'

Our drinks arrived: a lemonade on a white paper coaster for me, a whiskey and water for my dad. He hadn't answered my question and I thought maybe he wouldn't. But then he sighed. 'Son,' he said, 'sometimes in life you get to a fork in the road. Your mother and I, we got to a fork in the road. She wanted to go one way, I wanted to go another. She won.'

My brow shot up. 'You mean Mummy wants all the people in the house? She actually wants them?'

'Wants them?' he asked grimly, as though my question was somehow ridiculous when it clearly wasn't.

'Does she want to live with all these people?'

'Christ, I don't know. I don't know what your mother wants any more. And here, take my advice. Never marry a woman. They might look good, but they destroy you.'

None of this was making any sense at all. What did marrying women – something I had no earthly intention of ever doing, but also something about which I thought there was no other option; if you didn't marry a woman then who would you marry? – have to do with the people upstairs?

I stared at him, willing him to say something clear and enlightening. But my father didn't have the emotional intelligence or, indeed, since his stroke, the vocabulary to be clear or enlightening. He pulled a cigar from the pocket of his jacket and spent some time preparing it to be smoked. 'Are you not keen on them, then?' he said eventually.

'No,' I replied. 'I'm not. Will they ever go?'

'Well, if I had anything to do with it . . .'

'But it's your house. Surely you have everything to do with it.'

I caught my breath, worried I'd pushed him too far.

But he just sighed. 'You'd have thought so, wouldn't you?'

His obtuseness was killing me. I wanted to scream. I said, 'Can't you just tell them to go? Tell them we want our house back. That we want to go to school again. That we don't want them here any more?'

'No,' said my father. 'No. I can't.'

'But why?'

My voice had risen an octave and I could see my father recoil.

'I told you,' he snapped. 'It's your mother. She needs them. She needs *him*.'

'Him?' I said. 'David?'

'Yes. David. Apparently he makes her feel better about her pointless existence. Apparently he gives her life "meaning". Now,' he growled, opening up a newspaper, 'you said you wouldn't talk. How about you stick to your word?'

21

Miller Roe stands outside the house on Cheyne Walk, staring at his phone. He looks even more rumpled than he'd looked that morning in the café on West End Lane. He straightens when he sees Libby and Dido approach and he smiles.

'Miller, this is Dido, my colleague—' She corrects herself: 'My *friend*. Dido, this is Miller Roe.'

They shake hands and then all turn to face the house. Its windows glow golden in the light of the evening sun.

'Libby Jones,' says Dido, 'good grief. You own an actual mansion.'

Libby smiles and turns to open the padlock. She feels no sense of ownership as they cluster together in the hallway, looking around themselves. She still expects the solicitor to appear, striding ahead of them authoritatively.

'I see what you mean about all the wood,' says Miller. 'You know, this house used to be full of stuffed animal heads and hunting knives. Apparently there were actual thrones, just here . . .' He indicates the spots on either side of the staircase. 'His and hers,' he adds wryly.

'Who told you about the thrones?' asks Dido.

'Old friends of Henry and Martina, who used to come here for raucous dinner parties in the seventies and early eighties. When Henry and Martina were socialites. When their children were tiny. It was all very glamorous, apparently.'

'So, all those old friends,' Dido continues, 'where were they when everything turned dark?'

'Oh God, they weren't proper friends. They were parents of the children's friends at school, transient neighbours, cosmopolitan flotsam and jetsam. Nobody who really cared about them. Just people who remembered them.'

'And their thrones,' says Libby.

'Yes.' Miller smiles. 'And their thrones.'

'And what about extended family?' Dido asks. 'Where were they?'

'Well, Henry had no family. He was an only child, both parents were dead. Martina's father was estranged, her mother remarried and was living in Germany with a second family. Apparently she kept trying to come over and Martina kept putting her off. She even sent one of her sons over, in 1992; he came and knocked at the door every day for five days and nobody ever replied. He said he heard noises, saw curtains moving. The phone line rang dead. The mother was racked with guilt that she hadn't tried harder to access her daughter. Never got over it. Can I . . . ?' He's veering to the left, towards the kitchen.

Libby and Dido follow him.

'So, this is where the children were taught,' he says. 'The drawers were full of paper and textbooks and exercise books.'

'Who taught them?'

'We don't know. It wouldn't have been Henry Lamb. He failed all his O levels and didn't go into higher education. Martina didn't have English as her first language, so it was unlikely to be her. So, one of the mystery "others", we imagine. And most likely a woman.'

'What happened to all the schoolbooks?' Libby asks.

'I have no idea,' says Miller. 'Maybe they're still here?'

Libby looks at the big wooden table in the middle of the room with its two sets of drawers on each side. She holds in her breath and pulls them open in turn. The drawers are empty. She sighs.

'Police evidence,' says Miller. 'They may well have destroyed them.'

'What else did they take as police evidence?' Dido asks.

'The robes. Bedclothes. All the apothecarial stuff, the bottles and trays and what have you. Soap. Face cloths. Towels. Fibres, of course, that sort of thing. But really, there was nothing else. No art on the walls, no toys, no shoes.'

'No shoes?' Dido repeats.

Libby nods. It was one of the most shocking of all the details in Miller's *Guardian* article. A house full of people and not one pair of shoes.

Dido glances around. 'This kitchen', she says, 'would have been the absolute height of kitchen chic back in the seventies.'

'Wouldn't it just?' agrees Miller. 'Top of the range, too. Virtually everything that had been in the house – before they sold everything – was bought from Harrods. The archivist in their sales department let me see the sales invoices, going back to the date Henry bought the house. Appliances, beds, light shades, sofas, clothes, weekly flower deliveries, hair appointments, toiletries, towels, food, everything.'

'Including my cot.'

'Yes, including your cot. Which was bought, if I recall, in 1977, when young Henry was a newborn.'

'So I was the third baby to sleep in it?'

'Yes. I guess so.'

They head towards the small room at the front of the house and Dido says, 'What's your theory? What do you think happened here?'

'In a nutshell? Strange people move in with wealthy family. Strange things happen and everyone dies, apart from some teenage children who are never heard of again. And of course, the baby. Serenity. And there was evidence that someone else lived here once. Someone who developed the herb garden. I spent an entire month tracking down every apothecary in the UK and abroad who might have been living in London at that time. Nothing. Not a trace.'

The room in which they stand is wood-panelled and wood-floored. There is a huge stone fireplace on the far wall and the remains of a mahogany bar on the other.

'They found equipment in here,' Miller says gravely. 'The police thought it was torture equipment at first, but apparently it was homemade callisthenics equipment. The bodies of two of the suicide victims were found to be very lean and hyper-muscled. This was clearly the room where they exercised. Possibly to mitigate against the negative effects of never leaving the house. So again, I spent a month hunting down every teacher of callisthenics I could find, to see if anyone knew about this technique being used in Chelsea in the eighties and early nineties. Again – nothing.' He sighs, and then turns suddenly to Libby. 'Did you find the secret staircase? To the attic?'

'Yes, the solicitor showed me when he brought me here.'

'Did you see the locks? On the children's doors?'

Libby feels a tremor pass through her. 'I hadn't read your article then,' she says, 'so I didn't look. And last time I came . . .' She pauses. 'Last time, I thought I heard someone up there and freaked out and left.'

'Shall we go and look?'

She nods. 'OK.'

'There's one of these secret staircases in my parents' house,' says Dido, clutching the handrail as they ascend the narrow staircase. 'Always used to give me the heebie-jeebies when I was little. I used to think that a cross ghost was going to lock both doors and I'd be trapped in there forever.'

At this, Libby quickens her pace and emerges slightly breathlessly on to the attic landing.

'You OK?' Miller asks kindly.

'Mm,' she murmurs. 'Just about.'

He puts his hand to his ear. 'Hear that?' he says.

'What?'

'That creaking?'

She nods, her eyes wide.

'That's what old houses do when they get too hot, or too cold. They complain. That's what you heard the other day. The house complaining.'

She contemplates asking him if houses also cough when they get hot, and decides against it.

Miller takes his phone from his pocket and fixes the camera ahead of him, filming as he goes. 'God,' he says in a loud whisper. 'This is it. This is it.'

He angles his camera towards the door of the first room on the left. 'Look,' he says.

She and Dido both look. There is a lock attached to the outside of the room. They follow him to the next door. Another lock. And another and another.

'All four rooms, lockable from the outside. This is where the police think the children slept. This is where they found some traces of blood and the marks on the walls. Look,' he says, 'even the toilet had a lock on the outside. Shall we?'

He has his hand on the handle of one of the rooms.

Libby nods.

When she'd first read Miller's article, she'd skimmed over the paragraphs about the attic rooms, unable to stomach the thought of what it suggested. Now she just wants to get it over with.

It's a good-sized room, painted white with flashes of yellow around the skirting boards, bare floorboards, tattered white curtains at the windows, thin mattresses in the corners, nothing more. The next room is the same. And the next. Libby holds her breath when they get to the fourth bedroom, convinced that behind the door there will be a man. But there is no man, just another empty, white room with white curtains and bare floorboards. They are about to close the door behind them when Miller stops, takes his camera to the furthest end of the room and aims it at the mattress.

'What?'

As he nears the mattress, he pulls it away from the wall slightly and zooms in on something wedged there.

'What is it?'

He picks it up and shows it first to his camera and then to himself. 'It's a sock.'

'A sock?'

'Yes. A man's sock.'

It's a red and blue sock, an odd blast of colour upon the blank canvas of the attic bedrooms.

'That's weird,' says Libby.

'It's more than weird,' says Miller. 'It's impossible. Because look.' He turns the sock over and shows it to Libby and Dido.

The sock bears the Gap logo.

'What?' says Dido. 'I don't get it.'

'That's the *current* Gap logo,' he says. 'They've only been using that logo for the past couple of years.' He locks his gaze with Libby's. 'This sock is new.'

22

Lucy calls Michael at five o'clock on Friday afternoon from a payphone around the corner. He answers immediately. 'I thought it might be you,' he says, and she can hear the lascivious smile behind his voice.

'How are you?' she asks brightly.

'Oh, I'm just great, and how are you?'

'I'm just great too.'

'Did you buy yourself a phone yet? This is a land-line number, no?'

'Someone I know is getting me one,' she lies smoothly. 'Something reconditioned. Should be getting it tomorrow.'

'Good,' says Michael, 'good. And since I realise that

this is not a social call, I guess you'll want to know how I got on with your little *request*.'

She laughs lightly. 'I would quite like to know,' she says.

'Well,' he continues, 'you are going to fucking love me, Lucy Lou, because I have got you the full monty. Passports for you, for Marco, your girl and even your dog. In fact, I paid so much for the passports that they threw the dog's in for free!'

She feels the ever-present bile curdle her lunch. She doesn't want to think about how much money Michael spent on the passports and how much he will want in return. She forces a laugh and says, 'Oh! How kind of them!'

'Kind, my ass,' he says. And then he says, 'So, wanna come over? Come and collect them?'

'Sure!' she says. 'Sure. Not today. But maybe tomorrow, or Sunday?'

'Come Sunday,' he says. 'Come for lunch. It's Joy's day off Sunday so we'll have the place to ourselves.'

She feels the bile rise from her stomach to the base of her throat. 'What time?' she manages to ask breezily.

'Let's say one. I'll put some steaks on the barbecue. You can make that thing you used to make, what was it? With the bread and tomatoes?'

'Panzanella.'

'That's the one. God, you used to make that so well.'

'Oh,' she says, 'thank you. I hope I've still got the magic touch.'

'Yeah. Your magic touch. I really, really miss your magic touch.'

Lucy laughs. She says goodbye, she says she'll see him on Sunday at 1 p.m. Then she puts down the phone, runs to the toilet and throws up.

23

In the summer of 1990, when I had just turned thirteen, I came upon my mother one afternoon on the landing. She was placing piles of clean bedding in the airing cupboard. Once upon a time we'd had our laundry taken away once a week in a small van with gold lettering on the side and then returned to us a few days later in immaculate bales wrapped in ribbon or hanging from wooden hangers under plastic sheets.

'What happened to the laundry service?' I asked.

'What laundry service?'

Her hair had grown long. She had not, as far as I was aware, had it cut in the two years since the other people had moved in with us. Birdie wore her hair

Lisa Jewell

long, and so did Sally. My mother had worn her hair in
a bob. Now it was past her shoulder blades and parted
in the middle. I wondered if she was trying to be like
the other women, in the same way that I was trying to
be like Phin.

'Remember? That old man who came in the white
van to collect our laundry, and he was so tiny you
used to worry that he wouldn't be able to carry it all?'

My mother's gaze panned slowly to the left, as
though remembering a dream, and she said, 'Oh yes. I
forgot about him.'

'How come he doesn't come any more?'

She rubbed her fingertips together, and I looked
at her with alarm. I knew what the gesture meant,
and it was something I'd long suspected, but this
was the first time I'd had it confirmed to me. We were
poor.

'But what happened to all Dad's money?'

'Shhh.'

'But I don't understand.'

'Shhh!' she said again. And then she pulled me gently by the arm into her bedroom and sat me on her
bed. She held my hand in hers and she stared hard
at me. I noticed she wasn't wearing any eye make-
up and wondered when that had stopped. So many
things had changed so slowly over such a long period
of time that it was hard sometimes to spot the joins.

'You have to promise, promise, promise,' she said, 'not to talk to anyone else about this. Not your sister. Not the other children. Not the grown-ups. Nobody, OK?'

I nodded hard.

'And I'm only telling you because I trust you. Because you're sensible. So don't let me down, OK?'

I nodded even harder.

'Dad's money ran out a long time ago.'

I gulped.

'What, like, all of it?'

'Basically.'

'So, what are we living on?'

'Dad's been selling stocks and shares. There's still a couple of savings accounts. If we can live on thirty pounds a week we'll be OK for at least a couple of years.'

'Thirty pounds a week?' My eyes bulged. My mother used to spend thirty pounds a week on fresh flowers alone. 'But that's impossible!'

'It's not. David's sat down with us and worked it all out.'

'David? But what does David know about money? He doesn't even have a house!'

'Shhh.' She put her finger to her lips and glanced warily at the bedroom door. 'You'll have to trust us, Henry. We're the grown-ups and you're just going to have to trust us. Birdie's bringing money in with her fiddle lessons. David's bringing money in with his exercise classes. Justin's making loads of money.'

'Yes, but they're not giving any to us, are they?'

'Well, yes. Everyone is contributing. We're making it work.'

And that was when it hit me. Hard and clear.

'Is this a commune now?' I asked, horrified.

My mother laughed as though this was a ridiculous suggestion. 'No!' she said. 'Of course it isn't!'

'Why can't Dad just sell the house?' I asked. 'We could go and live in a little flat somewhere. It would be really nice. And then we'd have loads of money.'

'But this is not just about money, you do know that, don't you?'

'Then what?' I said. 'What is it about?'

She sighed, softly, and massaged my hand with her thumbs. 'It's, well, it's about me, I suppose. It's about how I feel about myself and how I've felt so sad for so long and how all of this' – she gestured around her grand bedroom with its swagged curtains and glistening chandelier – 'doesn't make me happy, it really doesn't. And then David came and he's shown me another way to live, a less selfish way. We have *too much*, Henry. Can you see that? Way, way too much, and when you have too much it drags you down. And now the money has virtually gone it is a good time to change, to think about what we eat and what we use and what we spend and how we fill our days. We have to give to the world, not keep taking from it. You know, David . . .' I heard her voice ring like a spoon against a wine glass when she said his name. '. . . he gives nearly all his money to charity. And now, with his guidance, we are doing the same. To give to needy people is so good for the soul. And the life we lived before, it was wasteful. So wrong. Do you see? But now, with David here to guide us, we can start to redress the balance.'

I allowed myself a moment to absorb the full meaning of what had been said.

'So, they're staying,' I said eventually. 'Forever?'

'Yes,' she replied with a small smile. 'Yes. I hope so.'

'And we're poor?'

'No. Not poor, darling. We're unburdened. We're free.'

24

Libby, Miller and Dido search the house from top to bottom looking for a possible means of entry for the mystery sock man. There is a large glazed door at the back of the house, which opens on to stone stairs down to the garden. It is bolted from the inside and, it transpires when they try to open it, also locked. Wisteria grows thickly across the cracks between the door and the doorframe, indicating that it has not been opened in many weeks, maybe even years.

They push at the dusty sash windows, but they're all locked. They peer into dark corners looking for secret doors but there are none.

They go through all the keys on Libby's bunch one

by one and finally find the one that unlocks the glazed door. But still the door doesn't budge.

Miller peers downwards through the glass to the outside of the door. 'It's been padlocked,' he says, 'from the outside. Do you have a small key on that bunch?'

Libby finds the smallest key that she can and passes it to Miller.

'How would you feel if I were to take out a pane of glass?'

'Take it out?' she says. 'With what?'

He shows her his elbow.

She winces. 'Go on then.'

He uses the tattered chintz curtain to soften the impact. The glass cracks and comes out in two perfect pieces. He puts his arm through the hole and unlocks the padlock with the tiny key. Finally the door opens, ripping apart the knots of wisteria.

'Here,' says Miller, striding out on to the lawn. 'This is where the drugs were grown.'

'The drugs that killed Libby's parents?' asks Dido.

'Yes. *Atropa belladonna*. Or deadly nightshade, in other words. The police found a big bush of the stuff.'

They walk to the bottom of the garden, shady and cool under the canopy of a tall acacia tree. There is a bench here, curved, to follow the shadow of the tree, and facing the back of the house. Even during the hottest summer that London has known in over twenty years, the bench is damp and mildewed. Libby lays her fingertips gently on to the armrest. She pictures Martina Lamb sitting here on a sunny morning, a mug of tea resting where Libby's fingers lie, watching the birds wheel overhead. She pictures her other hand going to cup her pregnant bump, smiling as she feels her baby kick and roll inside her.

And then she pictures her a year later taking poison with her dinner, then lying down on the kitchen floor and dying for no good reason at all, leaving her baby all alone upstairs.

Libby snatches her hand back and turns abruptly to look at the house.

From here they can see the four large windows that span the back of the drawing room. They can see another four smaller windows above, two in each of the back bedrooms, plus a smaller window in the middle that sits at the top of the landing. Above that are eight narrow windows with eaves, two for each attic bedroom, and a tiny circular window in between where the bathroom is. And then a flat roof, three chimney stacks and the blue sky beyond.

'Look!' says Dido, reaching on to her tiptoes and pointing wildly. 'Look! Is that a ladder there? Or a fire escape?'

'Where?'

'There! Look! Just tucked behind that chimney stack, the red one. Look.'

Libby sees it, a glint of metal. She follows it down with her eyes to a brickwork ledge, then a lip above the eaves, then a drainpipe that attaches itself to another brickwork promontory on the side of the house, a short hop across to the adjoining garden wall, then down to a kind of concrete bunker, then to the garden.

She spins round. Behind is dense foliage, bounded by an old brick wall. She pushes an obvious path through it, her feet finding the bare patches in the weeds. The growth is laced with old spider webs which catch on her clothes and in her hair. But she keeps moving. She can feel this course, it's already in her, she knows what she's looking for. And there it is, a battered wooden gate, painted dark green, hanging off its hinges, and leading into the overgrown back end of the garden of the house behind.

Miller and Dido stand behind her, peering across her shoulder through the wooden gate. She pushes the gate as hard as she can and peers into the neighbour's garden.

It's scruffy and unmanicured. There's a wonky sundial in the middle of the lawn, and some dusty gravelled paths. There's no furniture, no children's toys. And there, down the side of the house, a pathway that seems, from here, to lead directly to the street.

'I've got it,' she says, touching the padlock that has been snapped open with bolt cutters. 'Look. Whoever it is that's been sleeping in the house has been getting in through this gate, across the garden, up on to that concrete thing over there' – she leads them back into the garden – 'up on to the garden wall, up the drainpipe on to that platform, see, up there, then up there on to the ledge, and then on to the roof and to the ladder. We just need to work out where that ladder goes.'

She looks at Miller. He looks back at her. 'I'm not very agile,' he says.

She looks at Dido, who puffs out her cheeks and says, 'Oh, come on.'

They head back into the house and back up to the attic rooms. And there it is, a small wooden trapdoor in the ceiling in the hallway. Miller puts Libby on his shoulders and she pushes at it.

'What can you see?'

'A dusty tunnel. And another door. Push me up higher.'

Miller grunts and gives her another boost. She clings on to a wooden slat and pulls herself up. The heat is intense up here, and she can feel her clothes sticking to her body with sweat. She crawls along the tunnel and pushes the next wooden trapdoor and is immediately hit by full, glorious sunshine. She's on a flat roof, where there are some dead plants in pots and two plastic chairs.

She puts her hands on her hips and surveys the view from up here: in front is the sun-baked greenery of Embankment Gardens, beyond that the dark belt of the river. Behind her she can see the grid of narrow streets that stretches between here and the King's Road; a beer garden filled with drinkers, a patchwork of back gardens and parked cars.

'What can you see?' she hears Dido bellow from below.

'I can see everything,' she says, 'absolutely everything.'

25

Marco looks at Lucy through narrowed eyes. 'Why can't we come?' he says. 'I don't understand.'

Lucy sighs, adjusts her eyeliner in the small hand mirror she's using and says, 'Just because, OK? He's done me a huge favour and he's asked me to come alone and so I'm going alone.'

'But what if he hurts you?'

Lucy stops herself flinching. 'He's not going to hurt me, OK? We had a very twisted marriage but we're not in that marriage any more. Things move on. People change.'

She can't look at her son while she lies to him. He would see the fear in her eyes. He would know what she was about to do. And he would have no idea why she was about to do it because he had no idea about her childhood, about what she'd run away from twenty-four years ago.

'You need a code,' says Marco authoritatively. 'I'll call you and if you're scared you just say, *How's Fitz?* OK?'

She nods and smiles. 'OK,' she says. She pulls him to her and kisses him behind his ear. He lets her.

Stella and Marco stand in the kitchen and watch her leave a few minutes later.

'You look pretty, Mama,' says Stella.

Lucy's stomach sinks. 'Thank you, baby,' she says. 'I'll be back at about four. And I will have passports and we can start planning our trip to London.' She smiles broadly, showing all her teeth. Stella hugs her leg. Lucy detaches her after a moment and leaves the building without turning back.

Fitz's shit is still there. It has twice as many bluebottles on it. She finds it strangely reassuring.

Michael opens the door; he has sunglasses on his head and is wearing loose shorts and a bright white T-shirt. He takes her bag of groceries from her, the tomatoes and bread and anchovies she picked up on the way over, and he swoops in to kiss her on both cheeks. Lucy can smell beer on his breath.

'Don't you look pretty?' he says. 'Wow. Come in, come in.'

She follows him into the kitchen. Two steaks sit on paper on the counter, a bottle of wine sits in a silver wine bucket. He's listening to Ed Sheeran on the Sonos sound system and seems to be in very high spirits.

'Let me get you a drink,' he says. 'What would you like? G & T? Bloody Mary? Wine? Beer?'

'I'll have a beer,' she says, 'thank you.'

He passes her a Peroni and she takes a sip. She should have had a big breakfast, she realises, feeling the first mouthful already heading straight to her head.

'Cheers,' he says, holding his bottle to hers.

'Cheers,' she echoes. There is a bowl of his favourite ridged crisps on the counter and she takes a large handful. She needs to be sober enough to stay in control but drunk enough to go through with what she came here to do.

'So,' she says, finding a chopping board in one of the drawers and a knife in another, taking the tomatoes out of the shopping bag. 'How's the writing going?'

'God, do not ask,' he says, rolling his eyes. 'It has not been a *productive week*, let's put it that way.'

'I guess that's how it goes, isn't it? It's a psychological thing.'

'Hm,' he says, passing her a serving dish. 'On the one hand. On the other hand, all the best writers just get on with it. It's like deciding not to go for a jog because it's raining. It's just an excuse. So, I must try harder.' He smiles at her and for a moment he seems almost humble, almost real, and for a moment she thinks maybe today won't pan out how she thought it would pan out, that maybe they will simply have lunch and talk and then he will give her the passports and let her go with nothing more than a hug on his doorstep.

'Fair enough,' she says, feeling Michael's hyper-sharpened knife sliding through the soft tomatoes like they are butter. 'I suppose it's just a job, like any other. You have to show up and get it done.'

'Exactly,' he says, 'exactly.' He downs the second half of his beer and drops the empty bottle in the re-cycling bin. He pulls another from the fridge and then holds one out to Lucy. She shakes her head and shows him her bottle, still nearly full.

'Drink up,' he says. 'I have a beautiful Sancerre chilling here for you, your favourite.'

'Sorry,' she says, bringing the bottle back to her lips. 'I've been on the wagon for quite a long time.'

'Oh yeah?'

'Not deliberately,' she replies. 'Just haven't had the money.'

'Well, let's call this Operation Get Lucy off the Wagon, shall we? Come on. Drink up.'

And there it is, that edge, so close to friendly, yet just a degree towards aggression. Not a light-hearted request, but a command. She smiles and downs half the bottle.

He watches her intently. 'Good girl,' he says, 'good girl. And the rest.'

She smiles grimly and necks the rest, almost choking on it as it goes down too fast.

He beams at her, shark-like, and says, 'Oh, good girl. *Good girl.*'

He takes the empty bottle from her and then turns to pull two wine glasses from a cupboard. 'Shall we?' he says, gesturing towards the door into the garden.

'Let me just finish this.' She indicates the tomatoes still only half chopped.

'Finish that later,' he instructs. 'Let's have a drink first.'

She follows him out to the patio, holding the bowl of crisps and her handbag.

He pours two large glasses of wine and pushes one across the table towards her. They toast each other again and then he pinions her with his eyes. 'So, Lucy Lou, tell me, tell me everything. What have you been doing for the past ten years?'

'Ha!' she says shrilly. 'Where on earth do you want me to start?'

'How about you start with the man who gave you your daughter?'

Lucy's stomach flips. She'd known from the moment

Michael set his eyes upon Stella that he would have been thinking about her having sex with another man.

'Oh, really,' she says, 'not much to tell. It was a disaster. But I got Stella out of it. So, you know.'

He leans towards her, fixes her with his hazel eyes. He is smiling but it doesn't reach his eyes. 'No,' he says. 'I really don't know. Who was he? Where did you meet him?'

She thinks of the passports sitting somewhere in this house. She cannot afford to make him angry. She cannot tell him that Stella's father was the love of her life, the most beautiful man she'd ever set eyes on, that he was an exquisite pianist whose music brought her to tears, that he'd broken her heart and that she was still carrying the shattered pieces of it around in her pockets even now, three years since she'd last seen him.

'He was an arsehole,' she says. Then she pauses and takes a large sip of wine. 'Just a pretty boy, a criminal, with nothing between his ears. I felt sorry for him. He didn't deserve me, and he certainly didn't deserve Stella.' She speaks the words with conviction, because while she looks Michael directly in the eye, little does he know that she is describing him.

This description seems to sate Michael for a moment. His smile softens and he looks real again.

'Where is he now, this idiot?'

'He did a runner. Went back to Algeria. Broke his mother's heart. His mother blames me.' She shrugs. 'But really, he was always going to disappoint her. He was always going to disappoint everyone. He was just one of those guys.'

He leans towards her again. 'Did you love him?'

She snorts derisively. 'God,' she says, still thinking of Michael. '*No*.'

He nods, as though giving her approval. 'And was there anyone else? Over the years?'

She shakes her head. It's another lie but an easier one to tell. 'No,' she says. 'No one. I've been living hand to mouth with two small children. Even if I had met someone, you know, it wouldn't have worked. Logistically.' She shrugs.

'Yeah. I can see that. And you know, Lucy' – he looks at her earnestly – 'you know, any time you'd asked, I would have helped. All you had to do was ask.'

She shakes her head sadly.

He says, 'Yeah. I know. Too proud.'

This is so far from the truth that it is almost funny, but she nods, knowingly. 'You know me so well,' she says, and he laughs.

'In so many ways we were the worst, worst combination of people. I mean, Jesus, remember the times we used to have? Christ we were *crazy*! But in other ways we were, God, we were fucking awesome, weren't we?'

Lucy makes herself smile and nod agreement, but she can't quite bring herself to say yes.

'Maybe we should have tried harder,' he says, topping up his glass already and then topping up Lucy's even though she's barely had two sips.

'Sometimes life just happens,' she says meaninglessly.

'That's true, Lucy,' he agrees as though she has just said something very profound. He takes a large gulp of wine and says, 'Tell me all about my boy. Is he clever? Is he sporty?'

Is he kind? she asks silently. *Is he good? Does he take good care of his little sister? Does he keep me grounded? Does he smell nice? Can he sing? Can he draw the most beautiful portraits of people? Does he deserve better than me and this shitty life I've given him?*

'He's pretty clever,' she replies. 'Average at maths and science, excellent at languages, art, English. And no, not sporty. Not at all.'

She looks at him steadily, searching his gaze for a shadow of disappointment. But he looks pragmatic. 'You can't win at everything,' he says. 'And boy is he good-looking. Any sign of an interest in girls yet?'

'He's only twelve,' Lucy says, somewhat brusquely.

'That's old enough,' he says. 'God, you don't think he might be gay, do you?'

She wants to throw her wine in Michael's face and

leave. Instead she says, 'Who knows? No signs of it. But as I say, he's not really interested in that sort of thing yet. Anyway,' she changes the subject, 'I should probably get back to the panzanella. Give it time to steep before we eat.'

She gets to her feet. He gets to his and says, 'And I should get the barbecue going.' She heads towards the kitchen but before she can walk away, he catches her hands in his and turns her to face him. She can see his eyes are swimming, that he's already losing focus and it's only half past one. He puts his hands on to her hips and pulls them towards him. Then he pushes her hair away from her ear, leans tight in towards her and whispers, 'I should never have let you go.'

His lips graze hers, briefly, and then he pats her on her bottom and watches her as she walks into the kitchen.

26

Shortly after my mother told me that David was making us give all our money to charity and that he was going to be living with us forever, I saw him kissing Birdie.

It was sickening to me at the time, on so many levels.

Firstly, as you know, I found Birdie physically repellent. The thought of her hard little lips against David's big generous mouth, his hands on her bony hips, her gross tongue chasing his around inside the dank cave made from their mouths. *Ouf.*

Secondly, I was something of a traditionalist and found the sight of adultery shocking to my core.

And thirdly: well, the third awful thing didn't strike me immediately. It couldn't have really, because the

179

implications of what I'd unwittingly seen were not entirely obvious. But I certainly felt something like dread pass through me at the sight of David and Birdie coming together, an innate sense that they might bring things out of each other that were better left buried away.

It happened on a Saturday morning. Sally was away taking photos on a film set somewhere. Justin had gone to set up a stall at a market to sell his herbal remedies. My mother and father were sitting in the garden in their dressing gowns reading the papers and drinking tea out of mugs. I'd slept until eight thirty, late for me. I've always been an early riser; I rarely slept later than nine even during my teenage years. I'd barely rubbed the sleep from my eyes as I emerged from my room when I saw them, clinging to each other in the doorway of David's room. She wore a muslin nightdress. He wore a black cotton robe with a belted waist. Her leg was jammed between his knees. Their groins were forced together. He had a hand to her pale, moley throat. She had a hand on his left buttock.

I immediately retreated into my bedroom, my heart pumping hard, my stomach well and truly turned. I put both my hands to my throat, trying to quell the nausea and the horror. I said the word *fuck* silently under my breath. Then I said it again, properly. I opened my door a crack a moment later and they had gone. I didn't know what to do. I needed to tell someone; I needed to tell Phin.

Phin flicked his blond curtains away from his face. He was, ludicrously, growing even more handsome as he passed through puberty. He was only fourteen and already six foot tall. He had never, as far as I was aware, had so much as a pimple. And if he had one, I would have noticed it, as studying Phin's face was virtually my hobby.

'I need to talk to you,' I hissed urgently into his face. 'It's really, really important.'

We walked to the end of the garden where a curved bench caught the morning sun. With the trees in blossom and full leaf we could not be seen from the house. We turned to face each other.

'I just saw something,' I said. 'Something really, really bad.'

Phin narrowed his eyes at me. I could tell he thought I was going to say that I'd seen the cat eating out of the butter dish or something equally babyish and banal. I could tell he had no faith in my ability to impart genuinely shocking news.

'I saw your dad. And Birdie . . .'

The expression of indulgent impatience shifted, and he looked at me in alarm.

'They were coming out of Birdie and Justin's room. And they were kissing.'

He jolted slightly at these words. I'd made my impact. Finally, after two years, Phin was really looking at me.

I saw a muscle in Phin's jaw twitch. 'Are you fucking lying to me?' he asked, almost growling.

I shook my head. 'I swear,' I said. 'I saw it. Just now. About twenty minutes ago. I swear.'

I saw Phin's eyes fill very quickly with tears and then I saw him trying very hard to force them to go away. Some people tell me I lack empathy. This might be true. It hadn't occurred to me for a moment that Phin might be upset. Shocked. Yes. Scandalised. Disgusted. But not upset.

'I'm sorry,' I said. 'I just . . .'

He shook his head. His beautiful blond hair fell across his face and then parted again to reveal an expression of grim, heart-breaking bravery. 'It's fine,' he said. 'I'm glad you told me.'

There was a beat of silence. I couldn't work out what to do. I had Phin's full attention. But I'd hurt him. I looked at his big, suntanned hands twisted together in his lap and I wanted to pick them up, caress them, hold them to my lips, kiss the pain away. I felt a terrible surge of physical desire rising through me, from the very roots of me, an agonising longing. I turned my gaze quickly from his hands to the ground between my bare feet.

'Will you tell your mum?' I said eventually.

He shook his head. The hair fell again and hid his face from me.

'It would kill her,' he said very simply.

I nodded, as though I knew what he meant. But really, I didn't. I was only thirteen. And I was a young thirteen. I knew that I'd found the sight of Birdie and David kissing passionately in their nightclothes disgusting. I knew that it was wrong that a married man should be kissing a woman who was not his wife. But I couldn't quite extrapolate those feelings beyond me. I could not imagine how that might make another person feel. I did not really understand why Sally would want to die because her husband had kissed Birdie.

'Will you tell your sister?'

'I'm not fucking telling anybody,' he snapped. 'Christ. And you mustn't either. Seriously. Don't tell anyone. Don't do anything unless I tell you to. OK?'

I nodded again. I was out of my depth and glad to follow Phin's lead.

The moment was falling away from me; I could feel it. I could tell Phin was about to stand up and go indoors and that he wasn't going to invite me to go in with him and that I would be left here on the bench staring at the back of the house with it all still blowing about inside me, all the wanting and the needing and the red raw desiring. And I knew that despite what had just happened, we'd go back to normal, back to the place of mutual polite reserve.

'Let's go out today,' I said breathlessly. 'Let's do something.'

He turned to look at me. He said, 'Have you got any money?'

'No. But I can get some.'

'I'll get some too,' he said. 'I'll meet you in the hall at ten.'

He stood then and he left. I watched him go, watched the shape of his spine under his T-shirt, the breadth of his shoulders, his big feet hitting the ground, the tragic hang of his beautiful head.

I found a handful of coins in the pockets of my father's Barbour. I took two pounds from my mother's purse. I combed my fringe and put on a jersey zip-up jacket that my mother had bought for me a few weeks before from a cheap shop on Oxford Street, which was about a hundred times nicer than anything I ever got bought from Harrods or Peter Jones.

Phin sat in his throne at the foot of the staircase with a paperback book in his hand. To this day, this is how I always picture Phin – except in my fantasies he lowers the book and he looks up at me and his eyes light up at the sight of me and he smiles. In reality he barely acknowledged my arrival.

He stood, slowly, then glanced around the house furtively. 'Coast clear.' He gestured for me to follow him through the front door.

'Where are we going?' I asked, chasing after him breathlessly.

I watched him raise his arm into a salute and move towards the kerb. A taxi pulled over and we got in.

I said, 'I can't afford to pay for taxis. I've only got two pounds fifty.'

'Don't worry about it,' he said coolly. He pulled a roll of ten-pound notes from his jacket pocket and cocked an eyebrow at me.

'Jesus! Where did you get that from?'

'My dad's secret stash.'

'Your dad has a secret stash?'

'Yup. He thinks no one knows about it. But I know everything.'

'Won't he notice?'

'Maybe,' he said. 'Maybe not. Either way there's no way of proving who took it.'

The taxi dropped us on Kensington High Street. I looked up at the building in front of us: a long façade, a dozen arched windows above, the words 'KEN-SINGTON MARKET' in chrome letters. I could hear music coming from the main entrance, something metallic, pounding, disturbing. I followed Phin inside and found myself in a terrifying rabbit warren of winding corridors, each home to multiple tiny shops, fronted by blank-faced men and women with rainbow hair, black rimmed eyes, ripped leather, white lips, shredded chiffon, fishnets, studs, platforms, nose piercings, face piercings, dog collars, quiffs, drapes, net petticoats, peroxide, pink gingham, PVC thigh-high boots, pixie boots, baseball jackets, sideburns, beehives, ballgowns, black lips, red lips, chewing gum, eating a bacon roll, drinking tea from a floral teacup with a black-painted pinkie fingernail held aloft, holding a ferret wearing a studded leather lead.

Each shop played its own music; thus the experience was of switching through channels on the radio as we walked. Phin touched things as we passed: a vintage baseball jacket, a silky bowling shirt with the word 'Billy' embroidered on the back, a rack of LPs, a studded leather belt.

I didn't touch anything. I was terrified. Incense billowed from the next little shop we passed. A woman sitting outside on a stool with white hair and white skin looked up at me briefly with icy blue eyes and I clutched my heart.

On the next stall a woman sat with a baby on her lap. I could not imagine that this was a good place for a baby to be.

We wandered the corridors of this strange place for an hour. We bought bacon rolls and very strong tea from a weird café on the top floor and watched people. Phin bought himself a black and white printed scarf of the type worn by men in the Sahara, and some seven-inch singles of music I'd never heard of. He tried to persuade me to let him buy me a black T-shirt with illustrations of snakes and swords on it. I declined, although part of me rather liked it. He tried on a pair of blue suede shoes with crêpey soles which he referred to as brothel creepers. He looked at himself in a full-length mirror, pulled his curtained hair away from his face and turned it into a quiff, rendering him suddenly into a beautiful 1950s heartthrob, Montgomery Clift crossed with James Dean.

I bought myself a bootlace tie with a silver ram's head. It was two pounds. It was slid into a paper bag by a man who looked like a punk cowboy.

We emerged an hour later into the normality of a Saturday morning, of families shopping, people getting on and off buses.

We walked for a mile into Hyde Park where we sat on a bench.

'Look,' said Phin, unfurling the fingers of his right hand.

I looked down at a small crumpled clear bag. Inside the small bag were two tiny squares of paper.

'What is that?' I asked.

'It's acid,' he replied.

I didn't understand.

'LSD,' he said.

I had heard of LSD. It was a drug, something to do with hippies and hallucinating.

My eyes widened. 'What. But how . . . ? Why?'

'The guy in the record shop. He just sort of *told* me he had it. I didn't ask. I think he thought I was older than I am.'

I stared at the tiny squares of paper in the tiny bag. My mind swam with the implications. 'You're not going to . . . ?'

'No. At least, not today. But some other time, maybe? When we're at home? You up for it?'

I nodded. I was up for anything that meant I could spend time with him.

Phin bought us sandwiches in a posh hotel overlooking the park. They came on plates with silver rims, and a knife and fork. We sat by a tall window and I wondered how we appeared: the tall, handsome man-boy, his tiny baby-faced friend in a scruffy jersey jacket.

'What do you think the grown-ups are doing now?' I asked.

'I couldn't give a shit,' said Phin.

'They might have called the police.'

'I left a note.'

'Oh,' I said, surprised by this act of conformity. 'What did it say?'

'It said me and Henry are going out, we'll be back later.'

Me and Henry. My heart leapt.

'Tell me what happened in Brittany?' I asked. 'Why did you all leave?'

He shook his head. 'You don't want to know.'

'No, I do want to know. What happened?'

He sighed. 'It was my dad. He took something that wasn't his. Then he said, oh, you know, I thought we were all supposed to be sharing everything, but this was like a family heirloom. It was worth about a thousand pounds. He just took it into town, sold it, then pretended he'd seen "someone" break into the house and steal it. Kept the money hidden away. The father found out through the grapevine. All hell let loose. We were turfed out the next day.' He shrugged. 'And other stuff too. But that was the main thing.'

I suddenly understood his lack of guilt about taking his father's money.

David claimed to be making a lot of money running his exercise classes, but really, how much money could you make out of a handful of hippies in a church hall twice a week? Could he have sold something of ours from under our noses? He'd already brainwashed my mother into letting him handle our family finances. Maybe he was taking money directly out of our bank account. Or maybe this was the money that my mother thought was going to charity to help poor people.

All my vague misgivings about David Thomsen began to coalesce into something hard and real.

'Do you like your dad?' I asked, fiddling with the cress on the side of my plate.

'No,' he said simply. 'I despise him.'

I nodded, reassured.

'How about you?' he said. 'Do you like your dad?'

'My dad is weak,' I replied, knowing with a burning clarity that this was true.

'All men are weak,' said Phin. 'That's the whole bloody trouble with the world. Too weak to love properly. Too weak to be wrong.'

My breath caught at the power of this statement. I immediately knew it to be the truest thing I'd ever heard. The weakness of men lay at the root of every bad thing that had ever happened.

I watched Phin peel two ten-pound notes from his wad to pay for the expensive sandwiches. 'I'm really sorry I can't pay you back,' I said.

He shook his head. 'My father's going to take everything you own and then break your life. It's the least I can bloody do.'

27

Libby, Dido and Miller lock the house up behind them and go to the pub. It's the pub Libby saw from the roof of the house. It's heaving but they find a high table in the beer garden and drag stools across from other tables.

'Who do you think it is?' says Dido, stirring her gin and tonic with her straw.

Miller replies, 'It's not someone homeless. There's not enough *stuff*. You know. If he was actually living there, there would be lots more things.'

'So you think it's someone who just comes occasionally?' says Libby.

'That would be my guess.'

'And so there *was* someone up there when I was here on Saturday?'

'That would also be my guess.'

Libby shudders.

'Look,' says Miller, 'here's what I think. You were born around June 1993?'

'June the nineteenth.' A chill goes through her as she says the date. How does anyone know? Maybe it was just made up. By the social services? By her adoptive mother? She feels her grasp on the certainty of herself start to slip and slide.

'Right. So your brother and sister would have known your date of birth given that they were teenagers when you were born. And if they somehow knew that the house was being held in trust for you until your twenty-fifth birthday, it would make sense that they might want to come back to the house. To see you . . .'

Libby gasps. 'You mean, you think it might be my brother?'

'I think it might be Henry, yes.'

'But if he knew it was me, and he was there, in the house, why didn't he come down and see me?'

'Well, that I do not know.'

Libby picks up her wine glass, puts it briefly to her lips and then puts it down again. 'No,' she says, forcefully. 'It doesn't make sense.'

'Maybe he didn't want to scare you?' suggests Dido.

'He could have left me a note?' she says. 'He could have got in touch with the solicitor and let them know he wanted to meet me? But instead, he's hiding out in the attic like a weirdo.'

'Well, maybe he *is* a weirdo?' says Dido.

'What did you find out about him?' Libby asks Miller. 'Apart from him being my brother?'

'Nothing, really,' says Miller. 'I know he went to Portman House School from the ages of three to eleven. His teachers said he was a clever boy, but a bit full of himself. He didn't really have any friends. And then he left in 1988, had a place offered to him at St Xavier's College in Kensington but didn't take it up. And that was the last anyone heard of him.'

'I just don't get it,' says Libby. 'Lurking around, slinking through tunnels and bushes, hiding upstairs when he knew I was downstairs. Are you *sure* it's Henry?'

'Well, no, of course not. But who else would know you were going to be there? Who else would know how to get into the house?'

'One of the others,' she answers. 'Maybe it's one of the others.'

28

Lucy checks the time on her phone when Michael is briefly distracted by a wasp that is bothering his plate. He flaps at it with his napkin, but it keeps coming back.

It's nearly three o'clock. She wants to be home by four. She needs the passports, but she also knows that in asking for the passports, she will be quickening the inevitable journey towards Michael's bed.

She starts to clear their plates. 'Here,' she says, 'let's get this stuff inside, that'll get rid of your annoying friend.'

His eyes are glassy and he smiles at her gratefully. 'Yup,' he says. 'Good plan, and let's get some coffee on too.'

She leads the way into the kitchen and starts to load the dishwasher. He watches her while the coffee machine grinds beans. 'You really kept your figure, Luce,' he says. 'Not bad for a forty-year-old mom of two.'

'Thirty-nine.' She smiles tightly and drops two forks into the cutlery basket. 'But thank you.'

The atmosphere is clumsy, slightly sour. They've left it too long for what comes next. They've drunk too much, eaten too much, sat for too long in the languorous air of the garden. Lucy says, 'I need to get back to the kids soon.'

'Oh,' says Michael lightly. 'Marco's a big boy. He can look after his little sister a while longer.'

'Yes, sure, but Stella gets a little anxious when she's not with me.'

She sees his jaw twitch a little. Michael does not like to hear about weakness in others. He abhors it. 'So,' he says with a sigh, 'I suppose you'll want the passports?'

'Yes. Please.'

Her heart thumps so hard under her rib cage that she can feel it in her ear canals.

He cocks his head and smiles at her. 'But don't rush off just yet? OK?'

He goes to his study and she can hear him opening and closing drawers. He returns a moment later, the passports in a felt drawstring bag in his hand. He waves it at her.

'I am nothing if not a man of my word,' he says, walking slowly towards her, his eyes on her, dangling the felt bag in front of him.

She can't work out what he's doing. Is he expecting her to snatch them from him? Chase him? What?

She smiles nervously. 'Thank you,' she says.

And then he is standing up against her, the small of her back hard against the kitchen counter, the felt bag clutched in his hand, his mouth heading towards the crook of her neck. She feels his lips against her throat. She hears him groaning.

'Oh, Lucy Lucy Lucy,' he says. 'God, you smell so good. You feel so . . .' He grinds himself against her. 'So good. You are . . .' He groans again and his mouth finds hers and she kisses him back. That is why she is here. She came here to fuck Michael and now she is going to fuck Michael and she has fucked him before and she can fuck him again, she really can, especially if she pretends he is Ahmed, pretends he is a stranger even, then yes, she can do this, she can do this.

She lets his tongue into her mouth and closes her eyes, tight, tight, tight. And his hands are pushing her up from behind, pushing her up on the counter and he takes her legs and he wraps them around his body, his hands gripping her ankles hard enough to make her wince, but she doesn't stop, she carries on because this is what she came here to do. Behind them the coffee machine bubbles and hisses. She knocks an empty glass and it rolls across the counter, smashes against the side of the kettle. She tries to move her hand away from the broken glass but Michael is pushing her closer towards it, his hands pushing up the fabric of her skirt, searching for the waistband of her knickers. She tries to move across the counter away from the glass, but she doesn't want to stop the momentum of what's happening, she needs it to happen so that it is done, so that she can pull on her underwear and take the passports and go home to her babies. She tries to focus on helping him take off her underwear, but she can feel a shard of glass under her small of her back, pressing into her flesh. She tries one last time to shift herself across the counter and then Michael suddenly pulls away and says, 'Fucking hell, will you stop fucking wriggling away from me. Fuck's sake,' and then he pushes down hard against her and she feels the glass pierce her skin and she jolts forward and shouts out in pain.

'What the fuck is it now? For fuck's sake!'

Almost in slow motion she sees his hand coming down towards her face and then she feels her teeth jolt inside her head, her brain slapping off the insides of her skull as he hits her.

And there is blood now, warm blood running from the small of her back. 'I'm hurt,' she says. 'Look. There was glass and . . .'

But he's not listening to her. Instead he forces her back on to the counter again, the glass piercing a new section of her back, and then he's inside her and his hand is over her mouth and this was not how it was going to be. It was going to be consensual. She was going to let him. But now she hurts and there is blood and she can smell the charred meat on his hand, see the blank fury on his face and she just wants the passports, she wants the fucking passports, she does not want this and her hand finds a knife; it's the knife she used to slice the tomatoes, the knife that cut through their skins like butter, and here it is in her hand and she plunges it into the side of Michael's body, into the space below the hem of his T-shirt, the soft, tender white part where the skin is like a child's skin and it goes in so easily she almost doesn't register that she's done it.

She sees his eyes cloud over briefly with confusion, then uncloud with realisation. He pulls out of her and staggers backwards. He gazes down at the blood pumping out of the hole in his side and covers it with his hands but the blood keeps pumping out. 'Fucking Christ, Luce. What the fuck have you done?' He gazes at her with wide, disbelieving eyes. 'Help me. Fuck.'

She finds tea towels and puts them into his hands. 'Hold them tight,' she says, breathlessly, 'hold them against it.'

He takes the cloths and presses them to his side and then she sees his legs buckle and he's falling to the floor. She tries to help him up again but he bats her away. It suddenly occurs to Lucy that Michael is dying. She envisages herself making a phone call to the emergency services. She imagines them arriving here, asking her what happened. She would tell them that he raped her. There would be evidence. The broken glass still embedded in her back would be proof. The fact that he still has his trousers around his ankles. Yes, they would believe her. They would.

'I'm calling an ambulance,' she says to Michael whose eyes are staring blindly into nothingness. 'Just keep breathing. Keep breathing. I'm calling them.'

She pulls her phone from her bag with shaking fingers, switches it on and is about to press the first digit when she realises this: she may well be believed, but she will not be released. She will have to stay in France, answer questions; she will have to reveal that she is here illegally, that she does not exist, and her children will be taken away from her and everything, absolutely everything will unravel, horribly, quickly, nightmarishly.

Her finger still rests on the screen of her phone. She

glances down at Michael. He is trembling. Blood still flows from his side. She feels sick and turns to face the sink, breathing hard.

'Oh God oh God oh God. Oh God oh God oh God.'

She turns back, looks at her phone, looks at Michael. She does not know what to do. And then she sees it; she sees the life pass from Michael's body. She has seen it before. She knows what it looks like. Michael is dead.

'Oh God. Oh God, oh God.' She drops to her haunches and feels for his pulse. There is nothing.

She begins to talk to herself.

'OK,' she says, standing up. 'OK. Now. Who knows you were here? Joy, he might have told Joy. But he would have told her that Lucy Smith was coming. Yes. Lucy Smith. But that is not my real name and now I am not even Lucy Smith. I am . . .' Her shaking hands find the little felt bag and she pulls out the passports. She flicks to the back and reads the text. 'I am Marie Valerie Caron. Good. Good. I am Marie Caron. Yes. And Lucy Smith does not exist. Joy does not know where I live. But . . .

'School!' she says. 'Michael knew where Marco went to school. But would he have told Joy? No. he would not have told Joy. Of course not. And even if he did, they only know Lucy Smith, not Marie Caron. And Stella is at a different school to Marco and no one apart from me and Samia knows where that is. So, what about the passport people? No. They would be somewhere so deeply buried away in the criminal underworld that no one would even think to look. The children: they knew I was here, but they would not tell anyone. Good. OK.'

She paces as she speaks. Then she looks down at Michael's body. Should she leave it? Leave it for Joy to find tomorrow morning. Or should she move him, clean everything? Hide his body? He is a big man. Where would she hide him? She would not be able to hide him completely, but maybe for just long enough for her and the children to get to London.

Yes, she decides, yes. She will clean everything. She will pull his body down into his wine cellar. She will cover it up with something. Joy will come tomorrow and think he has gone somewhere. She won't know he's missing until his body starts to smell. By which time Lucy and the children will be long gone. And everyone will just assume he was killed by someone from the shadier parts of his life.

She pulls open the cupboard beneath the sink. She takes out bleach. She opens a new roll of super-absorbent kitchen towel.

She starts to clean.

29

Chelsea, 1990

Phin and I sat on the roof of the house. Phin had found the roof. I had no idea it existed. To access the roof, one had to push open a trapdoor in the ceiling of the attic hallway, climb up into a low-roofed tunnel and then push open another trapdoor which opened out on to a flat roof with the most remarkable views across the river.

We were not, it seemed, the first to discover the secret roof terrace. There was already a pair of scruffy plastic chairs up there, some dead plants in pots, a little table.

I could barely believe that my father did not know about this space. He always complained about having a north-facing garden, that he could not enjoy the evening sun. Yet up here was a private oasis which caught the sun all day long.

The tiny squares of paper that Phin had been given at Kensington Market the week before turned out to be comprised of four even smaller squares of paper joined together. Each tiny segment had a picture of a smiling face on it.

'What if we have a bad trip?' I asked, feeling un-utterably foolish using such language.

'We should just have half each,' said Phin. 'To start off with.'

I nodded effusively. I'd have preferred to take none at all. I really wasn't that type of person. But it was Phin and I would, to use the parental cliché, have fol-lowed him off a cliff if he'd asked me to.

I watched him swallow down the tiny shred and then he watched as I did the same. The sky was water-colour blue. The sun was weak but up here, in this trap, it felt warm against our skin. We felt nothing for quite some time. We talked about what we could see: the people sitting in their gardens, the boats idling down the Thames, the view of the power station on the other side of the river. After half an hour or so I relaxed, thinking that the acid was clearly fake, that nothing was going to happen, that I'd got away with it. But then I felt my blood begin to warm beneath my skin; I glanced upwards into the sky and saw that it was filled with pulsing white veins that became luminous and multi-toned, like mother of pearl, the longer I stared at them. I realised that the sky was not blue at all but that it was a million different colours all conspiring together to create a pale blue and that the sky was conniving and lying, that the sky was in fact much cleverer than us and that maybe everything we considered to be insentient was in fact cleverer than us and laughing at us. I looked at the leaves in the trees and questioned their greenness. Are you really green? I asked myself. Or are you actually tiny little particles of purple and red and yellow and gold all having a party and laughing, laughing, laughing. I glanced at Phin. I said, 'Is your skin really white?'

He looked at his skin. He said, 'No. It's . . .' He looked at me and laughed out loud. 'I have scales! Look! I have scales. And you!' He pointed at me with great hilarity. 'You have feathers! Oh God,' he said, 'what have we become? We're creatures!'

We chased each other round the roof for a minute, making animal noises. I stroked my feathers. Phin unfurled his tongue. We both expressed shock and awe at the length of it. 'You have the longest tongue I have ever seen.'

'That's because I am a lizard.' He rolled it back in and then out again. I watched it keenly. And when it came out again, I leaned in and trapped it between my teeth.

'Ow!' said Phin, grabbing his tongue between his fingers and laughing at me.

'Sorry!' I said. 'I'm just a stupid bird. I thought it was a worm.'

And then we stopped laughing and sat in the plastic deckchairs and stared, stared, stared into the whirling aurora borealis above and our hands hung down side by side, our knuckles brushing every now and then, and each time I felt Phin's skin touch mine I felt as though his very being was penetrating my epidermis and bits of his essence were swirling into my essence, making a soup of me and him and it was too too tantalising, I needed to plug myself into him so that I could capture all of his essence and my fingers wrapped themselves around his fingers and he let me, he let me hold his hand, and I felt him pour into me like when we went on a canal boat once and the man opened the lock and we watched the water flow from one place to another.

'There,' I said, turning to look at Phin. 'There. You and me. We're the same person now.'

'We are?' said Phin, looking at me with wide eyes.

'Yes, look.' I pointed at our hands. 'We're the same.'

Phin nodded and we sat then for some time, I don't know how long, it might have been five minutes, it might have been an hour, our hands held together, staring into the sky and lost in our own strange chemically induced reveries.

'We're not having a bad trip, are we?' I said eventually.

'No,' said Phin. 'We're having a good trip.'

'The best trip,' I said.

'Yes,' he agreed. 'The best trip.'

'We should live up here,' I said. 'Bring our beds up here and live up here.'

'We should. We should do that. Right now!'

We both leapt to our feet and jumped down through the trapdoor into the tunnel above the attic. I saw the walls of the tunnel throbbing, like the inside of a body; I felt we were in a throat, maybe, or an oesophagus. We almost fell through the trapdoor into the hallway, and suddenly it felt like we were in the wrong place, like in *Doctor Who* when he opens the door to the Tardis and doesn't know where he is.

'Where are we?' I said.

'We're down,' said Phin. 'In down world.'

'I want to go back up.'

'Let's get the pillows,' said Phin. 'Quick.' He pulled me by the hand into his bedroom and we grabbed the pillows and we were about to climb back up into the tunnel when David appeared in front of us.

He was wet from the shower, his bottom half wrapped in a towel, his chest bare. I stared at his nipples. They were dark and leathery.

'What are you two up to?' he asked, his eyes switching forensically from Phin to me and back again. His voice was like a low rumble of thunder. He was tall and absolutely hard, like a statue. I felt my blood turn cold in his presence.

'We're taking pillows,' said Phin. 'To up.'

'Up?'

'Up,' repeated Phin. 'This is down.'

'Down.'

'Down,' said Phin.

'What the hell is wrong with you two?' said David. 'Look at me.' He grabbed Phin's jaw hard with his hand and stared into his eyes. 'Are you high?' he asked, turning his gaze to me. 'God, both of you. What the hell have you taken? What is it? Hash? Acid? What?'

Soon we were being ordered downstairs and my parents were being summonsed, and Phin's mum, and David was still in his towel and I still stared at his leathery nipples and felt my breakfast start to roil inside my gut. We were in the drawing room surrounded by staring oil portraits, looming dead animals nailed to the wall, four adults asking questions, questions, questions.

How? What? Where from? How did you pay for it? Did they know how old you are? You could have died. You're too young. What the hell were you thinking?

And it was at that precise moment that Birdie walked into the room.

'What's going on?' she asked.

'Oh, go away,' said Phin, 'this is nothing to do with you.'

'Don't you dare talk to a grown-up like that,' said David.

'That', said Phin, pointing at Birdie, 'is not a grown-up.'

'Phin!'

'She is not a grown-up. She is not even a human. She is a pig. Look. Look at her pink skin, her tiny eyes. She is a pig.'

A gasp went around the room. I stared at Birdie and tried to picture her as a pig. But she looked more like a very old cat to me, one of those bony cats with patchy fur and rheumy eyes.

Then I looked at Phin and saw that he was staring at his father and I saw him open his mouth wide and laugh and then I heard him say, 'So, that makes you a pig-kisser!'

He laughed uproariously.

'She's a pig and you are a kisser of pigs. Did you know that, when you kissed her, did you know she was a pig?'

'Phin!' Sally grimaced.

'Henry saw Dad kissing Birdie. Last week. That's why we took all Dad's money and went out without asking. Because I was cross with Dad. But now I know why he kissed her. Because . . .' Phin was now laughing so hard he could barely speak. '. . . he wanted to kiss a pig!'

I wanted to laugh too because Phin and I were the same person, but I couldn't feel it any more, that intense connection had gone, and now all I could feel was cold, hard horror.

Sally ran from the room; Phin followed her, then David, still in his bath towel. I looked at Birdie awkwardly.

'Sorry,' I said, for some strange reason.

She just gawped at me, before leaving the room too.

Then it was just me and my mother and my father.

My father got to his feet. 'Whose idea was it?' he said. 'The drugs?'

I shrugged. I could feel the trip passing from my being. I could feel myself drifting back to reality. 'I don't know.'

'It was him, wasn't it?'

'I don't know,' I repeated.

He sighed. 'There will be repercussions, young man,' he said gruffly. 'We will need to discuss them. But for now, let's get you a glass of water and something to eat. Something stodgy. Some toast, Martina?'

My mother nodded, and I followed her sheepishly to the kitchen.

I could hear voices raised overhead: Sally's glassy

vowels, David's boom, Birdie's whining. I could hear footsteps, doors opening and closing. My mother and I exchanged a glance as she posted bread into the toaster for me.

'Is that true?' asked my mother. 'What Phin said about David and Birdie?'

I nodded.

She cleared her throat but said nothing.

A moment later we heard the front door bang shut. I peered into the hallway and saw Justin, his hands filled with hessian bags, returning from his Saturday market stall. Soon enough his voice was added to the symphony of shouting coming from above.

My mother passed me the toast and I ate it silently. I remembered the strange dread I'd felt seeing Birdie and David kissing the week before, the sense of something putrid being unleashed into the world, as though they were keys and they'd unlocked each other. And then I thought of the feeling of Phin's hand in my hand on the roof, and thought that we were also keys unlocking each other, but letting out something remarkable and good.

'What's going to happen?' I asked.

'I have no idea,' said my mother. 'But it's not good. It's not good at all.'

30

Michael is in the cellar and Lucy has cleaned for over an hour. She collects a bin bag from the front door; it's filled with blood-sodden paper towels, a pair of Joy's latex gloves and every last trace of their meal: empty wine bottles, beer bottles, napkins, uneaten panzanella. She has dressed the cuts on her back with plasters from Michael's en suite and in her bag are three thousand euros taken from a drawer in his bedside cabinet.

She glances at the Maserati as she passes it on the driveway. She feels a strange wave of sadness pass over her: Michael will never drive another performance car. Michael will never book another spontaneous flight to Martinique, never pop the cork on another bottle of vintage champagne, never write his stupid book, never jump in his pool in all his clothes, never give a woman a hundred red roses, never fuck anyone, never kiss anyone . . .

Never hurt anyone.

The feeling passes. She drops the bin bag in a huge municipal bin by the beach. Adrenaline courses through her, keeping her centred and strong. She buys two bags full of snacks and drinks for the children. Marco texts her at 5 p.m. *Where are you?*

At the shops, she replies. *Be home soon.*

The children are cooperative. They look in the bag of snacks and treats with disbelief. 'We're going to England,' she tells them, mustering a light and whimsical tone. 'We're going to meet my friend's daughter, to celebrate her birthday.'

'The baby!' says Marco.

'Yes,' she says. 'The baby. And we're going to stay in a house I once lived in when I was a child. But first we're going on an adventure! First of all we're going to Paris! On the train! Then we're getting another train, to Cherbourg. Then we're going to get on a little boat to a little island called Guernsey and we're going to stay in a sweet little cottage for a night or two. Then we're getting another boat to England and driving to London.'

'All of us?' asks Stella. 'Even Fitz?'

'Even Fitz. But we need to pack, OK? And we need to get some sleep because we have to be at the station at five o'clock tomorrow morning! OK! So let's have something to eat, let's get nice and clean, let's pack and let's go to bed.'

She leaves the children packing and eating and goes to Giuseppe's room. The dog jumps up at her and she lets him lick her face. She looks at Giuseppe and wonders what to tell him. He is loyal, but he is old and can get confused sometimes. She decides to tell him a lie.

'I'm taking the children for a holiday tomorrow,' she says. 'We're going to Malta. I have friends there.'

'Oh,' says Giuseppe. 'Malta is a magical place.'

'Yes,' she agrees, feeling sad that she is misleading one of the kindest people she knows.

'But hot,' he says, 'at this time of year. So hot.' He looks down at the dog. 'You want me to look after him for you?'

The dog. She hadn't thought about the bloody dog. She panics momentarily and then she rallies and says, 'I'm bringing him. As an assistance dog. For my anxiety.'

'You have anxiety?'

'No. But I told them I did and they said I could bring my dog.'

Giuseppe won't question this. He doesn't entirely

know how the modern world works. It is roughly 1987 in Giuseppe's world.

'That's nice,' he says, touching the dog's head. 'You get a holiday, boy! A nice holiday! How long will you be gone?'

'Two weeks,' she replies. 'Maybe three. You can rent out our room, if you need to.'

He smiles. 'But I will make sure it's here when you get back.'

She takes his hand in hers. 'Thank you,' she says. 'Thank you so much.' She hugs him hard; she has no idea, no idea at all if she will ever see him again. She leaves his room before he can see her tears.

31

'I'm going to stay at the house tonight,' says Miller, placing his empty pint glass on the table. 'If that's OK with you?'

'Where will you sleep?'

'I'm not going to sleep.'

His face is set with resolve.

Libby nods. 'OK,' she says. 'That's OK.'

They walk back to the house and Libby unlocks the padlock again, pulls back the wooden hoarding again; they enter the house again. They stand for a moment, eyes cast upwards, listening out for movement. But the house is silent.

'Well,' says Libby, glancing at Dido, 'I guess we should get back.'

Lisa Jewell

Dido nods and Libby takes a step towards the front door. 'Are you going to be OK?' she says. 'Here? All by yourself?'

'Hey,' says Miller, 'look at me. Do I look like I'd be creeped out all alone in a dark, empty house where three robed cult members died?'

'Do you want me to stay too?'

'No. You go home, to your nice comfy bed.' He has his fingers splayed over his beard and looks at her with appealing puppy eyes.

Libby smiles. 'You want me to stay, don't you?' she says.

'No. No no no.'

Libby laughs and looks at Dido. 'Do you mind?' she asks. 'I'll be in tomorrow morning. I promise.'

'Stay,' says Dido. 'And come in whenever tomorrow. No rush.'

It's just starting to get dark as Libby meanders back to the house after walking Dido to the tube station. She absorbs the atmosphere of a hot summer's night in Chelsea, the throngs of blond teens in ripped denim hot pants and oversized trainers, the views through sash windows of beautiful rooms. For a moment she fantasises about living here, being part of this rarefied world, being, indeed, a Chelsea girl. She imagines the house on Cheyne Walk filled with antiques, with dripping crystal chandeliers and modern art.

But the moment she opens the door to number sixteen the fantasy dissipates. The house is tainted, blighted.

Miller is sitting in the kitchen at the big wooden table. He glances up as she walks in and says, 'Quick, look at this. Look.'

He is using his phone as a torch and looking at something inside the drawer. She peers inside.

'Look,' says Miller again.

At the very back of the drawer, in black pencil, someone has scrawled the words: 'I AM PHIN'.

32

Sally moved out of our house a few weeks later. Then a few days after that, Birdie moved into David's room. But Justin did not move out. He kept the bedroom he'd shared with Birdie.

I was never punished for the acid trip incident, and neither was Phin. But it was clear that Phin felt that the loss of his mother was worse than any punishment his father could have concocted. He blamed himself, first and foremost. Then after that he blamed Birdie. He despised her and referred to her as 'it'. Then he blamed his father. And then, unfortunately, and mainly sub-liminally, he blamed me. After all, I was the one who'd imparted unto him the terrible, fatal bullet of know-ledge which he'd used to inadvertently destroy his parents' marriage. If I hadn't told him then none of it would have happened: the shopping trip, the acid, the hideous afternoon of the pig-kissing revelations. And so that bond we'd made up on the roof that day, it didn't just fade, it kind of combusted in a cloud of toxic smoke.

It was hard not to agree that I'd brought it all upon myself. When I think of my intention when I told him what I'd seen, my keenness to scandalise and impress, my lack of empathy or appreciation of the way it might make him feel, I felt, yes, a sense of personal liability. And I did pay the price for that, I really did. Because in unwittingly destroying his parents' marriage, I'd unwittingly destroyed my entire life.

Shortly after Sally moved out, I came upon Justin sitting at the table on the terrace in the garden, sorting through piles of herbs and flowers. The fact that he had stayed under the same roof as his adulterous girlfriend struck me as sad and a little subversive. He carried on much as before, tending and harvesting his plants, turning them into little canvas bags of powder, tiny glass phials of tincture, tying on his little tags that said 'The Chelsea Apothecary'. He wore the same clothes and trundled about in the same way; there were no external tell-tales of any inner turmoil or heartbreak. Suffering as I was with my own sense of heartbreak at the end of my brief relationship with Phin, I was curious to get inside his head a little. And with the departure of Sally and the mating of Birdie and David, not to mention my own parents becoming smaller and smaller shadows of their former selves, he seemed oddly like one of the more normal people in the house.

I sat opposite him and he looked up at me genially.

'Hello, boy. How are things?'

'Things are . . .' I was about to say that things were fine, but then remembered that they were not fine at all. So I said, 'Weird.'

He looked at me more closely. 'Well,' he said. 'That's for sure.'

We fell silent for a moment. I watched him delicately picking buds from branches and laying them on to a tray.

'Why are you still living here?' I said eventually. 'Now that you and Birdie . . . ?'

'Good question,' he said, not looking up at me. He laid another bud down on the tray, rubbed his fingertips together and then laid his hands in his lap. 'I guess, because even though I'm no longer with her, she's still a part of me? You know, the part of love that isn't about sex, it doesn't automatically die. Or at least it doesn't have to.'

I nodded. This was certainly true for me. Although

there was a large probability that I might never get the chance to hold Phin's hand again, or even have another meaningful conversation with him, that did not diminish my feelings for him.

'Do you think you might get back together with her?'

He sighed. 'Yeah,' he said. 'Maybe. But maybe not.'

'What do you think of David?'

'Ah.'

His body language changed subtly. He drew his shoulders closer together, entwined his fingers.

'Jury's out,' he said finally. 'In some ways I think he's awesome. In other ways . . .' He shook his head. 'He freaks me out.'

'Yes,' I said louder and more fervently than I'd intended. 'Yes,' I said again, quietly. 'He freaks me out too.'

'In what way, exactly?'

'He's . . .' I cast my eyes to the sky, looking for decent vocabulary. 'Sinister.'

Justin emitted a rumble of laughter. 'Ha, yeah,' he said. 'Exactly spot on. Yeah. Sinister.

'Here.' He passed me a handful of small yellow daisy-shaped flowers and a roll of string. 'Tie them into little bundles, by their stalks.'

'What are they?'

'It's calendula. For soothing skin complaints. Brilliant stuff.'

Lisa Jewell

'And what's that?' I gestured towards the tray of tiny yellow buds.

'This is chamomile. For making tea. Smell that.' He passed me a bud. I put it to my nose. 'Isn't that just the nicest smell?'

I nodded and looped some string around the stems of the calendula, tying it in a bow. 'Is that OK?'

'Brilliant. Yeah. So,' he opened. 'I heard about you and Phin. The other week. You know, *tripping*.'

I flushed pink.

'Man,' he said, 'I didn't touch drugs 'til I was almost eighteen! And what are you? Twelve?'

'Thirteen,' I replied firmly. 'I'm thirteen.'

'So young!' he said. 'Hats off to you.'

I didn't understand this sentiment. It was so clearly a bad thing I'd done. But I smiled anyway.

'You know,' he said conspiratorially. 'I can grow anything out here. Virtually. Do you know what I mean?'

I shook my head.

'I don't just grow stuff that's good for you. I can grow other stuff. Anything you like.'

I nodded seriously. And then I said, 'Like drugs, you mean?'

He laughed his belly rumble laugh again. 'Well, yeah, I guess. Good ones.' He tapped his nose. 'And bad ones too.'

The back door opened at that moment. We both turned to see who it was.

It was David and Birdie. They had their arms looped around each other's waists. They glanced briefly in our direction and then went and sat at the other end of the garden. The atmosphere shifted. It felt like a cloud passing over the sun.

'Are you OK?' I mouthed at Justin.

He nodded. 'I'm cool.'

We sat for a while in the muffling blanket of their presence, chatting about different herbs and plants and what they could do. I asked Justin about poisons and he told me about *Atropa belladonna*, or deadly nightshade, which, legend has it, was used by Macbeth's soldiers to poison the incoming English army, and hemlock, used to kill Socrates at his execution. He also told me about using enchanting herbs, with spells, and aphrodisiacs like *Gingko biloba*.

'How did you learn all this?' I asked.

Justin shrugged. 'From books. Mainly. And my mum likes to garden. So you know, I was brought up around plants and the soil. So . . . natural progression, really.'

At this point we had not been given a day's teaching since Sally had left. We children had been freewheeling around the house, bored and restless. 'Read a book,' was the refrain to anyone complaining of having nothing to do. 'Do some sums.'

So I was ripe, I suppose, to learn something new and all that was on offer elsewhere was David's weird exercises or Birdie's fiddling.

'Are there any plants that can make people, you know, do things – against their will?'

'Well, there are hallucinogenics, of course, magic mushrooms and the like.'

'And you can grow these?' I asked. 'In a garden like this?'

'I can grow virtually anything, boy, anywhere.'

'Can I help you?' I asked. 'Can I help you grow things?'

'Sure,' said Justin. 'You can be my little apprentice buddy. It'll be cool.'

I do not know what sort of pillow talk occurred behind the dreadful door of David and Birdie's room; I didn't like to think too hard about anything that happened beyond that door. I heard things which even now, nearly thirty years later, make me shudder to think about. I slept with my pillow over my head every night.

In the mornings they would descend the stairs together, looking self-satisfied and superior. David was obsessed with Birdie's waist-length hair. He touched it constantly. He twisted it around his fingers and bunched it up in his hands; he ran his hands down it, twirled shanks as he talked to her. I once saw him pick up a strand and hold it to his nostrils, then breathe in deeply.

'Isn't Birdie's hair wonderful,' he said once. He looked across at my sister and Clemency who both wore their hair on their shoulders. 'Wouldn't you like to have hair like this, girls?' he asked.

'You know,' said Birdie, 'in many religions it is seen as highly spiritual for women to wear their hair long.'

Despite not being at all religious David and Birdie talked a lot about religion in the early days of their relationship. They talked about the meaning of life and the terrible disposability of everything. They talked about minimalism and feng shui. They asked my mother if it was OK if they repainted their bedroom white, if they could move their antique metal bedframe into another room and have their mattress on the floor. They abhorred aerosol cans and fast food and pharmaceuticals and man-made fibres and plastic bags and cars and aeroplanes. They were already talking about the threat of global warming and worrying about the impact of their carbon footprints. They were, looking back on it from the point of view of the end-of-days scenario currently playing out during this ominous heatwave of 2018, with the ocean full of plastic-choked sea creatures and polar bears sliding off melting ice caps, well ahead of their time. But in the context of 1990, when the world was just waking up to all that modern technology and throwaway culture had to offer and embracing it, they were an aberration.

And I might have had some respect for David and Birdie and the strength of their commitment to the planet if it hadn't been for the fact that David expected everyone else to live according to his will. It wasn't enough for him and Birdie to sleep on mattresses on the floor. We all must sleep on mattresses on the floor. It wasn't enough for him and Birdie to eschew cars and aspirin and fish fingers. We all must eschew cars and aspirin and fish fingers. It had become very clear to me that what I had predicted subliminally all those weeks ago when I saw David and Birdie kissing had come to pass. She had unlocked something terrible in David and now she wanted David to control everything.

We were no longer, it seemed, free.

33

It doesn't get dark until nearly ten. Libby and Miller talk to each other across the garden table in the encroaching darkness, not noticing that it has come until they can no longer see the whites of each other's eyes. Then they light candles which jump and dance in the breeze. They'd spent the last hour of daylight searching the house and this is what they talk about: the things they have found.

Apart from the words 'I AM PHIN' scrawled on the inside of the table drawer, they found the same words scrawled on the underside of the bath on the attic floor, on the skirting around one of the bed-room doors and inside a fitted wardrobe in one of the bedrooms on the first floor. They found a handful of musical strings in one of the smaller reception rooms downstairs and a music stand crammed into a corner cupboard. They found a pile of clean terry nappies, safety pins, nappy cream and Babygros in the wardrobe in the room where Libby had been found in her cot. They found a pile of books in a trunk in the back hallway, mouldy and grey, books about the healing properties of herbs and plants, books about medieval witchcraft, books of spells. The books were wrapped in an old blanket and covered over with upholstered cushions that must have once adorned a set of garden furniture.

They found a thin gold band ring wedged between the wooden floor and the skirting board. It had a hallmark which Miller photographed with his camera and then zoomed in on to. When they googled it they discovered that it was hallmarked in 1975, the year of Henry and Martina's wedding. A tiny thing, lost to the world, saved from the eyes of looters and detectives in its dark hiding place for twenty-five years or more.

Libby wears the ring now, on the ring finger of her left hand. *Her mother's ring.* It fits her perfectly. She twirls it as they talk.

They pause every couple of minutes, listening for the sound of footsteps in the undergrowth. Miller goes to the back of the garden now and then, looking for shadows, for signs of someone entering through the gate in the back wall. They bring out the upholstered cushions they'd found in the trunk and they blow out the candles and sit on the corner of the lawn furthest from the back door. They are talking in whispers when Miller suddenly stares at her with wide eyes and his finger to his lips. 'Shh.' Then his eyes swivel towards the back of the garden. There is something there. She sits up straight. There, at the back of the garden. And as they watch they see a man stalk across the lawn, a tall, slim man, with short hair, glasses reflecting the moonlight, white trainers, a shoulder bag. They watch him sling his shoulder bag on to the top of the bunker and then follow suit. They hear him shimmy up the drainpipe to the promontory on the first floor. Then they both move very quietly and watch him as he disappears up on to the roof.

Libby's heart hammers. 'Oh my God,' she whispers, 'oh my God. What do we do?'

'I haven't got a fucking clue,' Miller whispers back.

'Shall we confront him?'

'I don't know. What do you think?'

She shakes her head. She's half terrified and half desperate to see this man face to face.

She looks at Miller. He will keep her safe. Or he will at least give the impression of being able to keep her safe. The man they saw was smaller than him and wearing glasses. She nods now and says, 'Yes, let's go in. Let's talk to him.'

Miller looks vaguely petrified but quickly rallies and says, 'Yes. Right.'

The house is dark, lit only by the blur of streetlights from outside and the silver shimmer of the moon on the river. Libby follows Miller, reassured by the solid width of him. They stop at the foot of the staircase. Then they take each step slowly and surely, until they are on the first-floor landing. Here it is lighter, the moon visible through the large window overlooking the street. They both glance upwards and then at each other.

'OK?' whispers Miller.

'OK,' replies Libby.

The hatch in the ceiling of the attic floor is open and the bathroom door is shut. They can hear the sound of pee hitting a toilet bowl, the stop-start of it as it comes to an end, the tap running, a throat being cleared. Then the door is open and a man walks out and he is cute. That is Libby's first thought. A cute guy, with neatly cut fair hair, a youthful, clean-shaven face, toned arms, a grey T-shirt, narrow black jeans, trendy glasses, nice trainers.

He jumps a foot in the air and clutches his chest when he sees them standing there. 'Oh my fucking God,' he says.

Libby jumps too. And so does Miller.

They all stare at each other for a moment.

'Are you . . . ?' asks the man eventually, at the precise moment that Libby says, 'Are you . . . ?'

They point at each other and then both turn to look at Miller as though he might have an answer for them. Then the man turns back to Libby and says, 'Are you Serenity?'

Libby nods. 'Are you Henry?'

The man looks at them blankly for a moment but then his face clears and he says, 'No, I'm not Henry. I'm Phin.'

II

34

My mother, being German, knew how to do a good Christmas. It was her speciality. The house was festooned from the beginning of December with home-made decorations made of candied oranges and red gingham and painted pine cones and filled with the aroma of gingerbread, stollen and mulled wine. No tacky tinsel or paper garlands for her, no tin of Quality Street or Cadbury's selection boxes.

Even my father enjoyed Christmas. He had a Father Christmas outfit which he used to don every Christmas Eve when we were little, and I still can't explain how I could both know it was him, but also have no idea it was him, at the same time. Looking back on it now, I can see that it was the same sort of terrible self-deception that played a part in the way everyone felt about David Thomsen. People could look and see just a man, but in the same glance, the answer to all their problems.

My father didn't wear the outfit that Christmas Eve. He said we were all too old for it, and he was probably right. But he also said he didn't feel too well. My mother laid on the usual Christmas Eve celebration anyway. We sat around a (smaller than usual) Nordic pine and unwrapped our (fewer than usual) gifts while Christmas carols played on the radio and a fire crackled in the grate. After about half an hour, just before dinner, my father said he needed to go and lie down, he had a terrible headache.

Thirty seconds later he was on the floor of the drawing room, having a stroke.

We didn't know it was a stroke at the time. We thought he was having some kind of fit. Or a heart attack. Dr Broughton, my father's private physician, came to look him over, still in his Christmas Eve outfit of red woollen V-neck and holly-print bow tie. I remember his face when my father said that he no longer had private health cover, how quickly he left the house, how he dropped his unctuous demeanour like a brick. He sent him straight to hospital in an NHS ambulance and left without saying goodbye.

My father came home on Boxing Day.

They said he was fine, that he'd have some cognitive challenges for a while, some motor problems, but that his brain would fix itself, that he would be back to normal within weeks. Maybe sooner.

But, as with his first stroke, he never recovered properly. There was an even greater vacancy there. He used the wrong words. Or couldn't find any words at all. He spent whole days sitting in the armchair in his bedroom eating biscuits, very slowly. Sometimes he'd laugh at inappropriate junctures. Other times he wouldn't get the joke.

He moved slowly. He avoided stairs. He stopped leaving the house entirely.

And the weaker my father became, the closer to the mark David Thomsen stepped.

By the time I turned fourteen in May 1991, we had rules. Not just normal family rules like no feet on the furniture, or do your homework before you watch TV. Not the sort of rules we'd had for all our lives.

No, now we had crazy, despotic rules, written out in black marker on a large poster that was taped to the kitchen wall. I can still remember them to this day:

No haircuts WITHOUT PERMISSION of David and/or Birdie
No television

No visitors WITHOUT PERMISSION of
David and/or Birdie
No vanity
No greed
Nobody to leave the building without the
EXPRESS PERMISSION of David and/or Birdie
No meat
No animal products
No leather/suede/wool/feathers
No plastic containers
No more than four pieces of rubbish per day per
person, including food waste
No unnatural coloured clothes
No pharma
No chemicals
One wash or shower PER PERSON PER DAY
One shampoo per week
ALL RESIDENTS must spend a minimum of
two hours a day with David in the exercise room
ALL CHILDREN must spend a minimum of two
hours a day with Birdie in the music room
All food must be homecooked from
organic ingredients
No electric or gas heating
No shouting
No swearing
No running

This list of rules had started quite short and was added to at intervals as David's control of our household got stronger and stronger.

Sally, at this stage, still used to come to the house once or twice a week, to take the children out for tea. She was sleeping on a friend's sofa in Brixton and desperately trying to find some kind of accommodation big enough for them all to live in. Phin would be extra sullen after spending time with his mother. He would lock himself in his room and miss the next couple of meals. It was because of Phin, in fact, that a lot of the rules were put in place. David found his moods untenable. He could not bear the wasted food, or the door which he was unable to open at will. He could not bear anyone doing anything that did not directly correspond with his own view of the world. He could not bear teenagers.

Two new rules were added:

No locked doors
ALL MEALS to be attended by ALL
members of the household

One morning, shortly after the fifth time Phin had come back from spending the afternoon with his mother and broken the rule about '**No locked doors**', I went upstairs to find David removing the locks from inside

Phin's room, his jaw clenched, his knuckles tight around the handle of the screwdriver.

Phin sat on his bed, watching with his arms folded hard across his chest.

When at dinnertime Phin was still sitting on his bed with his arms folded, silent and deathly, David dragged him down by his – still folded – arms and threw him into a chair.

He forcibly pushed the chair into place and served Phin a large bowl of curried marrow and rice. Phin's arms remained crossed. David got to his feet, piled some curry on to a spoon and forced it to Phin's lips. Phin locked his lips together. I could hear the spoon hitting his teeth. The atmosphere was shocking. Phin, at this stage, was fifteen and a half, but looked much older. He was tall and he was strong. The situation looked as though it could turn violent very easily. But Phin stood his ground, his eyes boring a hole into the wall opposite, his whole face rigid with anger and determination.

Eventually David gave up trying to feed the spoon into his son's mouth and hurled it across the room, the curry forming an ugly yellow crescent across the wall, the spoon making an angry metallic scream as it hit the floor.

'Get to your room!' David shouted. 'Now!' A vein throbbed on his temple. His neck was tensed and puce.

I had never before seen a human being as engorged with rage as David at that moment.

'With pleasure,' hissed Phin.

David's hand appeared; then, almost in slow motion, as Phin passed him it connected with the back of his head. Phin turned; his eyes met his father's eyes, I saw true hatred pass between them.

Phin carried on walking. We heard his footsteps, sure and steady up the staircase. Someone cleared their throat. I saw Birdie and David exchange a look. Birdie's look, pinched and disapproving, said, *You're losing control. Do something*. David's look, dark and furious, said, *I intend to*.

The moment the meal was over I went to Phin's room.

He sat on his bed with his knees drawn tight to his chin. He glanced up at me. 'What?'

'Are you OK?'

'What do you think?'

I edged a little closer into the room. I waited for him to ask me to leave but he didn't.

'Did it hurt?' I asked. 'When he hit you?'

My parents, strange as they both were, had never hit me. I couldn't even imagine such a thing.

'Not really.'

I edged closer again.

Then, suddenly, Phin looked up at me and it was there again. He was seeing me. Properly.

'I can't stay here,' he said, shaking his head. 'I've got to get out.'

My heart skipped a beat. Phin was the only thing that kept any sense of possibility alive.

'Where will you go?'

'I don't know. To Mum's.'

'But—'

I was about to say that his mum was sleeping on a sofa in Brixton. But he interjected. 'I don't know, all right? I just have to get out of this place. I can't be here any more.'

'When?'

'Now.'

He looked at me through his ridiculous eyelashes. I tried to read his expression. I felt I saw a challenge there.

'Do you . . . Should I . . . come with you?'

'No! Fucking hell. No.'

I shrunk back into myself. No. Of course not.

'What shall I say? When the adults ask?'

'Nothing,' he hissed. 'Just nothing. Don't say anything.'

I nodded, my eyes wide. I watched him throw things into a drawstring bag: pants and socks, a T-shirt, a book, a toothbrush. He turned and saw me looking at him.

'Go,' he said. 'Please.'

I left the room and walked slowly to the back staircase where I sat on the third step down and closed the top door to just a crack, through which I watched Phin disappear through the hatch into the attic space with his bag. I couldn't imagine what he was doing or where he was going. For a moment I thought maybe he was planning to live on the roof. But although it was May, it was still cold: he couldn't possibly. Then I heard scuffling noises outside and dashed into Phin's bedroom, cupped my hands to the glass of his dormer window and watched the back garden. There he was: darting across the dark garden into the ink-black shadows of the trees. And then suddenly he was gone.

I turned to face his empty room. I picked up his pillow and held it to my face. I breathed him in.

35

It's still dark when Lucy leaves the Blue House the next morning. The children are wall-eyed and silent. She holds her breath as she hands over the cash for the train tickets to Paris to a woman who looks like she knows all of Lucy's deepest secrets. She holds it again as they board the train, and she holds it again when the inspector enters their carriage and asks to see their tickets. Every time the train slows down she holds her breath and scans the sidings for a flash of blue light, for the navy képi of a gendarme. At Paris she sits with the children and the dog in the quietest corner of the quietest café as they wait for their train to Cherbourg. And then it starts again: the stultifying fear at every stage, at every juncture. At lunchtime, as they board their next train, she imagines Joy at Michael's house starting to wonder where he is, and the adrenaline pumps so hard and fast around her body that she feels she might die of it. She mentally pans around Michael's house, looking for the thing she forgot, the huge red flag that will tell Joy to look in the cellar immediately. But no, she's certain, absolutely certain, she left not a clue, not a trace. She has bought herself time. At least a day. Maybe even three or four days. And even then, would Joy tell the police anything about her, the nice woman called Lucy, the mother of Michael's son, that would lead them to suspect her in any way? No, she would tell them about Michael's shady underworld connections, the rough-looking men who sometimes came to the door to discuss 'business'. She would lead them in an entirely different direction and when they eventually realised it was a dead end, Lucy would be nowhere to be found.

By the time the train pulls into Cherbourg that evening her heart rate has slowed and she finds enough appetite to eat the croissant she bought in Paris.

At the taxi rank they climb into the back of a battered Renault Scenic and she asks the driver to take them to Diélette. The dog sits on her lap and rests his chin on the half-open window. It is late. The children both fall asleep.

Diélette is a tiny harbour town, green and hilly. The

only people catching the late ferry to Guernsey are British holidaymakers, mostly families with small children. Lucy clutches the passports hard inside sweaty hands. Her passports are French, but she is English. Both children have different surnames to her on their passports. Stella is a different colour to her. They have huge grubby rucksacks and are so tired that they look unwell. And their passports are fake. Lucy is certain, utterly convinced that they will be stopped, pulled aside, asked questions. She planned this long and meandering journey back to London to dilute her trail, but still, as she shows the passports to the inspector at the ferry port her heart beats so hard she imagines he can hear it. He flicks through the passports looking from photo to person and back again, hands the passports back, gestures them through with his eyes.

And then they are on the sea, the churning, navy grey froth of the English Channel, and France is soon behind them.

She holds Stella on her knee at the back of the ferry so that the little girl can watch the country of her birth, the only home she has ever known, recede to a fairy-lit wreath on the horizon.

'Bye bye, France,' says Stella, waving her hand, 'bye bye France.'

36

Libby stares at Phin.

He stares at her. 'I used to live here,' he says, although no one has asked him to explain who he is. Then quickly, before Libby can form a response, he says, 'You're really pretty.'

Libby says, 'Oh.'

Then he looks at Miller and says, 'Who are you?'

'Hi.' Miller offers him a big hand. 'I'm Miller Roe.'

Phin peers at him questioningly. 'Why do I recognise that name?'

Miller makes a strange noise under his breath and shrugs.

'You're that journalist, aren't you?'

'Yup.'

'That article was such shit. You were wrong about everything.'

'Yup,' says Miller again, 'I kind of know that now.'

'I can't believe how pretty you are,' he says, turning back to Libby. 'You look so like . . .'

'My mother?'

'Yes,' he says. 'Like your mother.'

Libby thinks of the photos of her mother with her dyed black Priscilla Presley hair, her dark kohled eyes. She feels flattered.

Then she says, 'What are you doing here?'

Phin says, 'Waiting for you.'

'But I was here the other day. I heard you upstairs. Why didn't you come down then?'

He shrugs. 'I did. But by the time I'd got to the bottom of the stairs, you'd gone.'

'Oh.'

'Shall we . . . ?' Phin gestures at the staircase.

They follow him down the stairs and into the kitchen.

Phin sits on one side of the table; Miller and Libby sit on the other. Libby studies Phin's face. He must be in his early forties, but he looks much younger. He has extraordinarily long eyelashes.

'So,' he says, spreading his arms wide, 'this is all yours.'

Libby nods. 'Although, really, it should have been my brother and sister's, too?'

'Well, more fool them. Oh, and I suppose I should wish you a happy birthday. A little belated.'

'Thank you,' she says. 'How long since you were last here?'

'Decades.'

There is a long and very brittle silence. Phin breaks it by saying, 'I imagine you have some questions.'

Miller and Libby exchange a brief glance. Libby nods.

'Well,' says Phin, 'shall we get out of this place? I live just across the river. I have cold wine. And a terrace. And cats that look like cushions.'

They exchange another glance.

'I'm not going to kill you,' says Phin. 'And neither will my cats. Come. I'll tell you absolutely everything.'

Twenty minutes later, Libby and Miller follow Phin out of a sleek lift and into a marble-floored corridor.

His apartment is at the other end.

Lights turn on automatically as he leads them down his hallway to a living room with glass doors on to a terrace overlooking the river.

Everything is pale and just so. A huge white sheepskin is draped over the back of a very long cream sofa. There is an extravagant arrangement of lilies and roses in a vase that wouldn't look out of place in the showroom of Northbone Kitchens.

Phin uses a small remote control to open the doors

on to the terrace and invites them to sit on a pair of sofas around a low table. While he goes to fetch wine, Libby and Miller exchange a look.

'This place must be worth a couple of million,' says Miller.

'At least,' says Libby. She stands up and takes in the view across the river. 'Look!' she says. 'It's the house. We're completely bang opposite it.'

Miller joins her. 'Well,' he says drily, 'I think we can assume that that is not a coincidence.'

'Do you think he's been watching?'

'Yes, I totally think he's been watching. Why else would you choose an apartment with this view?'

'What do you think of him?' she whispers.

Miller shrugs. 'I think he's a bit . . .'

'Weird?'

'Yes, a bit weird. And a bit . . .'

But then Phin returns, a bottle of wine and three glasses in an ice bucket in one hand, a cat held against his chest with the other. He puts the bucket down on the table but keeps the cat in his arms. 'Meet Mindy,' he says, holding the cat's paw up in an approximation of a salute. 'Mindy, meet Libby and Miller.'

The cat ignores them and tries to wriggle out of Phin's embrace. 'Oh,' he says to the cat's retreating form, 'fine. Be a bitch, see if I care.'

Then he turns to them again and says, 'She's my

favourite. I always fall in love with the ones who can't bear me. It's why I'm single.'

He opens the wine and pours them each a large glass.

'Cheers,' he says, 'to reunions.'

They touch glasses and a slightly weighted silence follows.

'This is an incredible view,' says Miller. 'How long have you lived here?'

'Not long. I mean, they only just finished building these apartments last year.'

'Amazing, isn't it, being right opposite Cheyne Walk.'

Phin nods. 'I wanted to be close,' he says to Libby, 'for when you came back.'

Another Persian cat appears on the terrace. This one is horribly overweight and has bulging eyes. 'Ah,' says Phin, 'here he is. Mr Attention-seeker. He's heard I have visitors.' He scoops up the gigantic cat and rests it on his lap. 'This is Dick. I called him that because it was the only way I could make sure I got some.'

Libby laughs and takes a sip of wine. In another realm, this would constitute a brilliant night out: two handsome men, a warm summer's night, a glamorous terrace overlooking the Thames, a glass of cold white wine. But in this realm, everything feels warped and vaguely threatening. Even the cats.

'So,' says Miller, 'if you're going to tell us everything

about what really happened in Cheyne Walk, will it be off the record? Or can I be a journalist?'

'You can be whatever you like.'

'Can I record you?' Miller reaches for his phone in his back pocket.

'Sure,' says Phin, his fingers raking through the thick fur on the cat's back. 'Why not? Nothing to lose any more. Go for it.'

Miller fiddles with his phone for a while. Libby notices his hands shaking slightly, betraying his excitement. She takes another large sip of wine, to calm her own nerves. Then Miller lays his phone on the table and asks, 'So. You say I got everything wrong in my article. Can we start there?'

'Certainly.' The fat cat jumps down from Phin's lap and he absent-mindedly brushes hairs from his trouser legs with the sides of his hands.

'So, when I was researching the article, I came upon a man called David Thomsen. Thomsen with an E.'

'Yes,' says Phin. 'My father.'

Libby sees a kind of triumphant relief flood across Miller's face. He exhales and says, 'And your mother – Sally?'

'Yes, Sally is my mother.'

'And Clemency . . . ?'

'My sister, yes.'

'And the third body . . .'

'Was my father.' Phin nods. 'Spot on. Such a shame you didn't work all that out before you wrote your article.'

'Well, I kind of did. But I couldn't find any of you. I searched for months, without a trace. So, what happened to you all?'

'Well, I know what happened to me. But I'm afraid I have no idea what happened to my mother and Clemency.'

'You haven't stayed in touch?'

'Far from it. I haven't seen them since I was a teenager. As far as I'm aware my mother lives in Cornwall and I'm going to assume that my sister does too.' He shrugs and picks up his wine glass. 'Penreath,' he says.

Miller throws him a quizzical look.

'I'm pretty sure she lives in Penreath.'

'Oh,' says Miller. 'That's great, thank you.'

'You are very welcome,' he replies. Then he rubs his hands together and says, 'Ask me something else! Ask me what really happened on the night that everybody died.'

Miller smiles grimly and says, 'OK. So, what really happened then? On the night that everyone died?'

Phin looks at both of them, mischievously, then leans in so that his mouth is directly over the microphone on Miller's phone and says, 'Well, for a start, it wasn't suicide. It was murder.'

37

Phin was gone for a week. I could hardly bear the pointlessness of everything without him around. With him in the house, every journey to the kitchen was ripe with the possibility of seeing his face, every morning began with the thought of potential encounters. Without him I was in a dark house full of strangers.

And then, a week later, I heard the front door slam and voices rising from the hallway, and there was Phin, Sally behind him, talking in urgent tones to David, who stood with his arms folded across his stomach.

'I *did not* tell him to come. For God's sake. That's the last thing I would have done. It's bad enough *me* over-staying my welcome at Toni's. Let alone my teenage son.'

David said, 'Why didn't you call?'

'He told me you knew he was coming! How was I supposed to know? And I called you now, didn't I?'

'I thought he'd been killed. We've been worried sick.'

'*We*? Who the fuck is "we"?'

'Us,' said David. 'All of us. And please don't use that language in our home.'

'Phin tells me you hit him.'

'Oh, I did not *hit* him. For God's sake. It was a slap.'

'You slapped him?'

'Good God, Sal, you have no idea, no idea at all what it's like living with this child. He's rude. He steals. He takes drugs. He disrespects the other housemates . . .'

Sally put her hand up between them. 'Enough,' she said. 'He's a teenager. He's a good kid, but he's a teenager. It comes with the territory.'

'Well, that might be true in your slightly pathetic view of the world. But the rest of the world would disagree. There's no excuse for any of it. I would never have dreamed of behaving in such a way when I was his age. It's diabolical.'

I saw Sally's hand grip Phin's shoulder. I saw her cheeks hollow. Then she said, 'I'm looking at a flat tomorrow. In Hammersmith. Two bedrooms. We can start splitting access to the children.'

David looked sceptical. 'How are you going to pay for it?'

'I've been working, and saving.'

'Well, we'll see. But seriously, I don't think Phin's safe in your care. You're too soft on him.'

'I am not soft, David, I am loving. You might want to try it sometime.'

Sally stayed for a couple of hours. The atmosphere was toxic. Birdie didn't come down from her room, but I heard her ostentatiously coughing and sighing and pacing. When Sally finally left, Birdie swept down the stairs and threw herself into David's arms and whispered melodramatically, 'Are you OK, my darling?'

David nodded stoically. 'I'm fine.'

And then, looking straight at Phin, he narrowed his eyes and said the words that signalled the beginning of the nightmare real.

He said, 'Things are going to change around here. You mark my words.'

The first thing that changed was that Phin was locked into his bedroom whenever David or Birdie were unable to monitor him. Somehow the adults colluded to persuade us that this was normal, explicable, sane, even. *It's for his own safety* was the mantra.

He was allowed out to shower, to tend the garden, to help in the kitchen, for fiddle lessons, meals and exercise classes.

Since we already spent most of our free time in our rooms, this didn't at first feel quite as sinister as it looks written down like this. It's very odd, looking back, how accepting children can be of the oddest scenarios. But still, seeing it now, in black and white, it really is quite shocking.

I was sitting cross-legged on my bed one day shortly after Phin returned with his mother. I was reading a book that he'd lent me a few weeks earlier. I jumped at the sight of him because it was late evening and I'd assumed his door would be locked for the night.

'How . . . ?' I began.

'Justin brought me up after dinner,' he said. 'Accidently on purpose forgot to turn the lock properly.'

'Good old Justin,' I said. 'What are you going to do? You won't run away, will you?'

'No,' he said. 'No point now. My mum's moving into the flat next week and then I'm going to live with her. All this shit will be over.'

I felt as if he'd punched me in the throat. My voice cracked as I replied, 'But your dad – will he let you?'

'I don't give a fuck whether he lets me or not. I'll be sixteen in December. I want to live with my mum. There's not much he can do about it.'

'And what about Clemency?'

'She'll come too.'

'Do you think your dad and Birdie will move out, too? Once you and Clemency are gone?'

He laughed harshly. 'Er. No. No way. He's here now. Feet under the table. Got everything going his way.'

A small silence drew out between us. Then Phin said, 'Remember that night? When we went up on the roof? When we took the acid?'

I nodded effusively. How could I forget?

'You know there's another one. Still up there?'

'Another . . . ?'

'Tab. Another tab of acid. The guy at Kensington Market gave me two. We only had one.'

I let this fact percolate within me for a moment.

'Are you saying . . . ?'

'I guess. I mean, they all think I'm safely locked up. The girls are asleep. No one will come up now. You could go down and tell everyone you're going to bed, then bring up a glass of water. I'll wait here.'

Of course I did precisely as I was told.

We grabbed a blanket and put on jumpers. I went first through the hatch, Phin passed me the water and then followed up behind me. It was July but the air was damp and cool. Phin located the little bag where he'd left it in a plant pot. I didn't really want to take it. I hoped that it had somehow lost its toxicity during the many months it had sat out there, subject to the elements. I hoped that a sudden gust of wind would blow it away. Or that Phin would put it back and say, 'We don't need that. We have each other.'

We brushed some dead leaves from the plastic chairs and sat side by side.

Phin tipped the tab into the palm of his hand.

The sky was remarkable. Royal blue, burnt amber, lipstick pink. It doubled itself in the face of the river. In the distance, Battersea Bridge sparkled.

I saw Phin watch the sky too. It felt different from the last time we'd been up here. Phin felt different. More pensive, less rebellious.

'What do you think you'll end up doing?' he asked me. 'When you're grown-up?'

'Something to do with computers,' I said. 'Or film-making.'

'Or both, maybe?' he suggested.

'Yes,' I agreed happily. 'Making films with computers.'

'Cool,' he said.

'And what about you?'

'I want to live in Africa,' he said. 'Be a safari guide.'

I laughed. 'Where did that come from?'

'We did a safari when we were travelling. I was six. We saw hippos having sex. That's what I mainly remember. But I also just really remember the guide. This really cool English guy. He was called Jason.'

I noticed a hint of longing in his voice at this point.

It made me feel closer to him in a way I couldn't fully process.

'I remember saying to my parents that that's what I wanted to do when I grew up. My dad said I'd never make my fortune driving tourists round in a Land Rover. As if money was the only thing that matters . . .'

He sighed and glanced down into the palm of his hand. 'So,' he said, 'shall we?'

'Just a tiny bit,' I said. 'Like a really tiny bit.'

The next couple of hours unfolded like a beautiful dream. We watched the sky until all the different colours had consolidated to black. We talked remarkable nonsense about the meaning of existence. We giggled until we hiccupped.

At one point Phin said, 'You'll have to come, sometimes, when I move to Hammersmith. You'll have to come and stay.'

'Yes. Yes please.'

And then at some other point I said, 'What would you do if I kissed you?'

And Phin laughed and laughed and laughed until he got a coughing fit. He was doubled over with mirth and I watched him with a blind smile, trying to fathom the meaning of his response.

'No,' I said, 'really? What would you do?'

'I'd push you off this roof,' he said, still smiling. Then he spread his fingers apart and said, '*Splat.*'

I made myself laugh. Ha-ha. So funny.

Then he said, 'Come on, let's get out of here.'

'And go where?'

'I'll show you. Follow me.'

And I did follow him. Stupid, stupid boy that I was. I followed him back on to the attic landing and out of a window and then down the side of the house in some dreadful awe-inducing, nausea-inspiring act of daredevil insanity.

'What are you doing?' I kept asking, my fingernails dug into bare brick, my trouser legs breaking apart on juts of masonry. 'Where are we going?'

'It's my secret route!' he said, looking up at me with wild eyes. 'Let's go to the river! No one will know!'

By the time we landed flat-footed on the lawn I was bleeding from three different places, but I didn't care. I followed him as he stepped through the shadows to a gate that I had no idea existed at the foot of our garden. Suddenly, Narnia-like, we were in someone else's garden and then Phin grabbed my hand and hoiked me round two corners, through the magical gloom of Chelsea Embankment, across four lanes of traffic and on to the riverside. Here he let my hand drop. For a moment we stood, silently, side by side, and watched gold and silver worms wriggling across the surface of the water. I kept staring at Phin, who looked more beautiful than ever in the dark, moving light.

'Stop staring at me,' he said.

I stared at him harder.

'I mean it,' he said. 'Stop staring.'

But I stared harder still.

And then he pushed me, with both his hands, pushed me hard and into the black water and then I was under and my ears filled with echoing bubbles, and my clothes became heavy and attached themselves to my skin and I tried to scream but swallowed instead and my hands felt for the river wall and my legs kicked against thick, gloopy nothing. And then my eyes opened and I saw faces: a constellation of blackened faces circling mine and I tried to talk to them, tried to ask them to help me but they all turned away and then I was coming up, a pain around my wrist, Phin's face above, dragging me up the stone steps and on to the bank.

'You bloody loony,' he said and laughed, as though I was the one who had chosen to fall into the Thames, as though it was all just high jinks.

I shoved him. 'You fucking bastard!' I screamed, my not-yet-broken voice sounding shrill and unbearable. 'You absolute fucking bastard!'

I stormed past him, across four lanes of traffic, causing someone to hoot their horn at me, and to the front door of the house.

Phin chased me and approached me at the front door, breathlessly.

'What the fuck are you doing?'

I should have stopped there and then, I really should. I should have taken a deep breath and evaluated the situation and made a different decision. But I was so engorged with rage, not born just of being pushed into the freezing, filthy Thames, but of years of Phin blowing hot and cold at me, of giving me titbits of attention when it was in his interests to do so and totally ignoring me when it wasn't. And I looked at him, and he was dry and beautiful and I was wet and ugly, and I turned and very firmly pressed my fingertip into the doorbell.

He stared at me. I could see him deciding whether to stay or to run. But a second later the door opened and it was David and he looked from me to Phin and back again and his shoulders rose up and his mouth tightened and he looked like a caged animal about to pounce. Very slowly and thunderously he said, '*Get inside now.*'

Phin turned then and began to run, but his father was taller than him, fitter than him; he caught up with him before Phin had even made it to the corner of the street and felled him to the pavement. I watched with my chin tipped up defensively, my teeth chattering inside my child skull, my arms wrapped around my body.

My mother appeared at the door. 'What the hell is

going on?' she asked, peering over the top of my head. 'What on earth have you been doing?'

'Phin pushed me in the river,' I stuttered through my chattering teeth.

'Dear Jesus,' she said, pulling me into the house. 'Dear Jesus. Get in. Take off those clothes. What the hell . . .'

I didn't go in and take my clothes off. I stood and watched David drag his fully grown son across the pavement, like a fresh kill.

That's it then, I thought to myself, *that's it.*

38

On Wednesday morning, after two nights in a rather basic B & B, and a choppy crossing over the remainder of the English Channel, Lucy hires a car at Portsmouth and they begin the drive to London.

It was winter when she'd left England and in her mind it is always cold there, the trees are always bare, the people always wrapped up against inclement weather. But England is in the grip of a long hot summer and the streets are full of tanned, happy people in shorts and sunglasses, the pavements are covered in tables, there are fountains full of children and deckchairs outside shops.

Stella stares out of the window in the back of the car with Fitz on her lap. She's never left France before.

She's never left the Côte d'Azur before. Her short life has been lived entirely on the streets of Nice, between the Blue House, Mémé's flat and her nursery school.

'What do you think of England, then?' Lucy asks, looking at her in the rear-view mirror.

'I like it,' says Stella. 'it's got good colours.'

'Good colours, eh?'

'Yes. The trees are extra green.'

Lucy smiles and Marco gives her the next direction towards the motorway from the Google Maps app.

Three hours later London starts to appear in flashes of shabby high street.

She sees Marco turn to face the window, expecting Big Ben and Buckingham Palace and getting Dixie Fried Chicken and second-hand appliance stores.

Finally they cross the river and it is a glorious sunny day: the river glitters with dropped diamonds of sunlight; the houses of Cheyne Walk gleam brightly.

'Here we are,' she says to Marco. 'This is the place.'

'Which one?' he asks, slightly breathlessly.

'There,' says Lucy, pointing at number sixteen. Her tone is light but her heart races painfully at the sight of the house.

'The one with the hoarding?' says Marco. 'That one?'

'Yes,' she says, peering at the house whilst also keeping an eye out for parking.

'It's big,' he says.

'Yes,' she says. 'It certainly is.'

But strangely, it looks smaller to her now, through adult's eyes. As a child she'd thought it was a mansion. Now she can see it is just a house. A beautiful house, but still, just a house.

It becomes clear that there is no parking to be had anywhere near the house and they end up at the other end of the King's Road, in a space in World's End that requires downloading a parking app on to her phone.

It's thirty degrees, as hot as the south of France.

By the time they get to the house they are all sweating and the dog is panting.

The wooden hoarding is padlocked. They stand in a row and study the building.

'Are you sure this is the right house?' says Marco. 'How does anyone live here?'

'No one lives here at the moment,' she says. 'But we're going to go inside and wait for the others to arrive.'

'But how are we going to get in?'

Lucy breathes in deeply and says, 'Follow me.'

39

Libby awakes the next morning in a shaft of bright sunlight. She trails her hand across the floor beneath her bed and then across the top of the bedside table trying to locate her phone. It's not there. The night feels furry and unformed. She sits up quickly and scans the room. It is a small white room and she is on a very low wooden bed with an enormous mattress. And so is Miller.

She instinctively clutches the sheet to her chest before realising that she is dressed; she is wearing the top she had on the night before, and her underwear. She vaguely remembers pulling off her shorts while Miller was in the bathroom and ducking under the cover. She vaguely remembers swilling with toothpaste and

The Family Upstairs

can feel it still stuck to her teeth. She vaguely remembers a lot of things.

She is in Phin's flat.

She is in bed with Miller.

They are both dressed and sleeping top to toe.

Last night Phin poured them glass after glass of wine. And insisted, almost to the point of being a bit weird about it, that they stay.

'Don't go,' he'd said. 'Please. I only just found you. I don't want to lose you again.'

And she'd said, 'You're not going to lose me. We're virtually neighbours now. Look!' And she'd pointed across the river at the noble row of houses where number sixteen sat.

'Please,' he'd wheedled, his long eyelashes touching his perfectly coiffed eyebrows. 'It's got to be better than sleeping on those manky old mattresses over there. Come on. I'll make you a delicious breakfast in the morning! I've got avocado. That's what you millennials like, isn't it?'

'I prefer eggs,' Miller had replied.

'Are you actually a millennial?' Phin had asked him, eyes narrowed, slightly bitchy.

'Just,' Miller had replied. 'But I missed the avocado moment.'

Libby looks at the time on the alarm clock on the bedside table now and works out that if she leaves in eight minutes she'll still make it to work by nine o'clock. Which is late, for her, but fine in terms of the phone ringing and customers walking in off the street.

She slides her shorts back on and hauls herself off the low-slung bed.

Miller stirs.

She glances at him.

She sees the suggestion of a tattoo on his upper arm where the sleeve of his T-shirt has ridden up. She can't bear tattoos. Which makes dating particularly awkward in this day and age. But he looks sweet, she can't help observing. Soft and appealing.

She pulls her gaze from his sleeping form and tiptoes to the en-suite bathroom she vaguely remembers using very late last night. In the mirror she looks reasonably unscathed. The previous morning's blow dry has survived all the subsequent adventures. She swills again with toothpaste and gargles with tap water. She pulls her hair back into a ponytail and finds a can of deodorant in the bathroom cabinet.

When she comes back into the bedroom Miller is awake.

He smiles at her. 'Good morning,' he says. He stretches his arms above his head and she sees the full extent of his tattoo. It's some kind of Celtic thing. It could be worse.

'I'm going now,' she says, picking up her handbag.

'Going where?'

'Work,' she says.

'God, are you really? You don't think your boss would give you the morning off?'

She pauses. Of course she would give her the morning off. But Libby doesn't work like that. It makes her feel edgy just thinking about it.

'No,' she says. 'I want to go to work. I've got a big day. Some client meetings in the diary.'

'You don't want to let people down?'

'I don't want to let people down.'

'Well,' he says, throwing back the sheet, revealing the fact that he is wearing red and blue jersey boxer shorts and has solid rugby player legs, 'give me thirty seconds and I'll come with you.'

'You don't know where my phone is, do you?' she asks.

'No idea,' he says, hauling himself out of bed and pulling on his trousers.

His hair is nuts. His beard is also nuts. She stifles a smile. 'Are you going to, you know, check your reflection?'

'Should I?' He looks confused.

She thinks of the time and says, 'No. You look fine. Let's go and find our phones and get out of here.'

She puts her hand on the door handle and pushes

Lisa Jewell

it down. The door does not open. She pushes again. Again, it does not open. She pushes it four more times.

Then she turns to Miller and says, 'It's locked.'

40

David kept Phin shut up in his room for a week after the night he pushed me in the river. A whole week. I was glad in some ways because I couldn't bear to look Phin in the eye. He had pushed me in the river, but what I had done was much, much worse.

But mainly I just ached. I ached with remorse, with regret, with fury, with helplessness and with missing him. Phin's meals were brought to him and he was allowed toilet visits twice a day, his father hovering outside the door with his arms folded across his stomach like a malevolent bouncer.

The atmosphere in the house during those days was ponderous and impossible to read. Everything emanated from David. He radiated a terrible dark energy and everyone avoided angering him further, including me.

One afternoon during Phin's incarceration, I sat with Justin, sorting herbs with him. I glanced up at the back of the house towards Phin's window.

'Don't you think it's bad', I said, 'that David's locking Phin up like that?'

He shrugged. 'He could have killed you, mate. You could have died.'

'Yeah, I know. But he didn't. *I* didn't. It's just . . . *wrong.*'

'Well, yeah, it's probably not how I'd do things, but then I'm not a dad, I don't know what it's like to have kids. David's just doing "his job", I guess.' He made quotes in the air as he said these words.

'His job?' I said. 'What do you mean?'

'Well, you know, having ultimate control over absolutely everything.'

'I hate him,' I said, my voice breaking unexpectedly.

'Yeah, well, that makes two of us.'

'Why don't you leave?'

He glanced first at me and then at the back door. 'I intend to,' he whispered. 'But don't tell a soul, OK?'

I nodded.

'There's a smallholding. In Wales. This woman I met at the market told me about it. They're looking for someone to set up a herb garden. It'll be like here, free board and lodging and all that. But no fucking dick-swinging overlords.' He rolled his eyes towards the house again.

I smiled. *Dick-swinging overlord*. I liked it.

'When are you going?'

'Soon,' he said. 'Really soon.' He looked up at me, quickly. 'Want to come with?'

I blinked. 'To Wales?'

'Yeah. To Wales. You can carry on being my little apprentice buddy.'

'But I'm only fourteen.'

He didn't say anything, just nodded and continued tying the herbs.

It wasn't until a little later that the significance of what he'd said hit me. He was not inviting me to Wales to be his little apprentice buddy; he wasn't inviting me because he needed me. He was inviting me because he thought I'd be safer there than in my own home.

Justin disappeared two days later. He told nobody he was going and left so early in the morning that even David had yet to wake up. Having learned a lesson about telling tales from what had happened with Phin, I told nobody about the Welsh smallholding. I got the impression he didn't want anyone to know where he was going. I walked into his room later that day. He'd arrived with very little, and left with even less. I walked to the windowsill where all his books sat in a row.

The Modern Book of Witchcraft and Spells.

Wicca for Beginners.

Wicca Book of Herbal Spells.

I felt sure he'd left them for me on purpose.

I glanced out into the hallway and, having ascertained that there was nobody about, I bundled the books under my jumper.

I was about to run back to my bedroom when my eye was caught by something else on his bedside table. Something small and furry. I thought at first it was a dead mouse, but upon inspection I found it to be a disembodied rabbit's foot attached to a small length of chain. I had a vague idea that it was supposed to be lucky in some way, like heather and four-leaved clovers. I jammed it quickly into my pocket and ran to my bedroom where I slid everything under my mattress.

I always expected to hear from Justin again.

After the bodies were discovered and the police were investigating the deaths and trying to trace the Lambs' 'tragic missing children' I waited and I waited for Justin to suddenly appear on the six o'clock news to talk about his time in the house, about how David Thomsen used to lock his teenage son in his bedroom

and tell everyone what to eat and what to wear and where they could and couldn't go.

I've googled Justin since, many, many times, but found no trace of him, anywhere. I can only assume either that he died, that he emigrated somewhere obscure and remote or that he knew what had happened to us all but had decided to keep silent and not get involved. Whatever the truth, I was always secretly relieved. But once he was gone, I missed him. I hadn't liked him at first, but he'd turned out to be the least of my bloody problems.

Months passed. Summer turned to winter. I took over Justin's herb garden. David actively encouraged this as it fitted with his ideology. Children should be hard at work doing wholesome things. They should not be learning skills that might bring them into the evil ways of capitalism. He had no idea about the books under my bed or the very particular skill set I was developing. Each evening I brought whoever was cooking handfuls of fresh basil and fresh mint, and was petted and approved of. Birdie even ran me a bath one night when she saw me out in the rain covering over some delicate new seedlings.

'You're doing a good job,' she said, handing me a towel as I walked up the stairs. 'David's very pleased with you.'

David's very pleased with you.

I wanted to bite her, like a dog.

Predictably, Sally had not got the flat in Hammersmith and was still on the sofa in Brixton and was now talking about moving down to Cornwall.

She arrived one evening with Phin and Clemency in tow, three hours late after taking them to a friend's party for the afternoon where it was clear that she had been drinking heavily. I had seen adults drunk before, many times, when my parents were still sociable and threw parties every weekend. But I'm not sure I'd seen anyone quite as drunk as Sally that evening.

'I can't believe', I heard David say in a voice tense with anger, 'that you think there is a chance in hell that anyone would let these children live with you. Look at the state of you.'

'You!' said Sally. 'You can talk! Look at the state of you! Who do you think you are? You're pathetic. Pathetic. You and that ugly girl. And God knows who else you're fucking. God knows.'

I saw David trying to manhandle Sally towards the door. I could tell he really wanted to hit her and was trying his hardest not to.

But then my mother appeared. 'I'll make you a coffee,' she said, touching Sally's elbow, throwing David a warning glance. 'Come on. Let's get you sorted out.'

I feigned ignorance of the drama and appeared in the kitchen a moment later.

'Just getting some water,' I said, though nobody really cared. I pretended to leave but skulked quietly just inside the pantry door.

Sally was crying, silently, a handkerchief pressed to her face. I heard her say, 'Please keep them safe. Please keep them safe for me. I just don't know if I'll ever be able to . . .' The rest of her words were swallowed up by a river boat honking its horn beyond the front door. 'I'm so worried. Phin told me about being locked in his room and I can see, yes, that he did a bad thing. I mean God, I know, Henry could have died. But it's just so . . . cold? Isn't it? To lock a child away like that? He's such a cold man . . .'

'You know what David is like,' replied my mother. 'It's his way of keeping everything together. He saved us, Sally. He really did. Before he came, I could not see the point of living each day. But now I wake up each morning and I feel happy about my existence. About myself. I am not taking from the planet. I am not plundering the earth. I am not contributing to global warming. My children are not going to end up sitting behind glass-topped desks taking money from the poor. I just wish', she said, 'that David had come into our lives many years before.'

41

Libby bangs her fists against the door. Miller bangs his too. The door is a solid fire door. He goes to the window to see if there are any means of escape there, but it is sealed shut and leads only to a sheer ten-floor drop.

They search the room once again for their phones but fail to unearth them.

After half an hour they stop banging and sit defeated on the floor with their backs against the foot of the bed.

'Now what?' says Libby.

'Let's give it half an hour and then I'll try and kick it down.'

'Why don't you try and kick it down now?

'I'm not as strong as I look, you know. I've got an old back injury. I have to be careful.'

'Ten minutes then,' she says.

'OK, ten minutes.'

'What the hell do you think he's playing at?' she asks.

'I have literally no clue.'

'Do you think he's going to kill us?'

'Oh, I doubt it.'

'Then why has he locked us in here?'

'By accident, maybe?'

Libby glances at him disbelievingly. 'You don't really believe that, do you?' The alarm clock says that it is now 7.37 a.m. She's still trying to calculate how late she's going to be for work when they both sit up straight at the sound of a door banging. Then they hear a voice. It's Phin's voice and he's addressing one of the cats. They hear kissy-kissy sounds. They jump to their feet and start to pound on the bedroom door again.

A moment later the door opens and Phin is peering at them.

'Oh God,' he says, his hand clamped over his mouth. 'Oh God. I am so sorry. I have this terrible sleepwalking habit. I've walked in on house guests before – actually tried to get into bed with them once. So I locked you in before I went to bed. And then I woke up this morning stupidly early and decided to go for a run. Completely forgot about you two. I am so incredibly sorry. Come on now. Come. Let's have breakfast.'

'I can't have breakfast. I'm late for work.'

'Oh, just call them up, tell them what happened. I'm sure they'll understand. Come on. I got fresh orange juice and everything. It's a beautiful day again. We can eat on the terrace. Please.'

He was doing the thing again, the wheedling thing he'd done the night before. Libby felt trapped.

'Why didn't you tell us', she said, 'last night? Why didn't you tell us you were going to lock the door? Or tell us to lock it from the inside?'

'It was very late,' he replied, 'and I was very drunk, and very stupid.'

'You really freaked us out, you know. I was really scared.' Libby feels her voice cracking on her words, the tension of the last moments starting to fade.

'Please forgive me,' he says. 'I'm an idiot. I wasn't thinking. You were asleep and I didn't want to wake you. I just locked it. Mindlessly. Come on. Come and have something to eat.

She and Miller exchange a glance. She can tell he wants to stay. She nods. 'OK, then, but just a quick one. And Phin?'

He looks at her sweetly.

'Where are our phones?'

'Oh,' he says. 'Are they not in your room?'

'No,' she replies. 'Neither of them.'

'Well, you must have left them out last night. Let's find them.'

They follow him down the hallway and back into the open-plan living room. 'Oh,' he says lightly. 'Here they are. You left them charging in the kitchen. We must all have been very, very drunk last night to have been that organised. Go,' he says, 'go and sit on the terrace. I'll bring breakfast out to you.'

They sit side by side on the sofa. The sun is shining on the other side of the riverbank now, picking out the windows of the houses on Cheyne Walk.

She feels Miller move closer to her. 'It doesn't wash,' he hisses in her ear. 'I don't buy the "I was drunk so I locked you in your bedroom without telling you" story. And I don't buy the mobile phone thing either. I was drunk last night, but I remember my phone being in my hand when we went to bed. I smell a rat.'

Libby nods her agreement. 'I know,' she says. 'Something doesn't quite add up.'

She switches on her phone and calls Dido. It goes through to her voicemail. 'It's a long story,' she says. 'But I'm still in Chelsea. Would you be able to ask Claire to talk to the Morgans when they come in at ten? She has all the details. And the newest quotes are on the system. They just need to be printed off. And I'll be in way before my next meeting. I promise. I'm so sorry, I'll explain everything when I see you. And if I'm not in by ten thirty, call me. If I don't answer' – she looks quickly behind her where she can see Phin still behind the kitchen counter, slicing bread – 'I'm in Battersea in an apartment block directly opposite the house. OK? I don't know what number it is. But I'm about the tenth floor up. I'll see you soon. I'm sorry. And bye.'

She ends the call and looks at Miller.

He looks at her from the corner of his eye and smiles gently. 'I won't let anything bad happen to you,' he says. 'I'll make sure you get to work for your next meeting. Alive. OK?'

A wash of affection floods through her. She smiles and nods.

Phin appears with a tray and places it in front of them. Scrambled eggs, smashed avocado sprinkled with seeds, a pile of dark rye toast, a pat of white butter and a jug of iced orange juice. 'How good does this look,' he says, handing out plates.

'It looks amazing,' says Miller, rubbing his hands together before starting to pile toast on to his plate.

'Coffee?' offers Phin. 'Tea?'

Libby asks for coffee and tops it up with milk from a jug. She picks up a slice of toast but finds she has no appetite.

She looks at Phin. She wants to ask him something

about the story he'd told them last night but she can't quite get a grip on it; it keeps moving out of touching distance. Something to do with a woman called Birdie who played the fiddle. Something to do with a cat. Something to do with a list of rules and a pagan sacrifice and something really very bad to do with Henry. But it's all so vague that it's almost, she ponders, as though he'd never told them anything at all. Instead she says, 'Do you have any pictures of you all when you were children?'

'No,' he replies apologetically. 'Not a one. Remember, there was nothing in the house when we left. My father sold everything, every last shred. And whatever he didn't sell, he dumped on charity shops. But . . .' He pauses. 'Do you remember a song? From the eighties called . . . No, of course you won't, you're far too young. But there was a song by a band called the Original Version? It was number one for weeks the summer before we came to live in the house. Birdie, the woman I was telling you about last night. She was in the band for a while. Birdie and Justin both were. And the video was filmed in Cheyne Walk. Do you want to see it?'

Libby gasps. Apart from the photo of her parents in their evening clothes in Miller's *Guardian* article, this will be the closest she'll have been to getting a sense of the place she came from.

They move into the living room and Phin connects

his phone to the huge plasma TV screen. He runs a YouTube search and then presses play.

Libby recognises the song immediately. She never knew what it was called or who it was by, but she knows it very well.

The video opens with the band performing in front of the river. They are all dressed similarly in tweed and braces and caps and DM boots. There are many of them, probably about ten members in all. Two of them are women, one of whom plays the fiddle, the other some kind of leathery drum.

'There,' says Phin, pausing the video and pointing at the screen. 'That's Birdie. Her with the long hair.'

Libby stares at the woman on the screen. A scrawny thing, weak-chinned and serious. She holds her fiddle hard against her chin and stares at the camera imperiously. 'That's Birdie?' she says. She cannot equate this frail, unimpressive-looking woman with the woman in the story Phin told them last night, the sadistic woman who presided over a household of cruelty and abuse.

Phin nods. 'Yup. Fucking evil bitch.'

He presses play again and the band are now inside a house, a glorious, riotous house filled with oil paintings and overblown furniture, red velvet thrones, gleaming swords and polished panelling, swagged curtains, moose heads, stuffed foxes and glittering chandeliers. The camera follows the band as they skip through the house with their instruments, posing on an ornate carved staircase, charging down wood-panelled corridors, play-fighting with the swords, modelling a knight's helmet, astride the cannon in the front garden and in front of a huge stone fireplace full of burning logs.

'Oh my God,' says Libby. 'It was so beautiful.'

'Yes,' says Phin drily, 'wasn't it? And that bitch and my father systematically destroyed it.'

Libby's gaze returns to the image on the television screen. Ten young people, a house full of life and money and energy and warmth. 'I don't understand,' she says quietly, 'how it all turned out the way it did.'

42

The early afternoon sun is still hot against their skin as Lucy, the children and the dog walk around the corner to the block of flats behind number sixteen Cheyne Walk. They tiptoe quickly through the communal garden to the rickety door at the back and she gestures to the children to be silent as they pass through the woody area and out on to the lawn which is parched brown by the long hot summer.

She notices with surprise that the back door to the house is unlocked. A pane of glass is broken. The breaks in the glass look fresh. A shiver runs down her spine.

She puts her hand through the broken pane and turns the handle on the inside. The door opens and she breathes a sigh of relief that she won't have to scale the side of the house to get in through the roof.

'It's scary,' says Stella, following Lucy into the house.

'Yes,' agrees Lucy, 'it is, a bit.'

'I think it's awesome,' says Marco, running his hand across the top of a huge pillared radiator and gazing around the room.

As she shows the children around the house it feels to Lucy as if not one mote of dust or string of cobweb has moved since she was last here. It feels as though it has been in stasis waiting for her to come back. The smell, whilst musty, is also darkly familiar. The way the light slices through the dark rooms, the sound of her feet against the floorboards, the shadows across the walls. It is all exactly the same. She trails her fingertips across surfaces as they step through the house. In the space of a week she has revisited the two most significant houses of her life, Antibes and Chelsea, the two places where she was hurt, where she was broken, from where she was forced to escape. The weight of it all lies heavy in her heart.

After the tour of the house they sit out in the garden. The shadows cast by the overgrown foliage are long and cool.

Lucy watches Marco picking around the garden with a stick. He's wearing a black T-shirt and for a fleeting moment she sees him as Henry, tending his herb garden. She almost jumps to her feet to check his face. But then she remembers: Henry is a man now. Not a boy.

She tries to picture Henry, but she can't. She can only see him as she saw him that last night they were all together, the set of his jaw against the shock of what had happened, the candlelight flickering across his cheeks, the dreadful silence of him.

'What's this?' Marco calls to her.

Lucy puts her hand to forehead and peers across the garden.

'Oh,' she says, standing and moving towards him. 'It's an old herb garden. One of the people who used to live here grew medicine out here.'

He stops then and holds the stick like a staff between his feet and looks up at the back of the house. 'What happened in there?' he asks.

'What do you mean?'

'I mean, I can just tell. The way you've been since we got here. Your hands are shaking. And you always just said your aunt brought you to France because you were an orphan. But I'm starting to think that something really, really bad must have happened to make her bring you. And I think it happened in this house.'

'We'll talk about it later,' she says. 'It's a very long story.'

'Where are your mum and dad?' he says and she

can see now that bringing Marco here has opened up the dams to all the things he never thought to ask her before. 'Where are they buried?'

She pulls in her breath, smiles tightly. 'I have no idea. No idea at all.'

Lucy used to write it all down, constantly, when she was younger. She'd buy a lined notepad and a pen and she'd sit somewhere, anywhere, and she'd write it and she'd write it and she'd write it. Streams of consciousness. Phin tied to a pipe in his bedroom, the adults dead, the van waiting in the shadows with its engine rumbling and the long dark drive through the night, the shell-shocked silence, and then the waiting and the waiting for the thing to come and it never did come and now, twenty-four years later, she's still waiting for it to come and it's so close she can taste it on the back of her tongue.

This was the story she wrote over and over again. She'd write it and then she'd tear the pages from the notepad, screw them into a ball and toss them in a bin, into the sea, into a dank lightwell. She'd burn them or soak them or tear them into shreds. But she needed to write it down to make it into a story instead of the truth about her life.

And all the time the truth jangled at her nerves, squeezed at her stomach muscles, played drums on her heart, taunted her in her dreams, sickened her when she awoke and stopped her from sleeping when she closed her eyes at night.

She'd always known that the only thing that would bring her back to London, to this place where so many terrible things had happened, was the baby.

But where is she? She's been here, that much is clear. There is evidence around the house of recent activity. There are drinks in the fridge, used glasses in the sink, the hole in the back door.

Now she just has to wait for the baby to come back.

43

The next thing that happened was that my mother fell pregnant.

Well, clearly it wasn't my father's baby. My father could barely get out of his chair. And the announcement, when it came, was curiously unsurprising. Because by this stage it had already become hideously clear to me that my mother was obsessed with David.

I'd seen her the night he first arrived, pulling back from him, and I'd known then that it was because she was attracted to him. And I'd seen that initial attraction turn to infatuation as my father grew weaker and David's influence grew stronger. I could see that my mother was under David's spell entirely, that she was willing to sacrifice everything for David and his approval, including her family.

But lately I'd noticed other things too.

I heard doors opening and closing late at night. I saw a flush upon my mother's neck, felt loaded moments, heard things whispered urgently, smelled his smell on her hair. I saw Birdie regard my mother watchfully, saw David's eyes upon parts of mother's body that should be no concern of his. Whatever was happening between my mother and David was feral and alive and was spreading into every corner of the house.

The announcement was made as all announcements were made, over the dinner table. David made the announcement of course, and as he made it he sat between Birdie and my mother holding one of their hands each. You could almost see the proud swell of the blood under his epidermis. He was so pleased with himself. What a guy. Two birds on the go and now a bun in the oven. What. A. Guy.

My sister immediately burst into tears and Clemency ran from the table and could be heard throwing up in the toilet by the back door.

I stared at my mother in utter horror. While I wasn't entirely surprised by the development, I was surprised that she had allowed it to be announced so publicly, so happily. I could not believe that she hadn't felt that maybe a quiet tête-à-tête in a dark corner might not have been a better way to break such news to her children. Was she not embarrassed? Was she not ashamed?

It appeared not. She grabbed my sister's hand and said, 'Darling, you always wanted a little brother or sister.'

'Yes. But not like this! Not like this!'

So dramatic, my little sister. But on this occasion I couldn't say I blamed her.

'What about Dad?' I piped up hopelessly.

'Dad knows,' she said, now clutching my hand and squeezing that too. 'Dad understands. Dad wants me to be happy.'

David sat between Birdie and my mother watching us carefully. I could tell he was simply humouring our mother by allowing her to comfort us. I could tell he did not care one iota what we thought about him and his repulsive act of penetrating and impregnating our mother. He cared nothing about anything other than himself.

I looked at Birdie. She looked oddly triumphant, as if this was the result of some great masterplan of hers.

'I'm not able to bear children,' she said, as though reading my mind.

'So my mother is – what?' I found myself asking quite sharply. 'A human incubator?'

David sighed. He touched his lips with the side of his finger, a pose he affected frequently and which to this day still unnerves me when I see other people doing it. 'This family needs a focus,' he said. 'A heart. A reason. This house needs a baby. Your amazing mother is doing this for all of us. She is a goddess.'

Birdie nodded sagely in agreement.

Clemency returned at this point looking ashen and unwell. She flopped heavily into her chair and shuddered.

'Darling,' David said to her. 'Try to look at it this way. This will bring our two families together. You four will all have a little brother or sister in common. Two families' – he reached for their hands across the table – 'united.'

My sister burst into fresh tears and Clemency kept her hand pulled into a fist.

Birdie sighed. 'Oh, for goodness' sake, you two,' she hissed, 'grow up.'

I saw David throw her a warning look. She returned the look with a petulant toss of her head.

'It will take a few days to get used to the idea. I understand,' said David. 'But you have to trust me. This will be the making of us all. It really will be. This baby will be the future of our community. This baby will be everything.'

* * *

My mother grew in a way I could not have imagined was possible. She, who had always been so slender with her jutting hip bones and long narrow waist, was suddenly the biggest person in the house. She was fed constantly and told to do nothing.

The 'baby' apparently needed a thousand extra calories a day and while we all sat picking over mushroom biryanis and carrot soups, my mother gorged on spaghetti and chocolate mousse. Have I mentioned how thin we all were by this point? Not that any of us had been particularly overweight to begin with, apart from my father. But we were virtually emaciated by the time my mother was being fattened up like a ceremonial goat. I was still wearing clothes that had fitted me when I was eleven, and I was nearly fifteen. Clemency and my sister looked as though they had eating disorders and Birdie was basically a twig. I'll tell you for nothing that vegan food goes straight through you; nothing sticks to the sides. But when that food is offered in mean portions and you are constantly told not to be greedy by asking for seconds, when one cook hates butter, so there is never enough fat (and children must eat fat), another hates salt, so there is never enough flavour, and another refuses to eat wheat because it causes their stomach to swell like a whoopee cushion, so there is never enough starch or stodge, well, that makes for very thin, malnourished people.

One of our neighbours, shortly after the bodies were found and the press were buzzing around our house with microphones and handheld cameras, appeared on the news one night talking about how thin we had all looked. 'I did wonder', said the neighbour (whom I had never before seen in my life), 'if they were being looked after properly. I did worry a bit. They were all so terribly thin. But you don't like to interfere, do you?'

No, mysterious neighbour lady, no, you clearly do not.

But while we wasted away my mother grew and grew. Birdie made her maternity tunics out of black cotton, bales of which she'd bought cheap from a fabric sale months earlier, in order to make shoulder bags to sell at Camden Market. She had sold a grand total of two before being chased away by other stallholders who all had licences to sell, and had instantly given up on the project. But now she was sewing with a fervour, desperate to be a part of what was happening to my mother. David and Birdie soon took to wearing Birdie's black tunics too. They gave all their other clothes to charity. They looked utterly ridiculous.

I should have guessed that it wouldn't be long before we children were expected to dress like this too.

Birdie came into my room one day with bin bags. 'We're to give all our clothes to charity,' she said. 'We don't need them as much as other people. I've come to help you pack them away.'

In retrospect I can't believe how easily I capitulated. I never gave myself over to David's ethos, but I was scared of him. I'd seen him fell Phin on the pavement outside our house that awful night the year before. I'd seen him hit him. I knew he was capable of more and of worse. And I was equally scared of Birdie. She was the one who had unleashed the monster inside him. So while I often moaned or grumbled, I never refused. And thus I found myself at three o'clock on a Tuesday afternoon in late April emptying my drawers and cupboards into bin bags; there went my favourite jeans, there went the really nice hoodie from H&M that Phin had passed down to me when I'd admired it. There went my T-shirts, my jumpers and shorts.

'But what will I wear when I go out?' I asked. 'I can't go out in the nude.'

'Here,' she said, passing me a black tunic and a pair of black leggings. 'We're all to wear these from now on. It makes sense.'

'I can't go out in this,' I said, appalled.

'We're keeping our overcoats,' she replied. 'Not that you ever go out anyway.'

It was true. I was something of a recluse. What with all the 'household rules', the 'not going to school' and the fact that I had nowhere to go, I barely left the house.

I took the black robe and the leggings from her and held them to my chest. She stared at me meaningfully. 'Come on then,' she said. 'The rest.'

I looked down. She was referring to the clothes I was already wearing.

I sighed. 'Could I have a moment of privacy please?'

She looked at me suspiciously but then left the room. 'Be quick,' she called through the door. 'I'm busy.'

I climbed out of my clothes as fast as I could and folded them roughly into a pile.

'Am I allowed to keep my underwear?' I called through the door.

'Yes, of course you can,' she replied impatiently.

I stepped into the stupid black robe and leggings and observed myself in the mirror. I looked like a very small, very thin monk. I stifled the desire to laugh out loud. Then very quickly I ran my hand around the backs of my drawers, searching for something. My fingers found it and I stared at it for a moment. The bootlace tie I'd bought in Kensington Market two years ago. I'd never worn it. But I could not bear the thought that I never would. I slipped it under my mattress with Justin's witchcraft books and his rabbit's foot and then I opened the door. I passed my folded clothes to Birdie.

'Good boy,' she said. She looked, for a moment, as though she might touch my hair. But then she smiled instead and repeated, 'Good boy.'

I paused for a moment, wondering, as she seemed momentarily soft, if I could possibly ask the question I desperately wanted to ask. I drew in my breath and then blurted it out. 'Aren't you jealous?' I asked. 'Aren't you jealous about the baby?'

She looked broken then, for just a split second. I felt as if I suddenly saw right inside her, right into the runny yellow yolk of her. She flinched and then she rallied. She said, 'Of course I'm not. David wants a baby. I'm grateful to your mother for letting him have one.'

'But didn't he have to have . . . sex with her?'

I wasn't entirely sure I'd ever said the word *sex* out loud before and I felt my face begin to flush red.

'Yes,' she said primly. 'Of course.'

'But he's your boyfriend?'

'Partner,' she said, 'he's my partner. I don't own him. He doesn't own me. All that matters is his happiness.'

'Yes,' I said thoughtfully. 'But what about yours?'

She didn't reply.

My sister had turned thirteen a few days after my mother's pregnancy announcement. I would say, although it is not particularly my area of expertise, that she was blossoming into a very pretty girl. She was tall, like my mother, and now, a year since the 'no haircut' rule had been implemented, her dark hair hung to her waist and unlike Clemency's hair and Birdie's hair, which grew thin and scraggy at the ends, hers was thick and shiny. She was thin, as we all were, but she had a certain shape to her. I could imagine (not that I spent very long at all doing such a thing, I can assure you) that with another stone on her, she would have had a knock-out figure. And there was an interesting face with a certain impish charm to it starting to emerge from beneath the baby face I'd been used to seeing all her life. Almost beautiful.

I mention all of this, not because I think you need to know what I thought about my sister's looks, but because you may still be envisaging a little girl. But she was no longer a little girl.

She was, when the next thing happened, much closer to being a woman.

44

Libby arrives at work, breathless, two minutes late for her meeting with Cerian Tahany. Cerian is a local DJ and minor celebrity who is spending fifty thousand pounds on a new kitchen and every time she walks into the showroom a kind of low-level electric buzz starts up. Usually Libby would have been ultra-prepared for seeing her, would have had the paperwork ready, coffee cup set up, she would have checked her reflection and eaten a mint and tidied her skirt. Today Cerian is already seated and staring tensely at her phone when Libby arrives.

'I am so, so sorry,' she says. 'So sorry.'

'It's fine,' says Cerian, turning off her phone and sliding it into her handbag. 'Let's crack on, shall we?'

For an hour, Libby has no time to think about the events of the past day. All she can think about is Carrara marble worktops and cutlery drawers and extractor hoods and copper pendant lights versus enamel pendant lights. It's comforting to her. She loves talking about kitchens. She's good at kitchens. Then suddenly it's over and Cerian's putting her reading glasses back in her handbag and hugging Libby goodbye and as she leaves the atmosphere in the showroom deflates and diffuses and everyone kind of flops.

Dido beckons her into the back office.

'So,' she says, clicking the tab on a can of Diet Coke. 'What the hell happened?'

Libby blinks. 'I'm not entirely sure. It was all completely bizarre.'

Libby talks her through coming upon Phin on the top landing and walking across Albert Bridge to his stunning riverfront apartment in Battersea with its view directly across to the house. She tells Dido what she can remember of the story that Phin recounted to them on the terrace. And then she tells her about awaking this morning to find herself top to toe with Miller in a big double bed and Dido says, 'Well, I could have told you that was going to happen.'

Libby looks at her askance. 'What?'

'You and Miller. You have a connection.'

'We do not have a connection.'

'You do have a connection. Trust me. I'm brilliant at this stuff. I've predicted three marriages from virtually before the couples had even met each other. Seriously.'

Libby waves this nonsense away. 'We were drunk and rolled into bed with all our clothes on. Woke up this morning still with all our clothes on. Oh, and he has a tattoo and I do not like tattoos.'

'I thought everyone liked tattoos these days.'

'Yes, I'm sure they do, but I don't.'

Her phone vibrates then and she picks it up. 'Talk of the devil,' she says, seeing Miller's name flash up.

'Hi!'

'Listen,' he begins urgently. 'Something weird. I just opened up my file from last night, the recording of Phin's story. It's gone.'

'Gone?'

'Yes. It's been deleted.'

'Where are you?'

'I'm in a café in Victoria. I was just about to start transcribing it and it's not there.'

'But – are you sure it was there? Maybe you hadn't pressed record properly?'

'I totally pressed record properly. I remember, last night, I checked it. I listened to it. It was there. I'd even given the file a name.'

'So, you think . . . ?'

'It must have been Phin. Remember you said you thought you had your phone with you when you came to bed? Well, so did I. And my phone has a thumbprint recognition. I mean, he must have come into our room, when we were sleeping, and opened up my phone *using my actual thumb*, while I was sleeping. And taken your phone too. Then locked us in. And there's more. I've googled him. Phin Thomsen. No trace of him anywhere on the internet. I googled the flat he's living in. It's an Airbnb. According to their booking system it's been booked since the middle of June. Basically since . . .'

'Since my birthday.'

'Since your birthday.' He sighs and runs his hand down his beard. 'I have no clue who that guy is. But he is dodgy as fuck.'

'The story,' she says. 'Can you remember the story? Enough to work out the truth.'

He pauses, briefly. 'It's hazy,' he says. 'I can remember most of it. But the bits towards the end are really . . .'

'Me too,' she says. 'Really hazy. And I slept . . .'

'Like a dead person,' he finishes.

'And all day I've felt . . .'

'Really, really strange.'

'Really strange,' she agrees.

'And I'm starting to think—'

'Yes,' she interjects, 'me too. I think he drugged us. But why?'

'That,' says Miller, 'I do not know. But you should check your phone. Do you have a passcode?'

'Yes,' she replies.

'What is it?'

She sighs. Her shoulders slump. 'It's my birth date.'

'Right,' says Miller. 'Well, check your phone for anything weird. He might have left something on it. Spyware or something.'

'Spyware?'

'God, hell knows. He's odd. Everything about last night was odd. He broke into your house. He drugged us—'

'*Might* have drugged us.'

'Might have drugged us. At the very least he snuck into our room while we slept, used my fingerprint to access my phone, took your phone from your bag and then locked us in. I wouldn't put anything past this guy.'

'No,' she says softly. 'No, you're right. I will. I'll check it. I mean, he might even be listening to us now.'

'Yes. He might. And, buddy, if you're listening, we're on to you, you creepy fuck.' She hears him draw in his breath. 'We should meet up again. Soon. I've been researching Birdie Dunlop-Evers. She's got an interesting back story. And I think I might have found out more about the other guy who lived here: Justin, Birdie's boyfriend. When are you free?'

Libby's pulse quickens at the prospect of developments in the story. 'Tonight,' she says breathlessly. 'I mean, even . . .' She looks up at Dido who is staring intently at her. 'Now?' She aims the question at Dido who nods at her furiously and mouths *go, go.*

'I can meet you now. Anywhere.'

'Our café?' he says.

She knows exactly where he means. 'Yes,' she says. 'Our café. I can be there in an hour.'

Dido looks at her after she hangs up and says, 'You know, I think this might be a good juncture for you to take some annual leave.'

Libby grimaces. 'But—'

'But nothing. I'll take on the Morgans and Cerian Tahany. We'll say you're ill. Whatever the hell is going on here is more important than kitchens.'

Libby half opens her mouth to say something in support of the importance of kitchens. Kitchens *are* important. Kitchens make people happy. People need kitchens. Kitchens, and the people who buy them, have been her life for the last five years. But she knows that Dido's right.

She nods instead and says, 'Thank you, Dido.'

Then she tidies her desk, replies to two new emails in her inbox, sets her account to Out-of-Office auto-reply and heads away from St Albans High Street to the train station.

45

By May 1992 our household had curdled and trans-mogrified into something monstrous. The outside world, filled as it was with meat-eaters and fumes and germs that could not be fought off by sweaty exercise and pretty flowers alone, was sure to bring about the death of David's precious spawn. So nobody was allowed to go outside. We had vegetables delivered to our door weekly and our larder was filled with enough pulses, grains and beans to feed us for at least five years.

Then one day, shortly before my fifteenth birthday, David ordered us to surrender our shoes.

Our shoes.

Shoes, apparently, even shoes that were not made of dead animals, were bad, bad, bad. They were suggestive of dirty pavements and joyless trudges to evil offices where people made yet more money to lavish upon the already rich whilst leaving the poor in the shackles of government-manufactured deprivation. Poor people in India did not, apparently, wear shoes; therefore, neither should we. All of our shoes were collected together into a cardboard box and left outside the nearest charity shop.

From the day that David took our shoes until the night of our escape two years later, nobody set foot outside our house.

46

Miller is eating when Libby walks into the café on West End Lane.

'What's that?' she asks, hanging her handbag on the back of the chair and sitting down.

'Chicken and chorizo wrap,' he replies, wiping some sauce from the corner of his mouth. 'So good. So, so good.'

'It's four o'clock,' she says. 'What meal does this constitute?'

He ponders the question. 'Late lunch? Or early supper? Dunch? Linner? Have you eaten?'

She shakes her head. She's not eaten since breakfast on Phin's terrace this morning and neither has she wanted to. 'I'm not hungry,' she says.

He shrugs and bites into his wrap again.

Libby orders a pot of tea and waits for Miller to finish eating.

There is something strangely attractive about Miller's appetite. He eats as though there is nothing else he would rather be doing. He eats, she observes, mindfully.

'So,' says Miller, opening up his laptop, typing something into it and then turning it to face Libby. 'Meet Birdie Dunlop-Evers. Or Bridget Elspeth Veronica Dunlop-Evers, to give her her full name. Born in Gloucestershire in April 1964. Moved to London in 1982 and studied violin at the Royal College of Music. Used to busk at the weekends and then joined a band called Green Sunday with her then boyfriend, Roger Milton. Roger Milton, incidentally, went on to be the lead singer in the Crows.'

He looks at her expectantly.

She stares back blankly. 'Are they famous?'

He rolls his eyes. 'Never mind,' he continues. 'Anyway, she jobs about with her fiddle for a few years before auditioning for a band called the Original Version. She starts a relationship with a man called Justin Redding and brings him into the band as a percussionist. According to interviews from the time, she was quite controlling. Nobody liked her. They had their big number one in the summer of 1988 and then released one more single with her and Justin, but when that tanked, she blamed everybody else, had a hissy fit and left, taking Justin with her. And that is the end of Birdie Dunlop-Evers's internet life story. Nothing since. Just . . .' He uses his hand to describe something falling off a cliff.

'But what about her parents?'

'Nothing. She was one of eight children, from a big posh Catholic family. Her parents are still alive, as far as I can tell – at least, I've found nothing to suggest that they're not – and there are *dozens* of posh little Dunlop-Everses out there playing musical instruments and running vegan home-delivery services. But for whatever reason, her family didn't notice or maybe just didn't care that their fourth daughter disappeared off the face of the earth in 1994.'

'And what about her boyfriend? Justin?'

'Nothing. A couple of mentions of him during his brief phase as a percussionist on the two Original Version hit singles. But nothing else.'

Libby pauses to absorb this. How can it be possible for people to slip off the edge of existence like that? How can it be possible for no one to notice?

He turns the screen back to himself and types something in. 'So,' he says, 'then I started looking into Phin. I got in touch with the Airbnb owner and said I was investigating a murder case and needed the name of the last person to rent his apartment. He was very forthcoming, clearly wanted in on the excitement. Justin Redding.'

Libby looks at him, startled. 'What?'

'Phin, or whoever that guy was, used the name of Birdie's ex-boyfriend to check into an Airbnb.'

'Oh,' she says. 'Wow.'

'Yeah, right?' He types something else into his laptop. 'And last, but by no means least, I give you Sally Radlett.'

He turns the screen towards her again. There is an older woman, silver hair cut into a helmet, horn-rimmed glasses, watery blue eyes, a suggestion of a smile, a light blue blouse unbuttoned to the third button, a pale collarbone, echoes of beauty in the angles of her face. Underneath her photograph are the words 'Life Therapist and Coach. Penreath, Cornwall'.

'Right town. Right age. Looks like the right career area generally – you know, *life therapist*. Kind of bullshit thing you'd end up doing, isn't it? If you were in fact Sally Thomsen?'

He looks at her triumphantly. 'What do you think?' he says. 'It's her, isn't it?'

She shrugs. 'Well, yeah, I guess it could be.'

'And there's her address.' He points at the screen and she can see the question in his eyes.

'You think we should go?'

'I think we should, yes.'

'When?'

He raises an eyebrow, smiles and presses a number into his phone. He clears his throat and says, 'Hello, is that Sally Radlett?'

She can hear a voice down the line saying *yes*.

Then, as suddenly as he'd made the call, Miller ends it. He looks at Libby and says, 'Now?'

'But—' She's about to start foraging for a reason why she cannot possibly go now, but remembers that she has no reason. 'I need a shower,' she manages.

He smiles, turns the laptop back to face him again and starts to type. 'B and B?' he says. 'Or Premier Inn?'

'Premier Inn.'

'Excellent.' With a few more clicks he's booked them two rooms at a Premier Inn in Truro. 'You can shower when we get there.' He closes his screen and unplugs his laptop, slides it into a nylon case. 'Ready?'

She gets to her feet feeling strangely excited at the prospect of spending the rest of the day with him.

'Ready.'

47

I decided that the oncoming baby was the cause of all our ills. I saw my mother getting fatter, the rest of us getting thinner. And I saw David fluffing out his tail feathers, preening and strutting. Every pound my mother gained, every time the baby kicked or wriggled, David developed another layer of sickening self-belief. I tried to keep hold of what Phin had told me the day we went to Kensington Market, about David being thrown out of the last home he tried to infiltrate and take control of. I tried to imagine the humiliation for him of being caught red-handed stealing from his hosts. I tried to remind myself that the man who'd turned up homeless and penniless on our doorstep four years earlier, was the same man swaggering now about my house like a puffed-up turkey.

I could not bear the thought of that baby coming into existence. I knew that David would use it to cement his role as the god of our warped little universe. If the baby didn't come, my mother could stop eating all the time, and we'd be able to bring germs into the house again. And, more importantly, there'd be absolutely no reason whatsoever for us to have anything more to do with David Thomsen. There'd be nothing to connect us, nothing to link us.

I knew what I had to do and it does not cast me in a good light. But I was a child. I was desperate. I was trying to save us all.

The drugs were surprisingly easy to administer. I made sure to cook for my mother as much as possible. I made her herbal teas and vegetable juices. I laced everything I gave her with the things listed in the chapter in Justin's book entitled 'Natural Termination of Unwanted Pregnancies'. Tons of parsley, cinnamon, mugwort, sesame seeds, chamomile and evening primrose oil.

As I passed her a glass of juice she would stroke my hand and say, 'You are being such a good boy, Henry. I feel very blessed to have you taking care of me.' And I would flush a little and not reply because in some ways I *was* taking care of her. I was making sure that she didn't get shackled to David for evermore. But in other ways I was not taking care of her in the least.

And then one day, when she was about five months pregnant and the baby was proper and real and had begun kicking and wriggling and moving about, my mother came downstairs and I heard her talking to Birdie in the kitchen and she said, 'The baby has not moved. Not today at all.'

The consternation grew over the course of the day and I felt a terrible dark sickness in the pit of my belly, because I knew what was coming.

Of course no doctors were called, no trips to A & E were embarked upon. Apparently David Thomsen was a fully qualified gynaecologist on top of all his other myriad skills. He took charge of everything, sent people running off for towels and water and pointless homeopathic tinctures.

It took five days for the baby to come out after it had died.

My mother wailed for hours. She stayed in her room with David and Birdie and the baby, making noises that could be heard throughout the house. We four children huddled silently together in the attic room unable to properly process what had just happened. And then finally, much later that day, my mother brought the baby downstairs wrapped in a black shawl and David made a grave for the baby at the far end of the garden and the baby was buried in the dark of night with lit candles all around.

I sought out my father that night. I sat opposite him and I said, 'Did you know that the baby died?'

He turned and stared at me. I knew he wouldn't answer the question because he couldn't speak. But I thought there might be something in his eyes to let me know what he was thinking about the events of the day. But all I saw in his eyes was fear and sadness.

'It was a little boy,' I said. 'They're calling him Elijah. They're burying him, now, in the back garden.'

He continued to stare at me.

'It's probably just as well, isn't it? Don't you think?'

I was seeking redemption for my sins. I decided to read approval into his silence.

'I mean, it probably would have died anyway, wouldn't it? Without medical assistance? Or even worse, Mum might have died. So, you know, maybe it was better this way.' I glanced at my reflection in the dark glass of the window behind my father. I looked young, and foolish. 'It was very small.'

My voice caught on this last word. The baby had been so very small, like a strange doll. My heart had ached at the sight of it. My baby brother.

'Anyway. That's what's been happening. And now, I suppose, we can all try and get back to normal.'

But that was the problem. Because there was no normal. My father's life was not normal. Our existence was not normal. The baby had gone, but I still didn't have any shoes. The baby was gone but my father still sat in a chair all day staring at the wall. The baby had gone but there was no school, no holidays, no friends, no outside world.

The baby was gone, but David Thomsen was still here.

48

It's nine o'clock. Lucy and the children are settled for the night in her parents' old bedroom. The walls of the room dance with candlelight. Stella is already asleep, the dog curled up in the crook of her knees.

Lucy opens a small can of gin and tonic. Marco opens a can of Fanta. They knock their cans together and say *Cheers* to London.

'So,' he says quietly. 'Are you going to tell me about the baby now?'

She sighs. 'Oh God.' She draws her hands down her face. 'I don't know. It's all so . . .'

'Just tell me. Please.'

'Tomorrow,' she says, stifling a yawn. 'I'll tell you tomorrow. I promise.'

Lisa Jewell

Marco finally falls asleep a few minutes later and then it is just Lucy, awake, in this blighted house that she swore she would never return to. She carefully lifts Marco's head from her lap and stands. At the window she watches the sun setting in the windows of the shiny new apartment blocks on the other side of the river. They weren't there when she lived here. Maybe if they had been, she ponders, someone might have seen them, someone might have known, someone might have rescued them and spared them all their sorry fates.

She falls asleep some time after 3 a.m., her mind stubbornly refusing to shut down for hours before, suddenly, she is in her dreams.

And then, just as suddenly, she is awake again. She sits up straight. Marco sits up too. Her phone tells her that they have all slept late into the morning.

There are footsteps overhead.

Lucy puts one hand over Marco's and touches her lips with tip of her index finger.

It's silent again and she begins to relax. But then she hears it again, the definite sound of footsteps, floorboards creaking.

'Mum . . .'

She squeezes his hand and gets slowly to her feet. She tiptoes across the room towards the door. The dog

322

awakes and raises his head, uncurls himself from Stella's body and follows her to the door. His claws are loud against the wooden floorboards and she picks him up. She can feel a growl forming in the back of his throat and shushes at him.

Marco stands behind her and she can hear his breathing hard and heavy.

'Stay back,' she hisses.

The growl in Fitz's throat is building and building. There's another creak overhead and then Fitz lets rip.

The creaking stops.

But then there comes the sound of footsteps, sure and steady, coming down the wooden staircase that leads to the attic bedrooms. She stops breathing. The dog starts barking again and struggling to get out of her arms. She pushes the door shut and throws her body against it.

Stella is awake now and stares at the door with wide eyes. 'What's going on, Mama?'

'Nothing, darling,' she whispers across the room. 'Nothing. Fitz is just being silly.'

The door on to the first-floor landing creaks, then bangs shut.

Adrenaline courses through her.

'Is it the baby?' Marco asks in an urgent whisper, his eyes wide with terror.

'I don't know,' she replies. 'I don't know who it is.'

Footsteps come up the landing and then there is someone breathing on the other side of the door. The dog goes quiet, his ears pinned back, his lips open over his teeth. Lucy moves away from the door and pulls it open a crack. Then the dog leaps out of her arms and forces his way through the crack of the door and there's a man standing outside their room and the dog barks and snaps around his ankles and the man looks down at the dog with a small smile, offers him his hand to sniff. Fitz quiets and sniffs his hand and then lets him stroke the top of his head.

'Hello, Lucy,' says the man. 'Nice dog.'

III

49

Libby lies stretched out on the hotel bed with its familiar strip of aubergine-coloured fabric draped across the foot. A Premier Inn hotel room is a happy place for Libby; she associates them with hen nights and city breaks and weddings in distant cities. A bed in a Premier Inn is familiar and comforting. She could stay here all day. But she has to meet Miller in the lobby at 9 a.m. She glances now at the time on her phone. Eight forty-eight. She pulls herself off the bed and has a very quick shower.

It had been a long journey from London the night before and she'd learned a lot about Miller in the five hours they'd spent together.

He'd been in a car accident when he was twenty-two

and spent a year in a wheelchair and being rehabilitated. He'd been very thin and sporty when he was
younger but never regained his former lithe physique. He has two older sisters and a gay dad and was
brought up in Leamington Spa. He studied politics at
university where he met his ex-wife, whose name was
Matilda, or Mati for short. He showed Libby a photo
of her on his phone. She was extraordinarily pretty
with dark red hair and full lips and a blocky, hipster
haircut that would look dreadful on 99 per cent of
other people.

'Why did you split up?' she'd said. Then added, 'If
you don't mind me asking?'

'Oh, my fault,' he'd said, putting a hand to his heart.
'My fault entirely. I prioritised everything over her. My
friends, my hobbies. But mainly my job. And mainly' –
he pauses to smile wryly – 'the *Guardian* article.' He'd
shrugged. 'Lesson learned though. I will never put my
work before my personal life again.

'And what about you?' he'd asked. 'Is there a Mr
Libby somewhere in the picture?'

'No,' she'd replied. 'No. That is an ongoing project.'

'Ah, but you're still young.'

'Yes,' she'd agreed, forgetting for once her usual
sense of running out of time to achieve all her arbitrary goals. 'I am.'

She redresses in yesterday's clothes and gets to the

lobby at two minutes past nine where Miller is already waiting for her. He has not changed or, it seems, showered. He looks dishevelled, every bit like a man who has not seen his own bed for forty-eight hours. But there is something pleasing to behold about his shagginess and his carewornness and she has to resist the temptation to arrange his hair for him, to straighten the neck of his T-shirt.

He has, of course, partaken of a hearty Premier Inn breakfast and is just downing the dregs of a coffee when she appears. Now he smiles at her, puts down his cup and together they leave the hotel.

Sally's practice is on the high street of Penreath in a small stone building. The shopfront houses a spa called the Beach. Sally's rooms are up a flight of stairs on the first floor. Miller rings the bell and a very young girl answers.

'Yes?'

'Hello,' says Miller. 'We're looking for Sally Radlett.'

'I'm afraid she's with a client at the moment. Can I help?'

The girl is pale and naturally blonde and shares the same well-formed bone structure as Sally. For a moment Libby thinks that this must be Sally's daughter. But that can't be right. Sally must be at least sixty, probably older.

'Erm, no, we really do need to speak to Sally,' says Miller.

'Do you have an appointment?'

'No,' he says, 'sadly not. It's something of an emergency.'

The girl narrows her eyes slightly and then turns her gaze to a leather Chesterfield sofa and says, 'Would you like to take a seat, while you're waiting? She won't be much longer.'

'Thank you so much,' says Miller and they sit side by side.

It's a tiny room; they are close enough to the girl, who is back behind her desk, to hear her breathing.

A phone call breaks the awkward silence and Libby turns to Miller and whispers, 'What if it's not her?'

'Then it's not her,' he says, shrugging.

Libby gazes at him for a split second. She realises that he doesn't see life the way she sees it. He's prepared to be wrong; he doesn't always need to know what's going to happen next. The thought of living life as Miller lives his life is strangely appealing to her.

A tall woman appears. She is wearing a grey short-sleeved dress and gold sandals. She says goodbye to a middle-aged man and then catches their eyes, giving them an uncertain look. She turns to the girl behind the desk and says, 'Lola?'

The girl looks at them and says, 'They asked for an emergency appointment.'

She turns back to them and smiles uncertainly. 'Hello?'

It is clear that she does not like people walking in asking for emergency appointments.

But Miller is unfazed and gets to his feet. 'Sally,' he says. 'My name is Miller Roe. This is my friend Libby Jones. I wonder if you might be able to spare us ten minutes or so?'

She glances back at the girl called Lola. Lola confirms that Sally's next appointment is not until eleven thirty. She beckons them into her office and then closes the door behind them.

Sally's consulting room is cosy in a Scandinavian style: a pale sofa with a crocheted blanket thrown across it, pale grey walls, a white-painted desk and chairs. The walls are hung with dozens of framed black and white photographs.

'So,' she says. 'What can I do for you?'

Miller glances at Libby. He wants her to start. She turns back to Sally and she says, 'I just inherited a house. A big house. In Chelsea.'

'Chelsea?' she repeats vaguely.

'Yes. Cheyne Walk.'

'Mm-hm.' She nods, just once.

'Number sixteen.'

'Yes, yes,' she says with a note of impatience. 'I don't—' she begins. But then she stops and narrows her eyes slightly.

'Oh!' she says. 'You're the baby!'

Libby nods. 'Are you Sally Thomsen?' she asks.

Sally pauses. 'Well,' she says after a moment, 'technically, no. I reverted to my maiden name a few years ago, when I started this practice. I didn't want anyone to . . . well. I was in a bad place for quite some time and I wanted a fresh start, I suppose. But yes. I was Sally Thomsen. Now listen,' she says, her tone suddenly becoming clipped and officious. 'I don't want to get involved in anything, you know. My daughter, she made me swear never to discuss anything about the house in Chelsea. Never to talk about it. She suffered from years of PTSD after what happened there, and really, she's still very damaged. It's not my place to say anything. And as much as I'm glad to see you here, alive and well, I'm afraid I'm going to have to ask you both to leave.'

'Could we, maybe, speak to your daughter? Do you think?'

Sally throws a steely gaze at Miller, the asker of this question. 'Absolutely not,' she says. 'Absolutely not.'

50

CHELSEA, 1992

My mother never really recovered from losing the baby.

She slowly withdrew from community life. She also withdrew from David. She began to spend more time with my father, just the two of them sitting quietly side by side.

I of course felt completely responsible for my mother's unhappiness. I attempted to remedy the situation by feeding her concoctions from Justin's books that claimed to cure people of melancholia. But it was virtually impossible to get her to eat anything, so nothing I did made any difference.

David seemed to have abandoned her. I was surprised. I would have expected him to want to be involved in her rehabilitation. But he was distant with her, virtually cold.

One day, shortly after my mother lost the baby, I asked David, 'Why aren't you talking to my mother any more?'

He looked at me and sighed. 'Your mother is healing. She needs to follow her own path towards that.'

Her own path.

I felt a wave of fury begin to build inside me. 'I don't think she is healing,' I responded. 'I think she's getting worse. And what about my father? Shouldn't he be getting some kind of care? Some kind of treatment? All he does is sit in that chair all day. Maybe in the outside world someone could do something for him. Maybe some kind of therapy. Maybe even electric shock therapy or something like that. There might be all sorts of medical advances being made for stroke victims that we don't even know about because we're all just *stuck in here* . . .' I'd begun to shout and as soon as the words were out of my mouth, I knew I'd passed into a bad place and then there it was, the cold, sharp skin of his hand, hard against the side of my jaw.

I tasted the metallic sting of blood inside my mouth, felt a numbness building up around my lips. I touched the blood with a fingertip and looked at David in horror.

He stared down at me, his big shoulders hunched

up around his ears, a vein throbbing on the side of his head. It was incredible how quickly this quiet, spiritual man could turn into a raging monster. 'You have no right to talk about these things,' he growled. 'You know nothing about anything. You are an infant.'

'But he's my father. And ever since you came you've just treated him like shit!'

His hand came back, this time across the other side of my face. I had always known this was going to happen. I had known from the moment I first saw him that David Thomsen would strike me if I confronted him. And here it was.

'You ruined everything,' I said in a nothing-to-lose-now rush of emotion. 'You think you're so powerful and so important but you're not! You're just a bully! You came into my home and you bullied everyone into being what you wanted us to be. And then you made my mum pregnant and now she's sad and you don't care, you don't care at all. Because all you care about is yourself!'

This time he hit me hard enough to throw me across the floor.

'Get up!' he yelled. 'Get up, and go to your room. You are in isolation for a week.'

'You're going to lock me up?' I said. 'For talking to you? For telling you how I feel?'

'No,' he snarled. 'I am locking you up because

I cannot bear to look at you. Because you disgust me. Now, you can either walk or I can drag you. What's it to be?'

I got to my feet and I ran. But I didn't run to the stairs, I ran to the front door. I turned the handle and I pulled and I was ready, ready to fly, ready to flag down a stranger and say, *God help us, we're trapped in a house with a megalomaniac. God help us please!* But the door was locked.

How had I not known this? I tugged and tugged and then turned to him and said, 'You've locked us in!'

'No,' he said. 'The door is locked. That is not the same thing at all. Now, shall we?'

I stamped up the back stairs to the attic floor, David following behind.

I heard the sound of the lock on my bedroom door turning.

I wailed and I cried like a terrible pathetic overgrown baby.

I heard Phin shouting at me through his bedroom wall: 'Shut up! Just shut up!'

I screamed for my mother but she didn't come.

Nobody came.

That night my face ached from where David had hit me and my stomach growled and I couldn't sleep and lay awake all night staring at the clouds passing over the moon, watching the dark shapes of birds in the treetops, listening to the house creaking and gasping.

I went a little mad, I think, over the course of the week that followed. I scratched marks into my walls with my fingernails until my nailbeds bled. I banged my head against the floor. I made animal noises. I saw things that weren't there. I think David's idea was that I would emerge from my imprisonment feeling subdued and ready to start afresh. But this was not the case.

When the door was finally unlocked a week later and I was once more allowed to roam around the house, I did not feel subdued. I felt monstrously consumed with righteous ire. I was going to finish David off for good.

There was something else in the air when I finally got my freedom back, a huge secret wafting about in the atmosphere, carried along by the dust motes and the sun rays, stuck in the strands of the spider webs in the high corners of the rooms.

As I joined everyone at the breakfast table that first morning out of isolation I asked Phin, 'What's going on? Why is everyone acting so weird?'

He shrugged and said, 'Isn't that how everyone always acts round here?'

I said, 'No. Weirder than usual. Like there's something going on.'

Phin was already ill by now, it was clear to me. His skin, once so smooth and flawless, looked grey and patchy. His hair flopped greasily to one side. And he smelled a little off, a little sour.

I mentioned it to Birdie. 'Phin seems ill,' I said.

She replied prissily, 'Phin is absolutely fine. He just needs more exercise.'

I would hear his father through the door of the exercise room imploring him to try harder. 'More – you can do it. Push back. Really push back. Come on! You're not even trying!' And then I'd see Phin leaving the exercise room looking wan and agonised, taking the steps up to the attic floor slowly as if each one caused him pain.

I said, 'You should come into the garden with me. The fresh air will help.'

He said, 'I don't want to go anywhere with you.'

'Well, you don't have to come with me. Go into the garden alone.'

'Don't you see?' he said. 'Nothing in this house will make me well. The only thing that will make me well is not being in this house. I need to leave. I need', he said, his eyes boring into mine, 'to leave.'

The house, it felt to me, was dying. First my father had faded, then my mother, now Phin. Justin had abandoned us. The baby was dead. I couldn't really see what the point of any of it was any more.

And then one afternoon I heard the sound of laughter coming from below. I peered down into the hallway and saw David and Birdie leaving the exercise room. They were both glowing with health. David swung an arm around Birdie's shoulders and drew her to him, kissed her hard on the lips with a sickening *mwah* noise. And it was them; I knew it clearly. It was them, draining the house, like vampires, of all of its decent energy, of all of its love and life and goodness, draining it all for themselves, feasting on our misery and our broken spirits.

Then I looked around myself at the bare walls where the oil paintings had once hung, at the empty corners where the fine pieces of furniture had once stood. I thought of the chandeliers that had once sparkled in the sunlight. The silver and the brass and the gold that had gleamed on every surface. I thought of my mother's wardrobe of designer clothes and handbags, the rings that used to adorn her fingers, the diamond earrings and sapphire pendants. All gone now. All gone to so-called 'charity', to help the 'poor people'. I estimated the value of all these lost possessions. Thousands of pounds, I suspected. Many thousands of pounds.

And then I looked down again at David, his arm circling Birdie, the two of them so free and unburdened by the things going on in this home. And I thought: You are not a messiah or a guru or a god,

David Thomsen. You are not a philanthropist or a do-gooder. You are not a spiritual man. You are a criminal. You have come to my house and you have plundered it. And you are not a man of compassion. If you were a man of compassion, you would be sitting now with my mother while she grieves for your lost baby. You would find a way to help my father out of his living hell. You would take your son to the doctor. You would not be laughing with Birdie. You would be too weighed down by everyone else's unhappiness. So, if you have no compassion then it follows that you would not have been giving our money to the poor. You would have been keeping it for yourself. And that must be the 'secret stash' that Phin had told me about all those years ago. And if that is the case, then where is it? And what are you planning to do with it?

51

Two weeks after David released me from my room, he announced my sister's pregnancy around the dinner table. She was barely fourteen.

I saw Clemency recoil from my sister, spring apart from her as though burned with hot oil. I saw my mother's face, the blank death look, and it was clear that she already knew. I saw Birdie. She smiled at me. And at the sight of those tiny little teeth I exploded. I leapt across the table and threw myself at David. I tried to hit him. Well, in fact, I tried to kill him. That was my main intent.

But I was small and he was big and Birdie of course came between us and I was somehow pulled away and back to my side of the table. I looked at my sister, at the strange smile playing on her lips, and I could not believe that I had never seen it before, had not seen that my stupid little sister had fallen for the whole thing, that she saw David as my mother saw David, as Birdie saw David. That she was *proud* that David had chosen her, and proud to be carrying his child.

And then it hit me.

David didn't just want our money. David wanted the house.

That was all he'd ever wanted from the moment he'd first set foot in it. And having a baby with my sister would secure his stake in it.

I went to my parents' bedroom the next day. I opened the cardboard boxes into which all their non-valuable possessions had been emptied when the furniture was given away. I could sense my father's eyes on me.

'Daddy,' I said, 'where's the will? The will that says what happens to the house when you die?'

I could see the suggestion of words forming in the base of his throat. He opened his mouth a millimetre or two. I moved closer to him. 'Dad? Do you know? Do you know where all the paperwork is?'

His gaze went from my face to the bedroom door.

'It's out there?' I asked. 'The paperwork?'

He blinked.

He did this sometimes when he was being fed. If

Mum said, 'Is that nice, darling?' he would blink and Mum would say, 'Good. Good,' and give him another mouthful.

'Which room?' I asked. 'Which room is it in?'

I saw his eyes move to the left a fraction. Towards David and Birdie's room.

'In David's room?'

He blinked.

My heart plummeted.

I could not possibly go into David and Birdie's room. They kept it locked, for a start. And even if they didn't, the consequences of being caught in there were unthinkable.

I referred once again to Justin's enormously useful book of spells.

'A Spell for Temporary Stupefaction'.

That sounded like exactly what I needed. It promised a few moments of general befuddlement and sleepiness, a 'small and unnoticeable fugue'.

It involved the use of deadly nightshade, *Atropa belladonna*, the poisonous plant that Justin had told me about all those months before. I'd been growing it, secretly, after finding some seeds in Justin's apothecarial chest. The seeds had needed to be soaked in water in the fridge for two weeks. I'd told the grown-ups I was experimenting with a new herb for Phin's *ennui*.

Then I'd taken the seeds and planted them in two

343

large pots. It had taken three weeks for the seedlings to show and the last time I'd looked they'd been in full bloom. According to the literature, *Atropa belladonna* was very difficult to grow and I'd felt incredibly pleased with myself when the first purple flowers had blossomed. Now I snuck to the garden and plucked a couple of sprigs, tucked them into the waistband of my leggings and ascended quickly. In my room I made up the tincture with chamomile leaves and sugar water. It was also supposed to contain two hairs from the back of a red cat and a puff of breath from an old woman's mouth, but I was an apothecary, not a wizard.

My herbal teas were much loved. I told David and Birdie that I'd been experimenting with a new blend: chamomile and raspberry leaves. They looked at me fondly and said that sounds delicious.

I apologised to Birdie as she drank hers that it was maybe a little sweet; I told her it was just a touch of honey, to balance out the rather bitter edge of the raspberry leaves. The spell had specified that the recipient of the spell needed to drink at least half a cup. So I sat and watched with an affectionate look on my face, as if I was desperately seeking their approval, so that they would keep drinking, even if they did not like the taste.

But they did like the taste and both of them drank their full cup.

'Well,' said Birdie a while later as we put away the washing up. 'That tea was super, super relaxing, Henry. I feel I could . . . In fact . . .' I saw her eyes roll back slightly in her head. 'I might have to go to bed,' she said.

I could see David struggling now, too, to keep his eyes open. 'Yes,' he said. 'Just a little nap.'

'Come on,' I said, 'let me help you both. Gosh, I'm so sorry. Maybe that tea had too much chamomile in it. Here, here.' I allowed Birdie to hold on to my arm.

She rested her cheek against my shoulder and said, 'I love your tea, Henry. It's the best tea ever.'

'Really, really good tea,' David agreed.

David fumbled for the key to their bedroom in the folds of his tunic. I saw as he did so that beneath his tunic, he wore a cross-body leather purse. I assumed that this must be where he kept all the keys to all the rooms in the house. He was having trouble putting the key in the lock so I helped him. Then I got them both on to the bed where they fell instantaneously into a deep sleep.

And there I stood. In David and Birdie's bedroom. I had not set foot in this room for years, not since David and Sally had still been together.

I looked around the room and could barely absorb what I was seeing. Piles of cardboard boxes over the tops of which spilt suggestions of clothing, of books, of possessions, the possessions we had been told were evil and bad. I saw two pairs of shoes in the corner of the room, his and hers. I saw alcohol, a half-drunk bottle of wine with the cork replaced, a glass with a dark sticky residue at the bottom, some of my father's very expensive whiskey. I saw a box of biscuits, a Mars Bar wrapper. I saw a slip of silky underwear, a bottle of Elvive shampoo.

But I ignored all this for now. I had no idea how long this state of 'temporary stupefaction' would last. I needed to find my father's paperwork and get out of there.

As my hands passed through the boxes I came upon my pencil case, not seen since my last day of primary school. I held it briefly in my hand and stared at it as a relic from another civilisation. I thought briefly of that boy in the brown knickerbockers, skipping from his last day at school, a triumphant tip to his chin as he imagined the brave new world about to be presented to him. I unzipped it, held it to my nose, inhaled the smell of pencil shavings and innocence; then I tucked it into my leggings to be secreted later in my own room.

I found a ballgown of my mother's. I found my father's shotguns. I found my sister's ballet leotard and tutu, the reason for the keeping of which I could not fathom.

And then, in the third box, I found my father's files:

grey marbled box files with fierce metal clips inside. I pulled one out that had written on the side 'Household Affairs' and flipped quickly through the contents.

And there it was, the last will and testament of Henry Roger Lamb and Martina Zeynep Lamb. I slipped this too into the waistband of my leggings. I would read it quietly, in my own room. I heard Birdie's breathing grow quicker and saw her leg twitch. I quickly pulled another box towards me. In here I saw passports. I picked them up and flicked to the back pages: mine, my sister's, my parents'. I felt a flame of fury build up inside of me. Our passports! This man had taken our passports! This seemed almost to surpass the sheer evil of locking us into our own home. To steal another human being's passport, their means to escape, to adventure, to explore, to learn, to take full advantage of the world – my heart pounded with rage. I noted that my own passport had expired, that my sister's had another six months to go. Useless to us now.

I heard David mumble under his breath.

The temporary stupefaction had been slightly too temporary and I wasn't sure I'd ever persuade them to drink a special 'new tea' again. This could be my one and only opportunity to uncover the secrets buried away in this room.

I found a packet of paracetamol. A packet of cough

sweets. A packet of condoms. And I found, buried underneath all of this, a pile of cash. I ran my fingers down the sides. It riffled satisfyingly, suggesting a good amount. A thousand, I estimated. Maybe more? I pulled a few ten-pound notes from the top of the pile and folded them into the paperwork held inside my elasticated waistband.

Birdie groaned.

David groaned.

I got to my feet, my father's will, my pencil case and five ten-pound notes clutched tightly against my stomach.

I left the room on tiptoe, shutting the door silently behind me.

52

Lucy's mind is spinning. The man's features come in and out of focus. For a moment he looks like one person, the next, another. She asks him who he is.

'You know who I am,' he says.

The voice is both familiar yet strange.

Stella has crossed the room and is clinging on to Lucy's leg with her arms.

Lucy can see Marco standing tall and strong beside her.

The dog accepts the man's affection happily, rolling now on to his back to allow him to tickle his belly.

'Who's a good boy,' says the man. 'Who's a very, very good boy.'

He glances up at Lucy and pushes his glasses up his nose with tip of his index finger. 'I would so love a dog,' he says. 'But you know, it's not fair, is it, leaving them at home all day when you're working. So, I make do with cats instead.' He sighs and then he stands up straight and looks her up and down. 'I love your look, by the way. I would never have thought you'd turn out so, you know, *bohemian*.'

'Are you . . . ?' she squints at him.

'I'm not going to tell you,' says the man playfully. 'You have to guess.'

Lucy sighs. She is so tired. She has travelled so far. Her life has been so long and so hard and nothing has ever, ever been easy. Not for one second. She has made terrible decisions and ended up in bad places with bad people. She is, as she has so often felt, a ghost, the merest outline of a person who might one day have existed but had been erased by life.

And now here she is: a mother, a killer, an illegal immigrant who has broken and entered into a property that does not belong to her. All she wants is to see the baby and to close the circle of her existence. But now there is a man here and she thinks he might be her brother, but how can he both be her brother and yet not be her brother? And why is she scared of him?

She glances up at the man, sees the shadow of his long eyelashes against his cheekbones. Phin, she thinks. This is Phin. But then she glances down at his hands: small and delicate, with narrow wrists.

'You're Henry,' she says, 'aren't you?'

53

I went to my mother after the announcement and said, 'You let your daughter have sex with a man the same age as you. That is just sick.'

She merely responded, 'It was nothing to do with me. All I know is that a baby is coming and that we should all be very happy.'

I had never and still to this day have never felt so entirely alone. I no longer had a mother nor a father. We had no visitors to the house. The doorbell never rang. The phone had been disconnected many months before. There was a time, in the days after my mother lost her baby, when someone came to our house and banged on the door, solidly, for half an hour every day for nearly a week. We were kept in our rooms while the person banged on the door. Afterwards my mother said it was her brother, my uncle Karl. I liked Uncle Karl, he was the type of boisterous young uncle who would throw children into swimming pools and tell off-colour jokes that would make all the adults tut. The last time we'd seen him was at his wedding in Hamburg when I was about ten years old. He'd worn a floral three-piece suit. The idea that he'd been at our door and that we had not let him in broke another small part of my heart. 'Why, though?' I asked my mother. 'Why didn't we let him in?'

'Because he wouldn't understand the way we choose to live. He is too frivolous and lives a life without meaning.'

I didn't respond to that because there was no response to be made. He would not understand. No one would understand. At least she could see that much.

Vegetables were delivered in a cardboard box once a week; cash was left in a hidden envelope by the front door. Once or twice the vegetable delivery man would ring on the bell and my mum would open the letterbox and the vegetable delivery man would say, 'No parsnips today, miss, replaced them with swedes, hope that's OK?' And my mother would smile and say, 'That is fine, thank you so much,' and after the bodies were found, this man would come to the police and tell them that he thought it was a closed convent and that

Lisa Jewell

my mother was a nun. He referred to this drop-off on his route as the 'nunnery'. He said he'd had no idea there were children living in the house. He'd had no idea there was a man.

I was very lonely by now. I tried to rekindle my friendship (or what semblance there had ever been of a friendship) with Phin, but he was still so angry with me for betraying him the night he pushed me into the river. And yes, I know I should have been angry with him for pushing me into the river in the first place, but we'd taken drugs, and I was annoying, I could see that I was annoying, and in a way I'd deserved to be pushed into the river and my fury afterwards was more to do with hurt pride and feelings than any sense that he'd put me in mortal danger. And also, I was in love with him and when you're in love, you'll forgive almost anything. It's a trait that I've carried with me into adult life, unfortunately. I always fall in love with people who hate me.

I came upon Clemency in the kitchen one afternoon shortly after the announcement of my sister's pregnancy.

'Did you know?' I said.

She flushed a little as obviously we'd barely spoken over the years and now we were talking about her best friend having sex with her father.

354

She said, 'No. I had no idea.'

'But you're so close. How could you not have known?'

She shrugged. 'I just thought they were exercising.'

'What do you think about it?'

'I think it's disgusting.'

I nodded, vehemently, as if to say *we are on the same page, good.*

'Has your father ever done anything like this before?'

'You mean . . . ?'

'The babies. Has he ever got people pregnant before?'

'Oh,' she said softly. 'No. Only my mum.'

I told her to come to my room and she looked scared for a minute, which hurt my feelings, but then I thought it was good. It was good to be scary if I was going to overthrow David and get us all out of this house.

In my room I pulled my mattress away from the wall and pulled out the objects I'd found in David and Birdie's room. I spread them across the floor and let her look at them. I told her where I'd found them.

'But how did you get in there?' she asked.

'I can't tell you,' I said.

I saw confusion sluice through her as she looked at the objects. 'Your pencil case?'

'Yes. My pencil case. And there was so much other stuff.' I told her about the silky underwear and the whiskey and the piles of cash. And as I told her I saw that I was breaking her. It was like the day I'd told Phin about seeing his dad kissing Birdie. I'd forgotten that I was talking to a child about her father, that there was a deep seam of shared genetic material, memories, connection there and that I was ripping it all apart with my words.

'He's been lying to us all along!' she said, rubbing her eyes with the heels of her hands. 'I thought we were doing all of this for the poor people! I don't understand. I don't understand!'

I looked her firmly in the eye. 'It's simple,' I said. 'Your father's taken everything of value from my parents and now he wants their house. Legally this house is held in trust for me and my sister until we're twenty-five. But look.' I showed her the will I'd pulled out of the box. It had a codicil added in David's handwriting. The house, he'd stated in cod legal language, was in the event of the deaths of my parents now to pass directly to David Sebastian Thomsen and his descendants. This codicil had been witnessed and countersigned by my mother and Birdie. It wouldn't stand a chance in hell of making it through a court of law but its intent was clear.

'And he's having a baby to secure his stake in the house.'

Clemency didn't say anything for a while. Then she said, 'What are we going to do?'

'I don't know yet,' I said, rubbing my chin as though there might be a wise man's beard there, but of course there was nothing of the sort. I didn't grow a beard until I was in my twenties and even then it was pretty unimpressive. 'But we are going to do something.'

She looked at me, wide-eyed. 'OK.'

'But', I said firmly, 'you have to promise me that this is our secret.' I gestured at the objects I'd purloined from David and Birdie's room. 'Do not tell your brother. Do not tell my sister. Do not tell anyone. OK?'

She nodded. 'I promise.' She was silent for a minute and then she looked up at me and said, 'He's done this before.'

'What?'

She dropped her gaze to her lap. 'He tried to get his grandmother to sign her house over to him. When she was senile. My uncle found out and kicked us out. That's when we moved to France.' She looked up at me. 'Do you think we should tell the police?' she said. 'Tell them what he's been doing?'

'No,' I said instantly. 'No. Because, really, he hasn't broken the law, has he? What we need is a plan. We need to get out of here. Will you help me?'

She nodded.

'Will you do whatever it takes?'

She nodded again.

It was a fork in the road, really. Looking back on it there were so many other ways to have got through the trauma of it all, but with all the people I loved most in the world facing away from me I chose the worst possible option.

54

Libby and Miller leave Sally's office ten minutes later.

'Are you OK?' he asks her as they emerge into the sweltering heat.

She manages a smile but then realises that she is about to cry and can do nothing to stop it.

'Oh God,' says Miller. 'Oh dear. Come on, come on.' He guides her towards a quiet courtyard and to a bench under a tree. He feels his pockets. 'No tissues, I'm sorry.'

'It's OK,' she says. 'I have tissues.'

She pulls a packet of travel tissues from her bag and Miller smiles.

'You are so exactly the sort of person who would carry a packet of travel-sized tissues around.'

She stares at him. 'What does that even mean?'

'It means . . . It just means . . .' His features soften. 'Nothing,' he says. 'It just means you're very organised. That's all.'

She nods. This much she knows. 'I have to be,' she says.

'And why is that?' he asks.

She shrugs. It's not in her nature to talk about personal things. But given what they've been through in the last two days she feels the boundaries that define her usual conversational preferences have been blown apart.

She says, 'My mum. My adoptive mum. She was a bit – well, *is* a bit chaotic. Lovely, lovely, lovely. But it was my dad who kept her on track. And he died when I was eight and after that . . . I was always late for everything. I never had the right stuff for school. I didn't used to show her the slips for trips and things because there was no point. She booked a holiday in the middle of my GCSEs. Emigrated to Spain when I was eighteen years old.' She shrugs. 'So I just had to be the grown-up. You know.'

'The keeper of the tissues?'

She laughs. 'Yes. The keeper of the tissues. I remember this one time I fell over in the playground and cut my elbow and my mum was just sort of flapping about looking for something in her handbag to clean it up with and this other mum came over with a handbag exactly the same size as my mum's and she opened it and pulled out an antiseptic wipe and a packet of plasters. And I just thought: Wow, I want to be the person with the magic handbag. You know.'

He smiles at her. 'You're doing really well,' he says. 'You know that, don't you?'

She laughs nervously. 'I'm trying,' she says. 'Trying to do the best I can.'

For a moment they sit in silence. Their knees touch briefly and then spring apart again.

Then Libby says, 'Well, that was a waste of time, wasn't it?'

Miller throws her a devious look. 'Well,' he says, 'not entirely a waste of time. The girl. Lola? She's Sally's granddaughter.'

Libby gasps. 'How do you know?'

'Because I saw a photo on Sally's desk of Sally with a younger woman holding a newborn. And then I saw another photo on her wall of Sally with a young girl with blond hair. And then I saw a child's drawing framed on the wall that said "I Love You Grandma".' He shrugs. 'I put it all together and hey presto.' Then he leans towards Libby and shows her something on the screen of his phone.

'What is it?' she asks.

'It's a letter addressed to Lola. It was poking out of

her handbag under her desk. I performed the classic kneeling-to-tie-my-shoelace manoeuvre. *Click.*'

Libby looks at him in awe. 'But what made you even think . . . ?'

'Libby. I'm an investigative journalist. This is what I do. And if my theory is correct, Lola must be Clemency's daughter. Which means that Clemency must live locally. And therefore, this address' – he points at his screen – 'is also Clemency's address. I think we might just have found the second missing teenager.'

A woman comes to the door of the smart bungalow. A well-behaved golden retriever stands at her side and wags his tail lazily at them. The woman is slightly overweight; she has a thick middle and long legs, a heavy-looking bosom. Her hair is very dark and cut into a bob and she wears gold hoop earrings, blue jeans and a pale pink sleeveless linen top.

'Yes?'

'Oh,' says Miller. 'Hello. Clemency?'

The woman nods.

'My name is Miller Roe. This is Libby Jones. We've just been talking to your mum. In town. She mentioned you lived close by and . . .'

She looks at Libby and does a double take. 'You look . . . I feel like I should know you.'

Libby bows her head and lets Miller do the honours.

'This is Serenity,' he says.

Clemency's hands go to the doorframe and grip it, momentarily. Her head rolls back slightly and for a moment Libby thinks she is about to faint. But then she rallies, puts her hands out to Libby and says, 'Of course! Of course! You're twenty-five! Of course. I should have thought – I should have known. I should have guessed you'd come. Oh my goodness. Come in. Please. Come in.'

The bungalow is beautiful inside: hardwood floors and abstract paintings, vases full of flowers, sunlight shining through stained-glass windows.

The dog sits at Libby's feet as Clemency gets them glasses of water and Libby strokes the crown of his head. He's panting in the muggy air and his breath smells bad but she doesn't mind.

Clemency returns and sits opposite them. 'Wow,' she says, staring at Libby. 'Look at you! So pretty! So . . . *real.*'

Libby laughs nervously.

Clemency says, 'You were just a baby when I left. I had no photos of you. No idea where you went or who adopted you or what sort of life you ended up having. And I could not picture you. I just could not. All I could see was a baby. A baby who looked like a doll. Not quite real. Never quite real. And oh . . .' Her eyes fill with tears then and she says, in a cracked voice, 'I am so, so sorry. Are you . . . ? Have you been . . . ? Has everything been OK for you?'

Libby nods. She thinks of her mother, with the man she calls her toyboy (although he's only six years younger than her), stretched out on the tiny terrace of her one bed apartment in Dénia (no room for Libby to stay when she comes to visit) in a hot pink kaftan, explaining over Skype that she'd been too busy to book flights to come and see Libby for her birthday and that by the time she'd looked online all the cheap ones had gone. She thinks of the day they buried her father, her hand in her mother's, looking up into the sky, wondering if he'd got there safely or not, worrying about how she was going to get to school now as her mother couldn't drive.

'It's been fine,' she says. 'I was adopted by lovely people. I've been very lucky.

Clemency's face brightens. 'So, where do you live now?'

'St Albans,' she replies.

'Oh! That's nice. And – are you married? Any children?'

'No. Just me. Single. Live alone. No kids. No pets. I sell designer kitchens for a living. I'm very . . . Well, there's not really a lot to say about me. At least, there wasn't until . . .'

'Yes,' says Clemency. 'Yes. I should imagine it's all been a bit of a shock to the system.'

'Putting it mildly.'

'And how much do you know?' she asks circumspectly. 'About the house. About all of it.'

'Well,' Libby begins, 'it's all a bit complicated. First of all there was what my parents had always told me, which was that my birth parents had been killed in a car crash when I was ten months old. Then there was what I read in Miller's article, which was that my parents were members of a cult and there'd been some kind of suicide pact and I'd been looked after by gypsies. And then, well, two nights ago Miller and I were at the house, in Cheyne Walk, and this guy appeared. Quite late at night. He told us . . . ' She pauses. 'He told us he was called Phin.'

Clemency's eyes open wide and she gasps. 'Phin?' she says.

Libby nods uncertainly.

Clemency's eyes fill with tears. 'Are you sure?' she says. 'Are you sure it was Phin?'

'Well, he told us that was his name. He said you were his sister. That he hadn't seen you or your mother for years.'

She shakes her head. 'But he was so ill when I left him in the house. So ill. And we looked everywhere for him, me and my mum. Everywhere. For years and years. We went to every hospital in London. Wandered round parks looking at rough sleepers. Kept waiting and waiting for him to suddenly appear on our doorstep. And he never did and eventually ... well, we assumed that he must have died. Otherwise, why wouldn't he come back? Why wouldn't he come to find us? I mean, he would have, wouldn't he?' She pauses. 'Are you absolutely sure it was Phin?' she asks yet again. 'Tell me what he looked like.'

Libby describes the horn-rimmed glasses, the blond hair, the long eyelashes, the full mouth.

Clemency nods.

And then Libby tells her about the luxury apartment, the Persian cats. She repeats the joke about the cat called Dick, and Clemency shakes her head.

'No,' she says. 'This doesn't sound like Phin at all. It really doesn't.' She pauses for a moment, her eyes roaming around the room as she thinks. 'You know what I think?' she says eventually. 'I think it might be Henry.'

'Henry?'

'Yes. He was in love with Phin. Totally unrequited. Obsessive almost. He would just stare and stare at him. He dressed like him. Copied his hairstyles. He even tried to kill him once. Pushed him in the river. Held him under. Luckily Phin was stronger than Henry. Bigger. He managed to fight him off. Henry killed Birdie's cat, you know?'

'What?'

'He poisoned her. Cut off her tail. Threw the rest of her body into the river. So the signs were there all along. It's a terrible thing to say about a child, it really is, but in my opinion Henry had a streak of pure evil.'

55

I did not kill Birdie's cat. Of course I didn't. But yes, she did die because of me.

I was working on something with the belladonna, another sleeping draught, something a little stronger than the draught I'd given David and Birdie to get into their room. Something to bring about a slightly less temporary stupefaction. I tested it on the cat figuring if it didn't harm the cat then it was probably safe on humans. Sadly it did harm the cat. A lesson learned. I made the next draught much, much weaker.

As for the cat's tail, well, it sounds harsh when put like that: *cut off her tail*. I took it. It was beautiful, so soft and full of remarkable colours. I had nothing then, remember, nothing soft, it had all been taken. She didn't need it any more. So yes, I took the cat's tail. And – *fake news* – I did not throw the cat in the Thames. How could I have? I wasn't able to leave the house. The cat, in fact, remains to this day interred in my herb garden.

As for it being *me* who had pushed Phin into the Thames rather than the other way around: well, that is categorically not true. What might be true is that Phin pushed me in during a struggle that had ensued after I attempted to push him in. Yes. That might have been the case. He told me I was staring at him. I said, 'I am staring at you because you are beautiful.'

He said, 'You're being weird. Why do you always have to be so weird?'

I said, 'Don't you know, Phin? Don't you know that I love you?'

(Remember, please, before you judge me too harshly, that I had taken LSD. I was not of sound mind.)

'Stop it,' he said. He was embarrassed.

'Please, Phin,' I implored. 'Please. I've loved you since the minute I saw you . . .' And then I tried to kiss him. My lips brushed his and for a minute I thought he was going to kiss me back. I can still remember the shock of it, the softness of his lips, the tiny puff of breath that passed from his mouth into mine.

I put my hand to his cheek and then he broke away from me and looked at me with such undisguised disgust that it felt like a sword passing through my heart.

He pushed me and I nearly fell backwards. So I pushed him and he pushed me and I pushed him and he pushed me and in I went, and I know it wasn't deliberate. Which is why it was so much worse that I'd allowed his father to think that he'd pushed me in on purpose, that I let him be locked in his room for all those days and never told anyone that it was an accident. He never told anyone it was an accident either, because to have done so would have been to tell them that I'd kissed him. And, well, clearly there was no worse confession to make than that.

56

CHELSEA, 1993

One summer's night, towards the middle of June, I heard my sister begin to moo.

There was no other word for it.

She sounded entirely like a cow.

This went on for some time. She was in the spare bedroom, which had been readied for her. Clemency and I were ushered away from the door of the room and ordered to stay in our own rooms until we were told we could come back.

The mooing continued for many hours.

And then, at around ten minutes past midnight, there was the sound of a baby crying.

And yes. It was you.

Serenity Love Lamb. Daughter of Lucy Amanda Lamb (14) and David Sebastian Thomsen (41).

I didn't get to see you until later that day and I must confess that I quite liked the look of you. You had a face like a baby seal. And you stared at me unblinkingly in a way that made me feel seen. I had not felt seen for a long time. I let you hold my finger in your little hand and it was strangely nice. I'd always thought I hated babies, but maybe I didn't, after all.

And then, a few days later, you were taken away from my sister and moved to David and Birdie's room. My sister was brought upstairs and put back in the room she shared with Clemency. At night I could hear you crying downstairs and I could hear my sister crying next door. She was brought downstairs during the day to pump breast milk into a medieval-looking contraption which was then poured into medieval-looking milk bottles and then told to go back to her room.

And so everything changed again: the lines between the thems and the usses shifted a few degrees and my sister was once more one of us and it was this final act of cruelty that brought us back together.

57

Lucy steps towards him.

Her brother.

Her big brother.

She can see it now.

She stares deep into his eyes and says, 'Where've you been, Henry? Where've you been?'

'Oh, you know, here and there.'

A wave of fury starts to engulf her. All these years she has been alone. All these years she has had no one. And here is Henry, tall and fresh-faced and handsome and glib.

She punches him in the chest with two furled fists.

'You left her!' she cries. 'You left her! You left the baby behind!'

He grabs hold of her hands and he says, 'No! *You* left! It was you! I was the one who stayed. The only one who stayed! I mean, you ask where I've been. Where on earth have *you* been?'

'I've been . . .' she begins, and then she lets her fists unfurl and her arms drop. 'I've been in hell.'

They fall silent for a moment. Then Lucy steps back and calls Marco to her. 'Marco,' she says. 'This is Henry. He's your uncle. Henry, this is my son. Marco. And this is Stella, my daughter.'

Marco looks from his mother to Henry and back again. 'I don't understand. What does this have to do with the baby?'

'Henry was—' she begins. She sighs and starts again. 'There was a baby. She lived here with us all when we were children. We had to leave her here because . . . well, because we had to. And Henry is here, like me, to see the baby, now that she's grown up.'

Henry clears his throat and says, 'Um.'

Lucy turns to look at him.

'I've met her already,' he says. 'I've met Serenity. She was here. At the house.'

Lucy gasps softly. 'Oh my God. Is she OK?'

'She is,' he replies. 'Hale and hearty, pretty as a picture.'

'But where is she?' she asks. 'Where is she now?'

'Well, she is currently with our old friend Clemency.'

Lucy inhales sharply. 'Clemency! Oh my God. Where is she? Where does she live?'

'She lives, I believe, in Cornwall. Here, look.' Henry switches on his phone and shows her a little flashing dot on a map. 'There's Serenity,' he says, pointing at the dot. 'Number twelve, Maisie Way, Penreath, Cornwall. I popped a little tracking device on her phone. Just so we wouldn't lose her again.'

'But how do you know that's where Clemency is?'

'Aha,' he says, closing down the app displaying Serenity's location and opening up another app.

He presses an arrow on an audio bar. And suddenly there are voices. Two women, talking, quietly.

'Is that her talking?' asks Lucy. 'Is that Serenity?'

He listens. 'Yes, I believe it is,' he says, turning up the volume.

Another voice breaks in.

'And that,' he says, 'is Clemency. Listen.'

58

Clemency has asked Miller to leave them alone. She wants to tell Libby the story in private. So Miller takes the dog for a walk and Clemency tucks her long legs under her on the sofa and slowly begins.

'The plan was that we would rescue the baby. Henry would drug the grown-ups with this sleeping draught he'd made and we would steal the shoes that were in the boxes in David and Birdie's room, steal some normal clothes, take the money and the baby and then we'd take the key from my dad's pouch and run into the street and stop a policeman or a trustworthy-looking grown-up and we'd tell them there were people in the house who'd kept us prisoners for years. Then somehow we'd all find our way down here to my mum. We hadn't quite worked out how we'd contact her. A phone box, reverse the charges, a wing and a prayer.' Clemency smiles wryly. 'As you can see, we hadn't really thought it through very well. We just wanted to be gone.

'And then one day my dad announced he was going to throw a party for Birdie's thirtieth birthday. Henry called us into his room. He was kind of our unofficial leader by this point, I suppose. And he said we were going to do it then. During Birdie's birthday party. He said he'd offer to cook all the food. He asked me to make a little pocket for him to tuck into his leggings so that he could put his bottles of sleeping draught in there. And then we'd all need to act as if we were really very enthusiastic about Birdie's birthday party. Lucy and I even learned a special piece on the fiddle for her.'

'And Phin?' asks Libby. 'Where was Phin involved in all of this?'

Clemency sighs. 'Phin kept himself to himself generally. And Henry didn't want him involved. Those two . . .' She sighed. 'It was kind of toxic between them. Henry loved Phin. But Phin hated Henry. Plus of course, Phin was ill.'

'What was wrong with him?'

'We never really found out. I wondered if maybe he'd had cancer or something. It's why Mum and I always thought he might have, you know, passed away.

'Anyway,' she continues. 'The day of the party we were tense. All three of us. But we kept up the pretence of excitement about the stupid bloody party. And in some ways of course we *were* excited about the party. It was our freedom party. At the other end of the party lay a normal life. Or at least a *different* life.

'And we played our fiddle piece for Birdie, distracting the grown-ups while Henry cooked the food and it was so bizarre, the contrast between my father and Birdie and everyone else. We all looked so sickly, you know. But Birdie and my dad, they were both glowing with vitality and satisfaction. My dad sat with his arm slung around her shoulder, this look of absolute and utter dominion on his face.' Clemency kneads at the cushion on her lap. Her gaze is hard and tight. 'It was like,' she continues, 'like he'd "allowed" his woman a party, out of the bountiful depths of his heart, as if he was thinking: Look at the happiness I have created. Look how I can do whatever I want and yet people still love me.'

Her voice begins to break and Libby touches her knee gently. 'Are you OK?' she asks.

Clemency nods. 'I've never, ever told anyone any of this before,' she says. 'Not my mother, not my husband, not my daughter. It's hard. You know. Talking about my father. About the sort of man he was. And about what happened to him. Because in spite of everything, he was my father. And I loved him.'

Libby touches Clemency's arm gently. 'Are you sure you're OK to carry on?'

Clemency nods and straightens her shoulders. She continues. 'Normally we placed dishes in the centre of the table and served ourselves but that night Henry said he wanted to serve everyone as though they were customers in a restaurant. That way he could make sure that each plate ended up in front of the right person. Then my dad made a toast. He raised his glass around the table to each person and he said, "I know that life hasn't always been so easy for us all, particularly for those of us who have experienced a loss. I know sometimes it must feel hard to keep the faith, as it were, but the fact that we are all here, after all these years, and we are still a family, and now, in fact, a bigger family" – and as he said that he touched the crown of your head – "just shows how good we all have it and how lucky we all are." And then he turned to Birdie and he said . . .' Clemency pauses and pulls in her breath. 'He said, "My love, my life, mother of my child, my angel, my reason for living, my goddess. Happy birthday, darling. I owe everything to you," and then they kissed and it was long and wet and it made noises and I remember thinking . . .' She stops for a moment and throws a rueful look at Libby. 'I thought: *I really really hope you both die.*

'It took about twenty minutes for the draught to

start to take effect. Three or four minutes later all the grown-ups were unconscious. Lucy grabbed you from Birdie's lap and we moved into action. Henry told us we had about twenty minutes, half an hour, tops, before the draught wore off. We laid the grown-ups down on the kitchen floor and I searched through my dad's tunic for the leather pouch. At the top of the stairs I fumbled and fumbled through the bunch until I found the one that opened the door to David and Birdie's room.

'And, oh God, it was shocking. Henry had told us what to expect, but still, to see it there; what remained of Henry and Martina's beautiful things, hoarded away, the antiques and perfumes and beauty products and jewellery and alcohol. Henry said, "Look. Look at all this stuff. While we had *nothing*. This is evil. You are looking at evil."

'We were five minutes into the estimated thirty minutes. I found nappies, baby suits, bottles. Then I realised that Phin was standing behind me. I said, "Quick! Find some clothes. You need to be warm. It's cold out there."

'He said, "I don't think I can. I think I'm too weak."

'I said, "But we can't leave you here, Phin."

'He said, "I can't! I just can't. OK?"

'We were nearly ten minutes in by then so I couldn't spend any more time trying to persuade him. I watched

Henry filling a bag with cash. I said, "Shouldn't we leave that as evidence? For the police?"

'But he said, "No. It's mine. I'm not leaving it."

'You were crying now, screaming. Henry was shouting, "Make her shut up! For God's sake!"

'And then there was the sound of footsteps on the staircase behind us. A second later the door opened and Birdie appeared. She looked absolutely crazy and was barely coordinated. She stumbled into the room, her arms outstretched towards Lucy, going, "Give me my baby! Give her to me!"'

'And Birdie just lunged,' says Clemency. 'Straight at you. And Henry was losing the plot. Massively screaming at everyone. Phin was standing there looking as if he was about to pass out. And I just froze, really. Because I thought that if Birdie was awake then everyone else must be awake. That my father must be awake. That any moment everyone was going to appear and we were going to be locked in our rooms for the rest of our lives. My heart was racing. I was so terrified. And then, I don't know, I'm still not entirely sure what really happened, but suddenly Birdie was on the floor. She was on the floor and there was blood sort of dripping out of the corner of her eye. Like red tears. And her hair, just here.' Clemency points to a spot just above her ear. 'It was dark and sticky. And I looked at Henry and he was holding a tusk.'

Libby looks at her questioningly.

'It looked like a tusk. From an elephant. Or an antler. Something like that.'

Libby thinks of the pop video Phin had showed them. She thinks of the animal heads looming off walls and the stuffed foxes posed as though still alive atop enormous mahogany desks.

'And it had blood on it, like a streak of blood. And it was in Henry's hand. And we all stopped breathing. For some seconds. Even you. And it was just completely silent. We were listening for the others. We were listening to Birdie's breathing. It had been rattly. Now it had stopped. A tiny little dribble of blood ran from her hair, down her temple, into her eye . . .' Clemency describes it on her own face with a fingertip. 'I said, "Is she dead?"

'Henry said, "Shut up. Just shut up and let me think."

'I went to check her heartbeat and Henry pushed me. Pushed me so hard I fell backwards. He yelled, "Leave her, leave her!"

'Then he went downstairs. He said, "Stay here. Just stay here." I looked at Phin. He was clammy-looking. I could see he was about to faint. I moved him towards the bed. Then Henry came back. He was ashen. He said, "Something's happened. Something's gone wrong. I don't understand. The others. They're all dead. All of them."'

Clemency's last word comes out as a gasp. Her eyes fill with tears and she brings her hands to her mouth. 'All of them. My father. Henry's mum and dad. Dead. And Henry kept saying, "I don't understand, I don't understand. I hardly gave them anything. Such a tiny amount, not enough to kill a cat. I don't understand."

'And suddenly this whole thing, this amazing rescue mission, this thing we were going to do that was going to set us free, had totally trapped us. How could we run down the street looking for a friendly policeman now? We had killed four people. *Four people.*'

Clemency stops for a moment and catches her breath. Libby notices that her hands are trembling. 'And we had a baby to look after and the whole thing – the whole thing was just . . . God, do you mind if we go out in the back garden. I need a cigarette.'

'No. No, of course,' says Libby.

Clemency's back garden is all chipped slate beds and rattan sofas. It's late morning and the sun is moving overhead, but it's cool and shady at the back of the house. Clemency pulls a packet of cigarettes from a drawer in the coffee table. 'My secret stash,' she says.

There's a photo on the side of the packet of someone with mouth cancer. Libby can hardly bear to look at it. Why, she wonders, why do people smoke? When they know they might die of it? Her mother smokes. 'Her boys', she calls them. *Where are my boys?*

She watches Clemency hold a match to the tip of the cigarette, inhale, blow it out. Her hands immediately stop shaking. She says, 'Where was I?'

59

I know it sounds like it was all just a terrible disaster. Of course it does. Any situation involving four dead bodies is clearly far from ideal.

But what nobody seems to realise is that without me, Christ almighty, we might all still be there, middle-aged skeletons, having missed out on our entire lives. Or dead. Yes, let's not forget we could all be dead. And yes, absolutely, things did not go exactly according to plan, but we got out of there. *We got out of there.* And nobody else had a plan, did they? Nobody else was prepared to step up to the line. It's easy to criticise. It's not easy to take control.

Not only did I have four dead bodies to deal with, a baby and two teenage girls, I had Phin to deal with, too. But Phin was behaving deliriously and felt like a liability so, just to make things easier, I locked him in his bedroom.

Yes, I know. But I needed to think straight.

We could hear Phin wailing from his room upstairs. The girls wanted to go to him, but I said, 'No, stay here. We need to work together. Don't go anywhere.'

The first priority to me seemed to be Birdie. It was bizarre to see her there, so small and broken, this person who had controlled our lives for so long. She was wearing the top that Clemency had made her for her birthday, and a chain that David had given her. Her long hair was twisted up in a bun. Her pale eyes stared hard at the wall. One eyeball was brilliant red. Her feet were bare and bony, her toenails overlong and slightly yellow. I unclipped the chain from around her neck and put it in my pocket.

Clemency was crying. 'It's so sad,' she said. 'It's so sad! She's someone's daughter! And now she's dead!'

'It's not sad at all,' I said, harshly. 'She deserved to die.'

Clemency and I got her on to the attic floor and then the roof. She was very light. On the other side of the flat roof where I'd once sat holding Phin's hand, there was a sort of gulley. It was filled with dead leaves and led to the guttering that ran down the side of the building. We wrapped her in towels and sheets and rammed her in there. Then we covered her over with handfuls of dead leaves and then some pieces of old scaffolding wood that we found up there.

In the kitchen afterwards I stared dispassionately at the three dead bodies. I could not let my mind dwell on the reality of the situation. I had killed my own parents. My beautiful, stupid mother and my poor, broken father. I had to distance myself from the fact that because of me, my mother would never again run her hand through my hair and call me her beautiful boy, that I would never again sit in a members' club with my father silently drinking lemonade. There would be no family to return to for Christmas Day, no grandparents for any children I might have, no people to worry about as they got older, no one to worry about me as I got older. I was an orphan. An orphan and an inadvertent murderer.

But I didn't panic. I kept a check on my emotions and I looked at the three figures stretched out on the kitchen floor and I thought: They look like members of a cult. I thought: Anyone walking in here now would look at them in their matching black tunics and think they had killed themselves.

And it was obvious then what I needed to do. I needed to set the stage for a suicide pact. We arranged the party paraphernalia into something that looked a little less 'frivolous thirtieth birthday party' and more 'very serious last supper'. We got rid of the extra plates. We washed up all the pots and pans and threw away all the old food. We arranged the bodies so that they all lay in the same direction. I pressed their fingertips against the empty phials and then placed them on the table, one by each place setting as though they had taken the poisons in unison.

We didn't speak.

It felt strangely holy.

I kissed my mother's cheek. She was very cold.

I kissed my father's forehead.

And then I looked at David. There he lay, the man who, just as Phin had predicted months earlier, had broken my life. The man who'd destroyed us, beaten us, denied us food and freedom, taken our passports, impregnated my mother and my sister, tried to take our house. I had snuffed out his pathetic existence and I felt triumphant. But I also felt a terrible sense of disgust.

Look at you, I wanted to say, *just look at you, what an absolute loser you turned out to be.*

I wanted to stamp my foot into David's face and grind it to a bloody pulp, but I resisted the urge and made my way back up to Birdie and David's room.

We cleared out all the boxes. In one we found a stash of Birdie's stupid drawstring bags that she'd made to take to Camden Market and we filled them with as much stuff as we could conceivably fit in them. We found nearly seven thousand pounds in cash and divided it four ways. We also found my mother's jewellery and my father's gold cufflinks and platinum collar bones and a whole box full of whiskey. We poured the whiskey down the sinks and put the empty bottles with the champagne bottle by the front door. We put the jewels in our bags. Then we broke the boxes down and left them in a pile.

Once the house was clear of anything that might cast doubt upon the idea of it being a cult, we quietly left the house, by the front door, and we made our way to the river. It was early morning by now. It must have been around 3 a.m. A few cars passed by, but no one slowed or seemed to notice us. We stood by the river, at the very spot where Phin and I had tussled all those years before, where I'd ended up under water seeing apparitions in the murk. I was calm enough to appreciate my first moments of freedom in two years. After tossing the empty bottles, the silk underwear, the bottles of perfume and evening gowns into the river, in bags weighted down with stones, we stood for a moment and I could hear us all breathing, the beauty and peace of the moment briefly overshadowing the horror of it all. The air coming off the steely black surface of the river was thick with diesel and life force. It smelled of all the things we'd missed since the moment David Thomsen had walked into our house, since the day he and his family had come to live upstairs.

'Smell that,' I said, turning to the girls. 'Feel that. We did it. We really did it.'

Clemency was crying silently. She sniffed and wiped the tip of her nose against the heel of her hand. But I could tell that Lucy felt it too, the power of what we'd done.

If it wasn't for you, Serenity, she would have been weaker. She would have been mourning for her mummy, sniffing into the heel of her hand like Clemency. But because she had you, she knew that there was more at stake here than our identities as beloved children of a mother and father. She had a brave, almost rebellious tilt to her chin. I felt proud of her.

'We're going to be OK,' I said to her. 'You know that, don't you?'

She nodded and we stood for a minute or two until we saw the lights of a tug boat heading towards us and we dashed, fleet-footed, back across the road and towards the house.

And that was when it happened.

Clemency ran.

She was not wearing shoes. Only socks. She had large feet and the shoes belonging to my mother that

Birdie had kept were far too small, David's shoes far too big.

For a moment I watched her run. I let a beat or two of indecision and inaction pass, then I whispered loudly to Lucy: 'Get back in the house, get back in the house.' And I turned on my heel and I gave chase.

But I quickly realised that in doing so I was drawing attention to myself. A few souls wandered the streets: it was a Thursday night, young people were making their way home from night buses on the King's Road. What explanation would I give for myself, in a black robe, chasing a young terrified girl, also in a black robe, with no shoes on her feet?

I stopped on the corner of Beaufort Street. My heart, which had not experienced the shock of running for a very long time, thumped under my ribs like a piston until I thought I was going to throw up. I collapsed in upon myself, heard my breath enter and leave my body like a strangled farm animal. I turned and headed slowly back to the house.

Lucy was waiting for me in the hallway. You sat on her lap, feeding from her breast. 'Where is she?' she said. 'Where's Clemency?'

'Gone,' I said. Still somewhat out of breath. 'She's gone . . .'

60

Libby stares at Clemency. 'Where?' she asks. 'Where did you go?'

'I went to the hospital. I followed the signs to the A & E department. I saw people looking at me. But you know, at that time of night, in an emergency department, no one really notices. It's all just so mad, everyone drunk or off their heads. Everyone scared and preoccupied. I went to the desk and I said, "I think my brother's dying. He needs medical help."

'The nurse looked at me. She said, "How old is your brother?"

'I said, "He's eighteen."

'She said, 'And where are your parents?' And I just sort of clammed up. I can't really explain it. I tried to say some words, but they literally wouldn't leave my mouth. I just had this image in my mind of my father, dead, laid out like a freakish holy man. And Birdie on the roof wrapped up like a mummy. I thought: How can I tell people to come to that house? What would they say? What would happen to the baby? What would happen to Henry? And I just turned then, and I walked away. I spent the night moving from chair to chair in the hospital. Every time someone gave me a strange look or seemed like they were about to say something to me, I'd move on.

'The next morning I washed in the toilets and then I went straight to a shoe shop. I had a coat on; I'd tied my hair back. I was as inconspicuous as a child walking around in early April without shoes on could be. I had my bag full of money. I bought some shoes. I wandered around the city. Nobody looked at me. Nobody noticed me. I walked all the way to Paddington Station, just following street signs. Even though I'd been living in London for six years, I had no mental map of how it worked. But I managed to get there. And I bought a train ticket to Cornwall. Which was mad because I didn't have a phone number for my mother. I didn't have an address. I didn't even know the name of her town. But I had memories, things she'd talked about when she came to visit us just after she moved here. The last time we'd seen her. She'd mentioned a restaurant on the beach where she would take us when we came to visit, that sold blue ice cream and slushies. She said there were a lot of surfers, that she watched them from the window of her flat. She mentioned an eccentric artist who lived next door whose garden was full of phallic sculptures made of colourful mosaic. She mentioned fish and chips on the corner of her street and missing the fast train to London and having to go through eighteen stations.

'And so yes, I found my way to her. To Penreath, to her street, to her flat.'

Her eyes fill with tears at this memory and her fingers go back to the cigarette packet in front of her. She pulls out a fresh one; she lights it and inhales.

'And she came to the door and she saw me there.' Her voice cracks on every single word and she breathes in hard. 'She saw me there and she just pulled me in, pulled me straight in and held me in her arms for, oh, for so long. And I could smell the stale booze on her and I knew she wasn't perfect and I knew why she hadn't come for us but I knew, I just knew that it was over. And that I was safe.

'She took me in and she sat me on her sofa and her flat was, well, it was a mess, stuff everywhere. I wasn't used to that by now; I was used to living with emptiness, with nothing.

'She moved things from her sofa so I had somewhere to sit and she said, "Phin? Where is Phin?"

'And then of course, I stopped. Because the truth was that I'd run away and I'd left him there, locked in his room. And if I explained why he was locked in his room then I'd have to explain everything else. And I looked at her and she was so damaged and I was so damaged and I should have told her everything. But I just couldn't do it. So I told her that the adults had killed themselves in a pact. That Henry, Lucy and Phin were still at the house with you. That the police were coming. That it would all be OK. And I know it sounds ridiculous. But remember: remember where I'd been, what I'd been through. My allegiances were so skewed. We children had had no one but each other for years. Lucy and I were inseparable, as close as real sisters . . . well, up until she got pregnant.'

'Lucy?' says Libby. 'Lucy got pregnant?'

'Yes,' says Clemency. 'I thought . . . Did you not know?'

Libby's heart starts to race. 'Know what?'

'That Lucy was . . .'

But Libby already knows what she's about to say. Her hand goes to her throat and she says. 'Lucy was what?'

'Well, she was your mother.'

Libby stares hard at the photo of the mouth cancer on Clemency's cigarette packet, takes in every vile,

Lisa Jewell

disgusting detail, to try to block out the wave of sickness coming towards her. Her mother is not a beautiful socialite with Priscilla Presley hair. Her mother is a teenage girl.

'Who was my father?' she says after a moment

Clemency looks at her apologetically and says, 'It was . . . my father.'

Libby nods. She'd been half expecting this.

'How old was Lucy?'

Clemency's chin drops into her chest. 'She was fourteen. My father was in his forties.'

Libby blinks, slowly. ' And was it . . . ? Did he—?'

'No,' says Clemency. 'No. Not according to Lucy. According to Lucy it was . . .'

'Consensual?'

'Yes.'

'But she was so young. I mean, that's still legally rape.'

'Yes. But my father . . . he was very charismatic. He had a way, a way of making you feel special. Or a way of making you feel worthless. And it was always better to be one of the special ones. You know, I can see how it happened. I can see . . . But that's not to say I didn't hate it. I did hate it. I hated him for it. And I hated her.'

They fall silent for a moment. Libby lets the revelations of the last few minutes sink in. Her mother was a teenage girl. A teenage girl, now a middle-aged woman lost somewhere in the world. Her father was a dirty old man, a child abuser, an animal. And at this thought, Libby starts at the sound of a notification coming from her phone. It's a WhatsApp message from a number she doesn't recognise.

'Sorry,' she says to Clemency, picking up her phone. 'Can I just?'

There's a photo attached. The caption says, *We're waiting here for you! Come back!*

Libby recognises the location of the photo. It's the house in Cheyne Walk. And there, sitting on the floor, holding up her hands to the camera is a woman: slender, dark-haired, very tanned. She's wearing a sleeveless vest and has some tattoos encircling her sinewy arms. To her left is a beautiful young boy, also tanned and dark-haired, and a gorgeous little girl with gold-tinged curls, olive skin and green, green eyes. On the floor by their feet is a little brown, black and white dog, panting in the heat.

And in the foreground of the photograph, holding the camera at arm's length and beaming into the lens with very white teeth is the man who calls himself Phin. She turns the screen to face Clemency.

'Is that . . . ?'

'Oh my God.' Clemency brings a fingertip closer to

the screen and points at the woman. 'That's her! That's Lucy.'

Libby uses her fingertips on the screen to stretch out the woman's face. Lucy looks like Martina, the woman she'd briefly thought was her mother. She has the dark skin and the glossy black hair, but hers is singed rusty brown at the tips. Her forehead is lightly lined. Her eyes are dark brown, like Martina's. Like her son's. She looks weathered; she looks tired. She looks absolutely beautiful.

They get to Cheyne Walk five hours later.

At the door, Libby feels for the house keys in the pocket of her handbag. She could just let herself in; it's her house after all. And then she gulps as it hits her. It's not her house. It's not her house at all. The house was for Martina and Henry's baby. A baby that was never born.

She puts the keys back into her bag and she calls the number attached to the WhatsApp message.

'Hello?'

It's a woman. Her voice is soft and melodic.

'Is that . . . Lucy?'

'Yes,' says the woman. 'Who's this?'

'This is . . . this is Serenity.'

61

Lucy puts the phone down and stares at Henry.

'She's here.'

They go to the front door together.

The dog starts to bark at the sound of people outside and Henry picks him up and tells him to shush.

Lucy's heart races as her hand goes to the door handle. She touches her hair, smooths it down. She makes herself smile.

And there she is. The daughter that she had to leave behind. The daughter that she has killed to come back for.

Her daughter is average height, average build, nothing like the huge roly-poly baby she'd left behind in the Harrods cot. She has soft blond hair, but no curls. She has blue eyes, but not the pale aqua blue of the baby she'd had to abandon. She's wearing cotton shorts, a short-sleeved blouse, pink canvas plimsolls. She's clutching a grass-green handbag to her stomach. She's wearing small gold sleepers with crystal drops hanging from them, just one in each ear lobe. She's not wearing any make-up.

'Serenity . . . ?'

She nods. 'Or Libby. For my day job.' She laughs lightly.

Lucy laughs too. 'Libby. Of course. You're Libby. Come in. Come in.'

She has to resist the urge to put her arms around her. Instead she guides her into the hallway with just a hand against her shoulder.

Following behind Serenity is a big, handsome man with a beard. She introduces him as Miller Roe. She says, 'He's my friend.'

Lucy leads them all to the kitchen where her children sit waiting nervously.

'Kids,' she says, 'this is Serenity. Or actually Libby. And Libby is . . .'

'The baby?' says Marco, his eyes wide.

'Yes, Libby is the baby.'

'Which baby, Mama?' says Stella.

'She's the baby I had when I was very young. The

baby I had to leave in London. The baby I never told anyone about, ever. She's your big sister.'

Marco and Stella both sit with their jaws hanging open. Libby sort of waves at them. For a moment it is awkward. But then Marco says, 'I knew it! I knew it all along! From the minute I saw it on your phone! I knew it would be your baby. I just knew it!'

He gets to his feet and runs across the kitchen and for a moment Lucy thinks he is running away, that he is angry with her for having a secret baby, but he runs towards Libby and throws his arms around her waist, squeezes her hard, and over the top of his head Lucy sees Libby's eyes open with surprise but also with pleasure. She touches the top of his head and smiles at Lucy.

Then, of course, because Marco has done it, Stella follows suit and clings to Libby's hips. And there, thinks Lucy, there they are. Her three babies. Together. At last. She stands with her hands clasped to her mouth and tears fall down her cheeks.

62

I'm not completely heartless, Serenity, I promise.

Remember how I let you hold my finger the day you were born, how I looked at you and felt something bloom inside me? I still felt that, when you and I came face to face here two nights ago. You were still that baby to me; you still had that innocence about you, that total lack of guile.

But you had something else.

You had his blue eyes, his creamy skin, his long dark eyelashes.

You don't look much like Lucy.

You don't look anything like David Thomsen.

You look just like your dad.

And it's ridiculous looking back on it that I couldn't

see it when it was right there under my nose. When your blond curls came through and your bright blue eyes and your full lips. How did David not see it? How did Birdie not see it? How did anyone not see it? I guess because it was impossible to believe. Impossible even to conceive.

That my sister was sleeping with David and Phin at the same time.

I didn't find out until the day after Birdie's birthday party.

Lucy and I had not decided what to do yet. Phin was thrashing about in his room, so I tied him to a radiator, to keep him safe. For his own good.

Lucy was appalled.

'What are you doing?' she cried.

'He's going to hurt himself,' I said righteously. 'It's just until we decide what to do with him.'

She was holding you in her arms. You and she had not been apart for a moment since she'd taken you out of Birdie's arms the night before.

'We need to get him some help.'

'Yes. We do. But we also need to remember that we've killed people and that we could go to prison.'

'But it was an accident,' she said. 'None of us meant to kill anyone. The police would know that.'

'No. They wouldn't. We have no evidence of any

abuse. Of anything that happened here. We only have our version of events.'

But then I stopped. I looked at Lucy and I looked at you and I thought: There it is. There's the proof we need, if we did decide to ask for help, the evidence of the abuse is there. *Right there.*

I said, 'Lucy. The baby. The baby is proof that you were abused. You're fifteen. You were fourteen when the baby was born. They can do a DNA test. Prove that David was her father. You can say he raped you, over and over again, from when you were a young child. You can say that Birdie encouraged him. And then they stole your baby. I mean it's virtually true anyway. And then I can say . . . I can say I found the grown-ups like that. I could leave a faked note, saying that they were so ashamed of what they'd done. Of how they'd treated us.'

I was suddenly overcome with the feeling that we could get out of this. We could get out of here and not go to jail and Phin could get better and Lucy could keep her baby and everyone would be nice to us.

And then Lucy said, 'Henry. You know Serenity isn't David's, don't you?'

My God, what a gullible idiot, I *still* didn't see it. I remember thinking, 'Oh, well, then whose could it possibly be?'

And then it fell into place. I laughed at first. And

then I wanted to be sick. And then I said, 'Really? You? And Phin? Really?'

Lucy nodded.

'But how?' I asked. 'When? I don't understand.'

She dropped her head and said, 'In his room. Only twice. It was like, I don't know, a comfort thing. I went to him because I was worried about him. Because he seemed so ill. And then we just found ourselves . . .'

'Oh my God. You *whore!*'

She tried to placate me, but I pushed her away. I said, 'Get away from me. You're disgusting. You are sick and you are disgusting. You are a slut. A dirty, dirty slut.'

Yes, I laid it on with a trowel. I have rarely been as disgusted by another human being as I was by Lucy that day.

I couldn't look at her. I couldn't think straight. Every time I tried to think about something, tried to decide what to do next, my mind would fill with images of Lucy and Phin: him on top of her, him kissing her, his hands, the hands that I had held that day on the roof, all over my sister's body. I had never felt a rage like it, never felt such hatred and hurt and pain.

I wanted to kill someone. And this time I wanted to do it on purpose.

I went to Phin's room. Lucy tried to stop me. I pushed her away from me.

'Is it true?' I screamed at him. 'Is it true that you had sex with Lucy?'

He looked at me blankly.

'Is it?' I screamed again. 'Tell me!'

'I'm not telling you anything,' he said, 'until you untie me.'

He sounded exhausted. He sounded as if he was fading away.

I immediately felt my rage start to dissipate and went and sat down at the foot of his bed.

I dropped my head into my hands. When I looked up his eyes were closed.

There was a moment of silence.

'Are you dying, Phin?' I asked.

'I don't. Fucking. Know.'

'We need to get out of here,' I said. 'You have to get it together. Seriously.'

'I can't.'

'But you have to.'

'Fucking just leave me here. I want to die.'

It did occur to me, I have to confess, that I could put a pillow over his face and push down, hold my face next to his to draw in his dying breath, whisper soothing words into his ear, overpower him, snuff his life force, take his power for myself. But, remember, apart from my mother's unborn baby – and I have googled this extensively over the intervening years and really, it would be very hard to abort a healthy pregnancy using parsley – I never killed anyone deliberately. I am a dark person, Serenity, I know that. I don't feel the way that other people feel. But I am capable of great compassion and great love.

And I loved Phin more than I have ever loved any other person since.

I untie his wrist from the radiator, and I lay down next to him.

I said, 'Did you ever like me? Even for a minute?'

He said, 'I always liked you. Why wouldn't I like you?'

I paused to consider the question. 'Because of me liking you? Too much?'

'Annoying,' he said, and there was a note of wry humour in his fading voice. 'Very annoying.'

'Yes,' I said. 'I can see that. I'm sorry. I'm sorry for letting your dad think you'd pushed me in the Thames. I'm sorry for trying to kiss you. I'm sorry for being annoying.'

The house creaked and groaned around us. You were asleep. Lucy had set you down in the old cot in my parents' dressing room. I had been awake for thirty-six hours by this point and the silence, the sound of Phin's breathing, lulled me into an immediate and rapturous sleep.

When I awoke, two hours later, Lucy and Phin had gone, and you were still asleep in your cot.

63

Libby looks at Lucy, this woman surrounded by loving children whom she has brought all the way from France to England. She has even brought her dog. She clearly is not the sort of woman to leave behind people she loves. She says, 'Why did you leave me?'

Lucy immediately starts to shake her head.

'No,' she says, 'no. No. I didn't leave you. I never left you. But Phin was so ill and you were so healthy and well. So I put you down in your cot, waited until you fell asleep, and I went back to Phin's room. Henry was asleep and I managed to persuade Phin to stand up, finally. He was so heavy; I was so weak. I got him out of the house and we went to my father's doctor's house. Dr Broughton. I remembered being taken there when I was small, just around the corner. He had a bright red front door. I remembered. It was about midnight. He came to the door in a dressing gown. I told him who I was. Then I said' – she laughs wryly at a memory – 'I said, "I've got money! I can pay you!"

'At first he looked angry. Then he looked at Phin, looked at him properly and said, "Oh my, oh my, oh my." He went upstairs quickly, grumbling under his breath; then he came back down fully dressed in a shirt and trousers.

'He took us into his surgery. All the lights were off. He turned them on, two rows of strip lights, all coming on at once. I had to shield my eyes. And he laid Phin on a bed and he checked all of his vitals and he asked me what the hell was going on. He said, "Where are your parents?" I had no idea what to say.

'I said, "They're gone." And he looked at me sideways. As if to say, We'll get to that later. Then he called someone. I heard him explaining the situation to them, lots of medical jargon. Half an hour later a young man appeared. He was Dr Broughton's nurse. Between them they did about a dozen tests. The nurse went off into the middle of the night with a bag of things to take to a lab. I hadn't slept for two days. I was *seeing stars*. Dr Broughton made me a cup of hot chocolate. It was . . . crazy as it sounds, it was the best hot chocolate of my life. And I sat on the sofa in his consulting rooms and I fell asleep.

'When I woke up it was about five in the morning and the nurse was back from the lab. Phin was on a drip. But his eyes were open. Dr Broughton told me that Phin was suffering from severe malnutrition. He said that with plenty of fluids and some time to recover, he'd be fine.

'I just nodded and said, "His father's dead. I don't know where his mother lives. We have a baby. I don't know what to do."

'When I told him that we had a baby, his face fell. He said, "Good Lord. How old are you exactly?"

'I said, "I'm fifteen."

'He gave me a strange look and said, "Where is this baby?"

'I said, "She's at the house. With my brother."

' "And your parents? Where have they gone?"

'I said. "They're dead."

'He sighed then. He said, "I had no idea. I'm very sorry." And then he said, "Look. I don't know what's going on here and I don't want to get involved in any of this. But you have brought this boy to my door and I have a duty of care towards him. So, let's keep him here for a while. I have the room for him."

'And then I said I wanted to leave, to go back for you, but he said, "You look anaemic. I want to run some tests

on you before I let you back out there. Give you something to eat."

'So he fed me, a bowl of cereal and a banana. He
took some blood, checked my blood pressure, my teeth,
my ears, like a horse at market.

'He told me I was dehydrated and that I needed to
spend some time under observation and on fluids'

Then Lucy looks up at Libby and says. 'I'm so sorry,
so, so sorry. But by the time he said I was OK to leave
the house, it was all over. The police had been, social
services had been, you were gone.'

Her eyes fill with tears.

'I was too late.'

64

CHELSEA, 1994

I was the one who looked after you, Serenity. I stayed behind and gave you mashed-up bananas and soya milk and porridge and rice. I changed your nappies. I sang you to sleep. We spent many hours together, you and I. It was clear that Lucy and Phin weren't coming back and the bodies in the kitchen would start to decompose if I stayed much longer. I suspected that someone might have gone to the authorities by now. I knew it was time for me to go. I added a few lines to the suicide note. 'Our baby is called Serenity Lamb. She is ten months old. Please make sure she goes to nice people.' I placed the pen I'd written the note with into my mother's hand, removed it and then left it on the table next to the note. I fed you and put you in a fresh Babygro.

And then, as I was about to leave, I felt in the pocket of my jacket for Justin's rabbit's foot. I'd put it in there for luck, not that I believe in such things, and it had clearly brought me no luck at all since I'd taken it from Justin's room. But I wanted the best for you, Serenity. You were the only truly pure thing in that house, the only good thing to come out of any of it. So I took the rabbit's foot and I tucked it in with you.

Then I kissed you and said, 'Goodbye, lovely baby.'

I left through the back of the house, in one of my father's old Savile Row suits and a pair of his Jermyn Street shoes. I'd tied the bootlace tie around the collar of one of my father's old shirts and combed my hair into a side fringe. My bag was filled with cash and jewels. I strode out into the morning sun, feeling it golden upon my tired skin. I found a phone box and I dialled 999. In a fake voice I told the police that I was worried about my neighbours. That I hadn't seen them for a while. That there was a baby crying.

I walked up to the King's Road; all the shops were still shut. I kept walking until I got to Victoria Station and there I sat outside a scruffy café in my Savile Row suit and I ordered a cup of coffee. I had never had a cup of coffee before. I really wanted a cup of coffee. The coffee came and I tasted it and it was disgusting. I poured two sachets of sugar into it and made myself drink it. I found an anonymous hotel and paid for three nights. Nobody asked my age. When I signed the register I used the name *Phineas Thomson*. Thomson with an O. Not Thomsen with an E. I wanted to be almost Phin. Not completely Phin.

I watched the TV in my hotel room. There was a small news article at the end of the bulletin. Three bodies. A suicide pact. A cult. A baby found healthy and cared for. Children believed to be missing. Police search under way. The photos they had were our school photos from our last year at primary school. I was only ten and had a short back and sides. Lucy was eight and had a pageboy cut. We were unrecognisable. There was no mention of Phin or of Clemency.

I breathed a sigh of relief.

And so then what? What happened between then, sixteen-year-old me in my underwear on a nylon coverlet in a cheap hotel room watching the news, and middle-aged me now?

Do you want to know? Do you care?

Well, I got a job. I worked in an electrical repair shop in Pimlico. It was owned by a mad Bangladeshi family who couldn't care less for my back story so long as I turned up to work on time.

I moved into a bedsit. I bought coding books and a computer and studied at home alone at night.

By then there was a proper internet and mobile

phones and I left the electrical repair shop and got a job at a Carphone Warehouse on Oxford Street.

I moved into a one-bedroom flat in Marylebone, just before Marylebone became unaffordable. I started to dye my hair blond. I worked out. I built some bulk. I went to clubs at night and had sex with strangers. I fell in love, but he hit me. I fell in love again, but he left me. I got my teeth whitened. I got tropical fish. They died. I got a job at a new internet company. There were five of us at first. Within three years there were fifty of us and I was earning six figures and had my own office.

I bought a three-bedroom flat in Marylebone. I fell in love. He told me I was ugly and that no one would ever love me again and then he left me. I had a nose job. I had eyelash extensions. A tiny bit of filler in my lips.

Then in 2008, I went to the solicitor named on the letterhead of my parents' original last will and testament. For so long I'd tried to put Cheyne Walk and what happened there to the back of my mind, tried to forge a new life with a new (if slightly borrowed) identity. I wanted nothing to do with pathetic little Henry Lamb or his history. He was dead to me. But as I got older and more settled, I started to think of you, more and more; I wanted to know where you were and who you were and whether or not you were happy.

I knew from the news reports that it had been

assumed you were the child of Martina and Henry Lamb. My 'suicide note' had been taken at face value and no DNA tests had been run to disprove the assumption. And remembering the terms of my parents' will it occurred to me that maybe one day you would come back into my life. But I had no idea if the trust was still lodged with the solicitors. And if it was, whether David had done anything to alter its terms during the time he had my mother entirely under his control.

I was in my thirties by now. I was tall, blond, buff and tanned. I introduced myself as Phineas Thomson. I said, 'I'm looking for some information about a family I used to know. I believe you were their solicitors. The Lambs. Cheyne Walk.'

A young woman shuffled through some papers, clicked some buttons on her keyboard, told me that they managed a trust for the family but that she was not at liberty to tell me any more.

There was a cute boy there. I'd caught his eye when I sat in reception. I waited outside the office until lunchtime and then I caught up with him as he left the office. His name was Josh. Of course. Everyone's name is Josh these days.

I took him back to my flat and cooked for him and fucked him and, of course, because I was only using him, he fell totally in love with me. It took less than a month of pretending I loved him too, to get him to find the paperwork, copy it and bring it to me.

And then there it was, in black and white, just as my parents had decreed when I was a tiny baby and Lucy was not yet even in existence. Number sixteen Cheyne Walk and all its contents to be held in trust for the descendants of Martina and Henry Lamb until the oldest reaches the age of twenty-five. David had not managed to get his hands on it after all and neither, it seemed, had Lucy reappeared to make a claim. The trust was still sitting there, ready and waiting, waiting for you to turn twenty-five. Someone more cynical than you might think I came to find you simply as a way to get my hands on my own inheritance. After all, I had no proof I was Henry Lamb so there was no way I'd be able to claim it for myself, and with you in my life I'd stand a chance to get what was rightfully mine. But you know, it really wasn't about the money. I have plenty of money. It was about closure. And it was about you, Serenity, and the bond I shared with you.

So, in June this year I rented the Airbnb across the river. I bought a pair of binoculars and I kept watch from the terrace.

One morning I scaled the back of the house on Cheyne Walk and spent a whole day on the roof dismantling Birdie's skeleton from its mummified casing. Pulling apart her tiny little bones. Dropping them into a black plastic bag. By the dark of night, I dropped the bag into the Thames. It was surprisingly small. I spent the night on my old mattress and returned to the Airbnb the following morning. And then, four days later, there you were. You and the solicitor. Heaving back the hoarding. Opening the door. Closing it behind you again.

I breathed a sigh of relief.

Finally.

The baby was back.

65

Libby stares at Lucy. 'What happened to Phin? After you left him at Dr Broughton's? Did he, I mean, did he get better?'

'Yes,' says Lucy. 'He got better.'

'Is he still alive?'

'As far as I'm aware. Yes.'

Libby covers her mouth with her hands. 'Oh my God,' she says. 'Where is he?'

'I don't know. I haven't seen him since I was about eighteen. We were in France together for a few years. And then we lost touch.'

'How did you both end up in France?' asks Libby.

'Dr Broughton took us. Or at least, he got someone he knew to take us. Dr Broughton seemed to know everyone. He was one of those people – a facilitator, I suppose you'd call him. He always had a number he could ring, a favour he could call in, a man who knew a man. He was the private physician to some very high-profile criminals. I think he'd been woken in the middle of the night before, stitched up some gunshot wounds in his rooms.

'And once he saw that we were on the news he just wanted us gone and away. A week after I'd knocked on Dr Broughton's door, he said we were well enough to leave. A man called Stuart squashed us into the back of a Ford Transit van and took us through the Eurotunnel, all the way to Bordeaux. He took us to a farm, to a woman called Josette. Another contact of Dr Broughton's. She let us stay for months in return for working the farm. She didn't ask who we were or why we were there.

'Phin and I, we didn't . . . you know. What happened between us, before, it was only because of the situation we were in together. Once we were free from all of that we fell back into being just friends. Almost like brother and sister. But we talked about you all the time, wondering how you were, who was looking after you, how pretty you were, how good you were, how amazing you'd grow up to be, how clever we were to have made you.'

'Did you ever talk about coming back for me?' asks Libby, pensively.

'Yes,' replies Lucy. 'Yes. We did. Or at least, I did. Phin was more circumspect, more worried about his future than the past. We didn't talk about the other stuff. We didn't talk about our parents, about what had happened. I tried to, but Phin wouldn't. It was like he'd just completely blanked it all out. Shut down. It was as if none of it had ever happened. And he got so well over that first year. He was tanned and fit. We both were. And Josette had an old fiddle she didn't play, and she let me use it. I'd play for her, in the winter, and then in the summer when her farm filled up with students and itinerants, I'd play for them too. She let me take the fiddle into the local town and I'd play on Friday nights and Saturday nights and I started to earn some money. I saved it up thinking that I'd use it to get Phin and me back to London, to come and find you.'

'Then one morning, about two years later, I woke up and Phin was gone. He left me a note that said, "Off to Nice".' Lucy sighs. 'I stayed in Bordeaux for the rest of that summer, saved up until I had enough money for a coach to Nice. I spent weeks sleeping on the beach at night and trying to find Phin by day. Eventually I gave up. I had Josette's fiddle. I played every night. I made enough money for a room in a hostel. I turned nineteen, twenty, twenty-one. And then I met a man. A very rich man. He swept me off my feet. He married me. I had a baby. I left the very rich man and met a very poor man. I had another baby. The poor man left me and then—' She stops then and Libby studies her expression. There's something unknowable, almost unthinkable in it. But the look passes and she continues.

'And then it was your birthday and I came back.'

'But why didn't you come back before?' Libby asks Lucy. 'When you turned twenty-five? Did you not know about the trust?'

'I knew about it, yes,' she says. 'But I had no proof that I was Lucy Lamb. I had no birth certificate. My passport was fake. I was in a terrible, terrible marriage with Marco's father. It was all just . . .' Lucy sighs. 'And then I thought, you know, if Henry doesn't come for the house and I don't come for the house, then it will automatically go to the baby, to you, because everyone thought you were my parents' baby. And I thought that's what I'll do. I'll wait until the baby is twenty-five and I'll come back for her then. When I got my first smartphone a few years ago, the first thing I did was put a reminder into the calendar, so I wouldn't forget. And every minute of every day since then I've been waiting for this. I've been waiting to come back.'

'And Phin?' says Libby, desperately. 'What happened to Phin?'

Lucy sighs. 'I can only assume he went somewhere

that he would not be found. I can only assume that that is what he wanted.'

Libby sighs. There it is. Finally. The whole picture. Apart from one piece.

Her father.

IV

66

Libby sits with her thumb over her phone. She's on her banking app where she's been refreshing her balance every fifteen minutes, since nine o'clock this morning.

It's completion day on the house in Cheyne Walk.

They sold it a month ago, finally, after months of no viewings and then a flurry of offers when they lowered the price and then two abortive attempts at exchanging contracts until, at last, a cash buyer from South Africa, all done and dusted, signed and sealed within two weeks.

Seven million, four hundred and fifty thousand pounds.

But her balance still sits at £318. The last dregs of her last pay cheque.

She sighs and turns back to the screen of her computer. Her final kitchen project. A nice little painted Shaker-style one with copper knobs and a marble worktop. Newlyweds' first home. It's going to look beautiful. She wishes she'd still be around to see it. But she won't ever see it. Not now. Today is her last day at Northbone Kitchens.

It's also her twenty-sixth birthday. Her *real* twenty-sixth birthday. Not 19 June after all, but 14 June. So she's five days older than she thought. That's fine. Five days is a small price to pay for seven million pounds, a mother, an uncle and two half-siblings. And now she's not climbing some spurious ladder in her head to some arbitrary birthday, who cares if she gets there five days ahead of schedule?

She presses refresh again.

Three hundred and nine pounds. A PayPal payment she made a week ago has come out of her account.

It's a beautiful day. She glances across at Dido. 'Shall we go out for lunch? My treat.'

Dido looks up at her over the top of her reading glasses and smiles. 'Absolutely!'

'Depending on whether this payment comes through by then or not, it'll be either sandwiches and Coke, or lobster and champagne.'

'Lobster's overrated,' Dido says before lowering her glasses and returning her gaze to her computer screen.

Libby's phone buzzes at 11 a.m. It's a text from Lucy. She says, *See you later! We've booked it for 8 p.m.!*

Lucy's living with Henry now in his smart flat in Marylebone. Apparently they are not getting on at all. Henry, who has lived alone for twenty-five years, doesn't have the stomach for sharing his space with children, and his cats hate the dog. She's already been house-hunting. In St Albans. Libby herself has her eye on a beautiful Georgian cottage in half an acre just on the outskirts of town.

She presses refresh again.

Three hundred and nine pounds.

She checks her email, in case there's been some kind of notification of something having gone wrong. But there's nothing.

The money will go three ways once the inheritance tax has been taken care of. She'd offered to forgo any of the inheritance. It's not her house. She's not their sibling. But they'd insisted. She'd said, 'I don't need a third. A few thousand will be fine.' But still they'd insisted. 'You're their granddaughter,' Lucy had said. 'You have as much right to it as we do.'

At 1 p.m. she and Dido leave the showroom.

'I'm afraid it's still sandwiches.'

'Good,' she says. 'I'm in the mood for sandwiches.'

They go to the café in the park and take a table outside in the sunshine.

'I can't believe you're leaving,' says Dido. 'It's going to be so, well, I was going to say quiet, you've never been exactly loud, but it's going to be so . . . utterly devoid of Libby without you. And your lovely hair. And your neat piles.'

'My neat piles?'

'Yes, your . . .' She mimes a squared-off pile of paper with her hands. 'You know. All the corners aligned.' She smiles. 'I'm going to miss you. That's all.'

Libby glances at her and says, 'Didn't you ever think about leaving? After you got left the cottage? And all the other stuff? I mean, surely you don't have to work, do you?'

Dido shrugs. 'I suppose not. And there are times I'd just like to chuck it all in and spend all day at the stables with Spangles before he cops it. But, ultimately, I have nothing else. But you – now you have everything. Everything that kitchens can't give you.'

Libby smiles. There is a truth to this.

It's not just the money. It's not just the money at all.

It's the people whom she now belongs to, the family who've encircled her so completely. And it's the person she discovered she was underneath all the neat piles and careful planning. She was never really that person. She'd made herself into that person to counterbalance her mother's inconsistencies. To fit in at school. To fit in with a group of friends whose values she never really shared, not really, not deep down inside. There is more to her than arms' length friendships and stupidly proscriptive Tinder requirements. She is the product of better people than her fantasy birth parents, the graphic designer and the fashion PR with the sports car and the tiny dogs. How unimaginative she'd been.

She presses refresh on her phone, absent-mindedly.

She looks again. A stupid number sits there. A number that makes no sense whatsoever. It has too many zeros, too many everythings. She turns her phone to face Dido. 'Oh. My. God.'

Dido covers her face with her hands and gasps. Then she turns to face the front of the café. 'Waiter,' she says. 'Two bottles of your finest Dom Pérignon. And thirteen lobsters. And make it snappy.'

There is no waiter of course and the people at the table next to them throw them a strange look.

'My friend', says Dido, 'has just won the lottery.'

'Oh,' says the woman. 'Lucky you!'

'You know,' says Dido, turning back to her. 'You really don't have to go back to work after this. It's your birthday. And you've just been given eleventy squillion pounds. You could, if you wanted, take the rest of the day off.'

Libby smiles, screws up her paper napkin and drops it on the plastic tray. 'No,' she says. 'No way. I'm no quitter. And besides, I'm pretty sure I left some paper-work slightly askew.'

Dido smiles at her. 'Come on then,' she said, 'three and a half more hours of normality. Let's get it over with, shall we?'

67

Lucy has the flat to herself for another hour. She uses it to have a bath, to paint her fingernails, to dry her hair with a dryer and make it sit neatly over her shoulders, to moisturise, to put on make-up. She still doesn't take these things for granted. It has been a year since Henry found her in the house in Cheyne Walk, since he brought Serenity to them, since they were all reunited. For a year Lucy has lived with Henry in his immaculate flat in Marylebone, where she has slept on a double bed under soft cotton sheets and had nothing more to do with her days than walk the dog and prepare delicious meals. She and Clemency meet up once a month and drink champagne and talk about their children and music and Henry's idiosyncrasies and anything, in fact, other than what happened to them both when they were young. They will never be as close as they once were, but they are still the best of friends.

Marco is thirteen now and enrolled at a trendy private school in Regent's Park, which Henry has been paying for and where 'everyone vapes and takes ket' apparently. He has lost his French accent completely and, as he says, 'I now identify as a Londoner.'

Stella is six and in year one of a nice primary school in Marylebone where she has two best friends who are both called Freya.

Yesterday Lucy took the tube to Chelsea and stood outside the house. The hoarding has been taken down and the for-sale sign outside has been swapped for a sold sign. Soon the house will be alive with the sound of drills and hammers as it is taken apart and put back together again to suit the tastes and needs of another family. Soon, someone else will be calling it home and they will never know, never suspect for even a moment the truth about what happened within those walls all those years ago, how four children were imprisoned and broken and then released into the world, damaged, incomplete, lost and warped. It's hard for Lucy to remember the girl she was then, hard for her to accept an incarnation of herself that was so desperate for attention that she would sleep with both a father and a son. She looks at Stella sometimes, her tiny perfect girl, and tries to imagine her at thirteen years old giving herself like that just to feel loved. It makes her feel unimaginable pain.

Her phone pings and she experiences as she always does, and probably always will, a shiver of unease. Michael's murder has not been solved but has been widely accepted to have been the result of some unpaid debts to his associates in the criminal underworld. She saw one mention of herself in a French paper shortly after the murder hit the headlines:

Rimmer, who has been married twice, is believed to have a child with his first wife, a Briton known only by the name of 'Lucy'. According to Rimmer's house-keeper, he and his former wife recently had a brief reunion, but she is not considered to be a suspect in the case.

But she will never be truly relaxed about the possibility of being tracked down by some fresh-faced young detective, newly qualified and desperate to prove themselves. She will never, she suspects, be truly relaxed ever again.

But it's not a message from a rookie detective, it's a message from Libby: a screenshot of a page from her bank statement accompanied by the word *Kerching!*

Lisa Jewell

There it is, thinks Lucy, and a shiver of relief runs through her. The end of this phase of her life. The beginning of the next. Now she can buy a place of her own. At last. A place for her and her children and her dog. A forever place that no one will be able to take away from her. And then, she thinks, then she will be able to discover exactly what it is that she should be doing with her life. She would like, she thinks, to study the violin. She would like to be a professional musician. And now there are no barriers in her way.

The first half of Lucy's life was tainted and dark, one struggle after another. The second half will be golden.

She replies to Libby's message.

Champagne all round! See you later sweetheart. I cannot wait to celebrate with you. Everything.

Libby answers: *I can't wait to see you either. Love you.*

Love you too, she finishes, then adds a long row of kisses and switches off her phone.

Her girl is glorious: a gentle, caring soul, a blend of Stella and Marco in many ways but also so very much her father's child in the way that she walks her own path and makes her own rules, that she is so entirely and utterly herself. And she is growing and changing so much, leaving behind some of the tics and compulsions that held her back, letting life show her her journey rather than imposing a journey on to her life.

She has been worth every bad moment between leaving her in her cot and finding her again. She is an angel.

Lucy picks up her phone again and she scrolls through her contacts until she gets to the Gs. She composes a message:

Darling Giuseppe. This is your Lucy. I am missing you so much. I just wanted you to know that I am happy and healthy and well and so are the children and so is Fitz. I won't be coming back to France. I have a wonderful new life now and want to put down roots. But I will think of you always and forever be so grateful to you for being there for me when my life was out of control. I'd be lost without you. My love, always, Lucy.

68

In the restaurant in Marylebone that evening Libby's family awaits her.

Lucy, Marco, Stella and Henry.

Marco greets her with an awkwardly dramatic half-hug, his head knocking against her collarbone. 'Happy birthday, Libby,' he says.

Stella hugs her gently and says, 'Happy birthday, Libby. I love you.'

These two children, her brother and sister, have been the greatest gifts of all.

They are wonderful children and Libby puts that down entirely to the woman who raised them. She and Lucy have become very close, very quickly. The small age gap means that often Lucy feels like a great new friend, rather than the woman who gave birth to her.

Lucy gets to her feet. She circles Libby's neck with her arms and kisses her loudly in the vicinity of her ear. 'Happy birthday,' she says. 'Proper happy birthday. This time twenty-six years ago. God. I thought I was going to split in half.'

'Yes,' agrees Henry. 'She was mooing like a cow. For hours. We had our hands over our ears.' Then he gives her one of his cautious embraces.

Libby still can't work Henry out. Sometimes she thinks about Clemency saying that she thought he had a streak of pure evil, and a shiver runs across her flesh. She thinks of what he did, the execution of four people, the mummification of a young woman's body, the mutilation of a cat. But killing had never been his intention and Libby still believes that if the four children had turned themselves in to the local police that night and explained what had happened, how they'd been so mistreated, imprisoned, that it had been a terrible accident, that they would have been believed and rehabilitated. But that's not how it had been and they had all made fugitives of themselves and taken their lives off on unimaginable tangents.

Henry is odd, but then he is very open about the fact that he is odd. He still maintains that he did not intentionally lock them into the spare bedroom of his

Airbnb rental that night, that he did not take their phones and delete Miller's recording. He said, 'Well, if I did I must have been even drunker than I thought.' And Libby never did find a tracking or listening device on her phone. But then she never changed the passcode on her phone either.

He also denies that he has had cosmetic procedures to make him look like Phin. He says, 'Why would I want to look like Phin? I'm so much better looking than he ever was.' He is impatient with the children and slightly flustered by the sudden influx of people into his tightly controlled little world, often grumpy but occasionally hilarious. He has a vague grasp of the truth and seems to live very slightly on the edges of reality. And how can Libby blame him? After everything he's been through? She would probably live on the edges of reality too if her childhood had been as traumatic as his.

She opens his card to her and reads: 'Sweet Libby Jones, I am so proud to call you my niece. I loved you then and I'll love you always. Happy birthday, beautiful.'

He looks at her with a slight flush of embarrassment and this time she doesn't accept one of his cautious embraces. This time she throws her arms around his neck and squeezes him until he squeezes her back. 'I love you too,' she says into his ear. 'Thank you for finding me.'

And then Miller arrives.

Dido was right.

There was something there.

Despite the fact that Roe double-barrels horribly with Jones, that his mother is rather distant, that his stomach wobbles, that he has too much facial hair, no pets and an ex-wife, there was something there that amounted to more than all of that. And what is a tattoo other than a drawing on skin? It's not an ideology. It's a scribble.

Miller abandoned his story for Libby. After the night last summer when she was reunited with her family, he'd taken his notepad and he'd ripped out all the pages.

'But', she'd said, 'that's your livelihood, that's your career. You could have made so much money.'

He'd silenced her with a kiss and said, 'I'm not taking your family away from you. You deserve them much more than I deserve a scoop.'

Now Libby takes the empty seat next to him and greets him with a kiss.

'Happy Birthday, Lamb,' he says into her ear.

That's his nickname for her. She's never had a nickname before.

He passes her a fat envelope.

She says, 'What's this?'

He smiles and says, 'I would suggest opening it to find out.'

It's a brochure, glossy and thick, for a five-star safari lodge in Botswana called the Chobe Game Lodge.

'Is this . . . ?'

Miller smiles. He says, 'Well, yes, apparently. According to the very forthcoming man I spoke to on reception, their head guide is a man in his early forties called Phin. But he spells it with an F now. Finn. Finn Thomsen.'

'And is it? Is it him?'

'I'm ninety-nine per cent certain that it is. But there is only one way to find out for sure.'

He pulls some printed paper out of his jacket pocket and passes it to her. It's an email confirmation of a booking for a deluxe room for two at the Chobe Game Lodge.

'I can take my mum,' he says. 'If you don't want to come. She's always wanted to go on safari.'

Libby shakes her head. 'No,' she says. 'No. I want to come. Of course I want to come.'

She flicks through the papers, then back through the brochure. And then her eye is caught by a photo: a jeep filled with tourists looking at a pride of lions. She peers closer at the photo. She looks at the tour guide sitting at the front of the jeep, turning to smile at the camera. He has a thatch of thick, sun-burnished blond hair. His face is wide open; his smile is like the sun shining.

He looks like the happiest man in the world.

He looks like her.

'Do you think that's him?' she asks.

'I don't know,' says Miller. He glances across the table at Henry and Lucy, turns the brochure to face them. Their faces bunch up as they examine the photo. And then Lucy puts her fist to her mouth and Henry falls against the back of his chair.

Lucy nods, hard. 'Yes,' she says, her voice breaking. 'Yes, that's him. That's Phin. He's alive. Look at him! He's alive.'

69

He's alive. Phin is alive. My heart twists and roils and I feel dizzy. He is handsome as all damnation. Look at him there with his tan and his combats and his big shit-eating grin, sitting in a jeep in Africa with barely a care in the world. I bet he never thinks about me, bet he never thinks about any of us. Especially not you, Serenity. Especially not you. He wasn't interested in you when you lived in our house. He won't be interested in you now.

Lucy was clearly lying when she said that they talked about you all the time when they lived in France. Phin's not a baby person. He's not a 'family guy'. He lives inside himself. He's a loner. The only time, the *only time* I managed to get him out of himself was the first time we took the acid. The time we held hands, when I felt him passing into me, when I became Phin. He didn't become me, of course – who would want to become me? But I became him. I used to write it all over the house, whenever I could, like silent shouts into corners and nooks and hidden places. 'I AM PHIN'.

But how could I be Phin while Phin was there reminding me, *constantly*, of how much I was not Phin? With every careless flick of his fringe, shrug of his shoulders, brooding look across an empty room, slowly turned page of a cult novel.

It started as a love potion. It was supposed to make him love me. It didn't work. All it did was diminish him. Make him weaker. Less beautiful. And the weaker he got the stronger I became. So I kept giving it to him, the tincture. Not to kill him, that was never my intention, but just to dim his lights so that I could shine a little brighter. And that night, the night of Birdie's thirtieth birthday party, when Lucy told me that Phin was her baby's father, I went into his room to kill him.

But when he told me to untie him, I said, 'Only if you let me kiss you.' And I kissed him. With his hand still tied to the water pipe, his body almost broken, I kissed him, on his lips, on his face. He didn't fight. He let me do it. I kissed him for a long minute. I touched my finger to his lips, I ran my hands through his hair,

I did everything I'd dreamed of doing from the very first minute he'd walked into our house when I was eleven years old, when I hadn't known that I would ever want to kiss anyone.

I waited for him to push me off. But he didn't. He was compliant.

Then, when I'd kissed him enough, I untied him from the radiator and I lay down next to him.

I wrapped my arm around his warm body.

I closed my eyes.

I fell asleep.

When I woke up, Phin was gone.

I've looked for him ever since.

But now he's found.

I knew Libby's big bear would find him.

And he did.

I look up at Miller; I look at you.

I slap on my best jolly Uncle Henry smile and I say, 'Room for one more?'

Acknowledgements

Thank you to a trio of incredible editors; to my UK editor Selina Walker who worked through weekends and long into nights to splice, polish and rework my manuscript into something readable. Then to Lindsay Sagnette in the US who added a whole new layer of extra insight and clarity. And lastly, to Richenda Todd, who went way beyond the role of a copy editor and made me deal with lots of problematic issues I'd been trying to ignore because I couldn't work out how to fix them. You three have been a masterclass in the difference that a good editor can make. Thanks also to my amazing agent, Jonny Geller, who did not let me send my book into the world without it being the best it possibly could be. The harder you're made to work on an edit, the more your publishers care about you and your work. I am so, so lucky to have you all.

Thank you to Najma Finlay, my amazing UK publicist, who is heading off on maternity leave and won't be back until we have the next book to publicise; enjoy every minute of your time with your beautiful baby.

Thank you to Deborah Schneider, my incredible agent in the US, for . . . well, you know what for! What a year it has been!

Thank you to Coco Azoitei for the technical jargon I needed to explain what happens when someone tests a newly repaired fiddle and thank you to everyone on Facebook who offered information about family trusts. Any mistakes in either regard are entirely my own.

Thank you to my publishing teams in the UK, the US and all over the world for taking such good care of my work – and me! – with especial thanks to Ariele and Haley in the US, Pia and Christoffer in Sweden, Oda in Norway and Elisabeth and Tina in Denmark.

Thank you to all my audio publishers and the recording studios who produce work of such astoundingly high quality and thanks to all the actors and voice artists who read my words so beautifully.

Thanks to the librarians, the book shops, the festival organisers and anyone who has helped put my books into the hands of readers.

Thanks to my family (including my menagerie) who keep me grounded, at all times.

And lastly, thank you to the two double vodka and tonics that saw me through the last three chapters of this book late on a Friday night and helped me find the last few lines that I knew were hidden away in there somewhere. Cheers!

About the Author

Lisa Jewell was born in London in 1968. Her first novel, *Ralph's Party*, was the best-selling debut novel of 1999. Since then she has written another eighteen novels, most recently a number of dark psychological thrillers, including *The Girls*, *Then She Was Gone* and *The Family Upstairs* (all of which were Richard & Judy Book Club picks).

Lisa is a *New York Times* and *Sunday Times* number one bestselling author who has been published worldwide in over twenty-five languages. She lives in north London with her husband, two teenage daughters, one cat, one guinea pig and the best dog in the world.

Four deaths. An unsolved mystery.
And a family whose secret history is darker
than anyone can imagine ...

**Find out what happened to
The Family Upstairs ...**

PREPARE TO BE HOOKED

Turn over to read an extract ...

1

July 2018

Groggy with sleep, Rachel peered at the screen of her phone. A French number. The phone slipped from her hand on to the floor and she grabbed it up again, staring at the number with wide eyes, adrenaline charging through her even though it was barely seven in the morning.

Finally she pressed reply. 'Hello?'

'*Bonjour*, good morning. This is Detective Avril Loubet from the Police Municipale in Nice. Is this Mrs Rachel Rimmer?'

'Yes,' she replied. 'Speaking.'

'Mrs Rimmer. I am afraid I am calling you with some very distressing news. Please, tell me. Are you alone?'

'Yes. Yes, I am.'

'Is there anyone you can ask to be with you now?'

7

'My father. He lives close. But please. Just tell me.'

'Well, I am afraid to say that early this morning the body of your husband, Michael Rimmer, was discovered by his house-keeper in the basement of his house in Antibes.'

Rachel made a sound, a hard intake of breath with a *whoosh*, like a steam train. 'Oh,' she said. 'No!'

'I'm so sorry. But yes. And he appears to have been murdered, with a stab wound, several days ago. He has been dead at least since the weekend.'

Rachel sat up straight and moved the phone to her other ear. 'Is it – Do you know why? Or who?'

'The crime scene officers are in attendance. We will uncover every piece of evidence we can. But it seems that Mr Rimmer had not been operating his security cameras and his back door was unlocked. I am very sorry, I don't have anything more definite to share with you at this point, Mrs Rimmer. Very sorry indeed.'

Rachel turned off her phone and let it drop on to her lap.

She stared blankly for a moment towards the window where the summer sun was leaking through the edges of the blind. She sighed heavily. Then she pulled her sleep mask down, turned on to her side, and went back to sleep.

2

June 2019

I am Henry Lamb. I am forty-two years old. I live in the best apartment in a handsome art deco block just around the corner from Harley Street. How do I know it's the best apartment? Because the porter told me it was. When he brings a parcel up – he doesn't need to bring parcels up, but he's nosey, so he does – he peers over my shoulder and his eyes light up at the slice of my interior that he can see from my front door. I used a designer. I have exquisite taste, but I just don't know how to put tasteful things together in any semblance of visual harmony. No. I am not good at creating visual harmony. It's OK. I'm good at lots of other things.

I do not currently – quite emphatically – live alone. I always thought I was lonely before they arrived. I would return home to my immaculate, expensively renovated flat and my sulky Persian

LISA JEWELL

cats and I would think, oh, it would be so nice to have someone to talk to about my day. Or it would be so nice if there was some- one in the kitchen right now preparing me a lovely meal, unscrew- ing the cap from a bottle of something cold or, better still, mixing me something up in a cocktail glass. I have felt very sorry for myself for a very long time. But for a year now, I have had house guests – my sister Lucy and her two children – and I am never, ever alone.

There are people in my kitchen constantly, but they're not mixing me cocktails or shucking oysters, they're not asking me about my day; they're using my panini-maker to produce what they call 'toasties', they're making hot chocolate in the wrong pot, they're putting non-recyclables in my recycling bin and vice versa. They're watching noisy, unintelligible things on the smart- phones I bought them and shouting at each other when there's really no need. And then there's the dog. A Jack Russell terrier type thing that my sister found on the streets of Nice five years ago scavenging in bins. He's called Fitz and he adores me. It's mutual. I'm a dog person at heart and only got the cats because they're easier for selfish people to look after. I did a test online – *What's Your Ideal Cat Breed?* – answered thirty questions, and the result came back: Persian. I think the test was correct. I'd only ever known one cat before, as a child, a spiteful creature with sharp claws. But these Persians are in a different realm entirely. They demand that you love them. You have no choice in the matter. But they do not like Fitz the dog and they do not like me liking Fitz the dog and the atmosphere between the animals is horrendous.

My sister moved in last year for reasons that I barely know how to begin to convey. The simple version is that she was homeless.

The more complicated version would require me to write an essay. The halfway version is that when I was ten years old our (very large) family home was infiltrated by a sadistic conman and his family. Over the course of more than five years the conman took control of my parents' minds and systematically stripped them of everything they owned. He used our home as his own personal prison and playground and was ruthless in getting exactly what he wanted from everyone around him, including his own wife and children. Countless unspeakable things happened during those years, including my sister getting pregnant at thirteen, giving birth at fourteen, and leaving her ten-month-old baby in London and running away to the south of France when she was only fifteen. She went on to have two more children by two more men, kept them fed and clothed with money earned by busking with a violin on the streets of Nice, spent a few nights sleeping rough, and then decided to come home when (amongst many other things) she sensed that she might be in line for a large inheritance from a trust fund set up by our parents when we were children.

So, the good news is that last week that trust finally paid out and now – a trumpet fanfare might be appropriate here – she and I are both millionaires, which means that she can buy her own house and move herself, her children and her dog out, and that I will once more be alone.

And then I will have to face the next phase of my life.

Forty-two is a strange age. Neither young nor old. If I were straight, I suppose I'd be frantically flailing around right now trying to find a last-minute wife with functioning ovaries. As it is, I am not straight, and neither am I the sort of man that other men wish to form lengthy and meaningful relationships with, so that leaves me in the worst possible position – an unlovable gay man with fading looks.

Kill me now.

But there is a glimmer of something new. The money is nice, but the money is not the thing that glimmers. The thing that glimmers is a lost jigsaw piece of my past; a man I have loved since we were both boys in my childhood house of horrors. A man who is now forty-three years old, sporting a rather unkempt beard and heavy-duty laughter lines and working as a gamekeeper in Botswana. A man who is – *plot twist* – the son of the conman who ruined my childhood. And also – *secondary plot twist* – the father of my niece, Libby. Yes, Phineas impregnated Lucy when he was sixteen and she was thirteen and yes that is wrong on many levels and you might have thought that that would put me off him, and for a while it did. But we all behaved badly in that house, not one of us got out of there without a black mark. I've come to accept our sins as survival strategies.

I have not seen Phineas Thomsen since I was sixteen and he was eighteen. But last week at my niece's birthday party, my niece's boyfriend, who is an investigative journalist, told us that he had tracked him down for her. A kind of uber-thoughtful birthday present for his girlfriend. *Look! I got you a long-lost dad!*

And now here I am, on a bright Wednesday morning in June, cloistered away in the quiet of my bedroom, my laptop open, my fingers caressing the touchpad, gently guiding the cursor around the website for the game reserve where he works, the game reserve I intend to be visiting very, very shortly.

Phin Thomsen was how I knew him when we lived together as children.

Finn Thomsen is the pseudonym he's been hiding behind all these years.

I was so close. An F for a Ph. All these years, I could have found him if I'd just thought to play around with the alphabet. So clever of him. So clever. Phin was always the cleverest person I knew. Well, apart from me, of course.

I jump at the sound of a gentle knocking at my bedroom door. I sigh. 'Yes?'

'Henry, it's me. Can I come in?'

It's my sister. I sigh again and close the lid of my laptop. 'Yes, sure.'

She opens the door just wide enough to slide through and then closes it gently behind her.

Lucy is a lovely-looking woman. When I saw her last year for the first time since we were teenagers, I was taken aback by the loveliness of her. She has a face that tells stories, she looks all of her forty years, she barely grooms herself, she dresses like a bucket of rags, but somehow she still always looks lovelier than any other woman in the room. It's something about the juxtaposition of her amber-hazel eyes with the dirty gold streaks in her hair, the weightlessness of her, the rich honey of her voice, the way she moves and holds herself and touches things and looks at you. My father looked like a pork pie on legs and my lucky sister snatched all her looks from our elegant half-Turkish mother. I have fallen somewhere between the two camps. Luckily, I have my mother's physique, but sadly more than my fair share of my father's coarse facial features. I have done my best with what nature gave me. Money can't buy you love but it can buy you a chiselled jaw, perfectly aligned teeth and plumped-up lips.

My bedroom fills with the perfume of the oil my sister uses on her hair, something from a brown glass bottle that looks like she bought it from a country fayre.

'I wanted to talk to you,' she says, moving a jacket off a chair in the corner of my room so that she can sit down. 'About last week, at Libby's birthday dinner?'

I fix her with her a *yes, I'm listening, please continue* look.

'What you were saying, to Libby and Miller?'

Libby is the daughter Lucy had with Phin when she was fourteen. Miller is Libby's journalist boyfriend. I nod.

'About going to Botswana with them?'

I nod again. I know what's coming.

'Were you serious?'

'Yes. Of course I was.'

'Do you think – do you think it's a good idea?'

'Yes. I think it's a wonderful idea. Why wouldn't I?'

'I don't know. I mean, it's meant to be a romantic holiday, just for the two of them . . .'

I tut. 'He was talking about taking his mother; he can't have intended it to be that romantic.'

Obviously, I'm talking nonsense, but I'm feeling defensive. Miller wants to take Libby to Botswana to be reunited with the father she hasn't seen since she was a baby. But Phin is also a part of me. Not just a part of me, but nearly all of me. I've literally (and I'm using the word 'literally' here in its most literal sense) thought about Phin at least once an hour, every hour, since I was sixteen years old. How can I not want to go to him now, *right now*?

'I won't get in their way,' I offer. 'I will let them do their own thing.'

'Right,' says Lucy, doubtfully. 'And what will you do?'

'I'll . . .' I pause. What will I do? I have no idea. I will just be with Phin.

And then, after that – well, we shall see, shan't we?

From the bestselling author of THE FAMILY UPSTAIRS

THE FAMILY REMAINS

THEIR SECRETS CAN'T STAY BURIED FOR EVER

LISA JEWELL

THE MILLION-COPY BESTSELLING AUTHOR

COMING JULY 2022

Available to pre-order now

Find out more about Lisa and her books online at

LisaJewellofficial

@lisajewelluk

@lisajewelluk

CB
SB